THE LIFE
AND
DEATH
OF
ROSE
DOUCETTE

Also by Harry Hunsicker

THE LEE HENRY OSWALD SERIES

Still River

The Next Time You Die

Crosshairs

THE JON CANTRELL SERIES

The Contractors

Shadow Boys

The Grid

THE ARLO BAINES BOOKS

The Devil's Country

Texas Sicario

THE LIFE
AND
DEATH
OF
ROSE
DOUCETTE

A NOVEL

HARRY HUNSICKER

OCEANVIEW (PUBLISHING
SARASOTA, FLORIDA

ISBN 978-1-60809-612-1

Published in the United States of America by Oceanview Publishing

Sarasota, Florida

www.oceanviewpub.com

10 9 8 7 6 5 4 3 2 1

To Alison

THE LIFE
AND
DEATH
OF
ROSE
DOUCETTE

CHAPTER ONE

We hadn't seen each other in three years.

A long time, but not long enough to forgive.

She'd reached out to me with the request to meet and suggested the location, a bar in a hotel where rooms started at seven hundred a night. Not a place either of us would have ever considered staying.

An odd choice, but my ex-wife was an odd woman. Or maybe I was the odd one, and I just didn't realize it. Introspection was never my strong suit.

The bar smelled of vanilla-scented candles and leather. It was dimly lit, decorated with oil paintings of fox-hunting aristocrats and Rubenesque women lounging about naked. An English gentleman's club transported to the plains of North Texas.

A waiter led me to her table in the corner.

She smiled as I approached. "Hello, Dylan."

"Rose."

Silence ensued, which I'd say was awkward but maybe, like the oddness, I was wrong about that too. I remained standing, trying not to stare too long into those eyes of hers. They were the color of mahogany and had always been a weakness of mine.

After a moment, she pointed to an empty chair. "Would you like to join me? It's been a while, hasn't it?"

"A little over a thousand days, but who's counting," I said, sitting down and sliding the chair so that my back was to the wall. Old habits for both of us. Rose was in a similar position against the wall perpendicular to mine.

The waiter took our order. Club soda for me, a martini for her.

When he left, I said, "Since when do you drink martinis?"

Back when we were together, she'd preferred merlot, and then only a glass or two a week. Her stepfather had been an alcoholic prone to violence, and that tended to stay with a person.

"I'd like to hire you," she said, ignoring my question. Her eyes fixed on mine as if she was trying to gauge my reaction.

"So much for the small talk, huh?"

I had left the police department and gone private around the time we split. My workload was typical for a cop turned PI— missing persons, asset retrieval, insurance cases.

Rose, however, had stayed on the force, and I couldn't imagine her ever leaving.

"And what's with meeting here?" I asked. "You working vice these days?"

Despite being a luxury hotel, the lodging of choice for presidents and pop stars, the bar had a reputation as a good place to hook up with a high-end call girl. When I'd been on the force—a patrol officer in those days—a county commissioner had died from a heart attack while in the missionary position with one in a room upstairs.

Last I heard, Rose was still a homicide detective with the Dallas Police Department, and a very good one at that. She taught classes at Quantico, consulted with other departments on cases they couldn't solve, and had a clearance rate in the nineties.

Vice would be a big step down, and Sergeant Rose Doucette never went backwards for anything or anyone.

"Still on the murder beat." She paused. "So how have you been? You look good."

"I'm upright. Beats the alternative." I debated what to say next. "You look . . . good too."

That last part sounded stiff, and I hoped she didn't notice.

The truth was she looked anything but good. Her skin, normally olive, was sallow; dark circles cupped her eyes. She'd always skewed petite, five-four or so, one ten-ish. Now the navy blazer she wore draped her shoulders like an oversized blanket, her cheeks hollow and sunken.

She was forty-two, a year younger than me, but she seemed used up, like there wasn't much gas left in the tank.

"I look like roadkill," she said with a chuckle. "But thanks for saying otherwise."

The waiter brought our drinks. While he fussed with cocktail napkins and a bowl of salted nuts, I watched Rose scan the room, eyes darting from one corner to the next, clearly uneasy. It was a little before lunch. Other than a pair of men at the bar wearing Dockers and golf shirts—business traveler chic—we were the only customers present.

The waiter departed.

"To old friends." She raised her glass, took a drink.

I tilted my club soda in her direction. "Interesting choice of words. Old friends."

"Does that mean there's no chance you'd ever think of me as a friend?" she asked. "You still hate me?"

I didn't reply because I wasn't sure. The line between hate and something else was as thin as a strand of hair.

The two guys at the bar left. The room felt lonely and cold.

"Thanks for meeting with me," she said. "Guess I'm the last person on earth you want to see. For what it's worth, you're still the most stand-up guy I know."

I wondered if I'd made a mistake coming here. "Tell me why you need a PI."

Occasionally, an old colleague from the force would reach out for assistance with a matter that required someone with the skills of a police officer, but who wasn't burdened by the regulations associated with a badge.

I was usually happy to oblige, especially if it meant helping someone who was getting a raw deal from the system. I liked to think of myself as a GPS for justice, a way to get that particular concept back on the right road when it got lost.

"I'm in a bind, Dylan. I need help." She took another drink. "From someone I trust."

I looked at her more closely.

In addition to the fatigue, there was something else wrong that I couldn't identify, an air about her that clouded the table like cigarette smoke. The way she held her arms, the angle of her head. The tendons along her jawline tight against her skin.

With a start, I recognized what it was, an emotion I'd never seen from her before.

Fear.

Rose Doucette, a twenty-year veteran of the Dallas Police Department, was afraid.

"What's going on?" I leaned forward.

"I never was one for taking a lot of crap from the boys upstairs. The job itself comes with enough already." She swirled her drink.

"I'm just trying to do the right thing. You know how I roll. I call 'em like I see 'em."

Rose was honest to a fault, which was part of what had attracted me to her.

But sometimes honesty required—oh, how should I put it—*delicate phrasing.* Or failing that, a sense of timing attuned to the political realities of a big city police department.

Like say if you were to find a dead county commissioner in a hotel room with a prostitute. There's a right way to handle that type of situation and a righter way.

Across the room, a waiter dropped a tray. The clang echoed in the empty bar, sharp and loud.

A pistol materialized in Rose's hand, seemingly out of nowhere. Her gaze swept the room, finger on the trigger.

"It's okay." I kept my voice low and even. "A guy just dropped something."

She took several deep breaths, and then holstered her gun. She stared at me for a few moments before speaking. "I need to show you. It's easier that way."

She stood, tossed some bills on the table.

"Let's take this one step at a time. Tell me what's wrong."

"Please, Dylan. Just trust me." She turned and strode toward the exit.

A moment later I followed, wondering what kind of man I was to ever trust her again.

CHAPTER TWO

R ose led me outside to the hotel pool.

It was the middle of August, the temperature in the nineties, the humidity not far below that. Sweat began to soak through my shirt.

"I caught a case," she said. "GSW, white male, early forties."

GSW was shorthand for gunshot wound.

"They found the body on the edge of the hotel property."

She was all business now, the fear from moments before gone as she entered the world in which she operated best—solving crimes.

The deck around the pool was covered in travertine tile. Rows of loungers flanked the water, teakwood topped with peach-colored cushions. Cypress trees pruned to a uniform height ringed the entire area.

A Latina woman in her thirties, a pair of cat-eye sunglasses perched on her nose, was in the shallow end with two preschool-age children, a boy and a girl, the only people outside. The kids were throwing a beach ball back and forth while the woman talked on her phone in Spanish.

"The weapon was next to the vic's body," Rose said. "So, we're looking at a suicide, right?"

I nodded, knowing there was more to come. She directed me to a three-sided, canvas cabana at the far end of the pool. A small refrigerator and two loungers were inside the cabana.

"The vic was staying at the hotel," she said. "He spent his last morning in this tent. Costs two fifty a day to rent. Can you imagine?"

"Rich people are different than you and me. Also, I think this is called a cabana."

"Whatever." She rolled her eyes. "To your first point, our guy wasn't rich, at least not as far as I can tell."

Rose and her younger brother had grown up in a two-bedroom house in a working-class neighborhood in northwest Dallas. Her stepfather had been a truck driver until the DWIs started to pile up. Her mother had played bingo and waited on the child support checks from Rose's father.

"The vic's name was Josh Gannon," she said. "That mean anything to you?"

"No. Should it?"

"He was four days out of Huntsville. Got off the bus and checked in here."

"I don't keep track of every hood in town. What was he in for?"

"Possession and possession with intent," she said. "Being a junkie basically."

I sat on one of the loungers in the cabana, trying to get a sense of what Josh Gannon had seen and felt during his last morning on earth. I also wondered how an ex-con just out of the penitentiary would have enough money to stay at this hotel.

"What's the catch?" I asked.

"The GSW. It was in his chest."

I looked up at her.

When a man used a gun for suicide, ninety-nine times out of a hundred it was a head shot, either to the temple or in the mouth. Women, on the other hand, tended to position the muzzle over the sternum and pulled the trigger with their thumb.

"So, you've probably got a murder," I said.

She nodded but didn't speak, her eyes locked on mine.

After a moment, I said, "What's the problem?"

She continued to stare at me, head tilted to one side like there was something she didn't want to talk about, at least not just yet.

Strange. Rose had never held back with me on a case before. She liked to talk through the details with someone else who was trained as an investigator. The process of speaking the words helped things come together in her mind.

"The powers that be strongly suggested I call this a suicide." She paused. "Somebody doesn't want this to be a murder."

"What's the other evidence say? Any legs on the suicide angle?"

The men-shoot-themselves-in-the-head theory was just that, a theory, one of many elements to consider. It was certainly not enough to hang a murder investigation on.

She pursed her lips, eyes half closed, her expression when she was angry.

I chose my next words with care. "Maybe it *was* a suicide. The guy was a druggie. Levelheaded-thinking, that's not their strong suit."

"You don't believe me either?"

"It's not a matter of believing you," I said. "Sometimes a cigar is just a cigar."

A bone of contention in our marriage; me not buying into her hunches 110 percent. She swore under her breath, shook her head slowly.

I wanted to say something more, something to diffuse the situation, but easing tensions in a nonexistent relationship didn't seem necessary. So, I stood there and sweated.

The ball that the children were playing with skipped out of the water and bounced off Rose's head.

"What the hell?" She looked over at the pool, frowning.

The mother approached, dripping wet. "Sorry. Could you throw it ba—"

Rose kicked the ball. Hard, like it was the head of her archenemy, and she wanted to send their brain into low earth orbit.

The ball flew across the pool, into the bushes.

One of the children began to cry. The mother, mouth agape, stared at us. Rose glared back. "What are you looking at?"

"It was an accident," the mother said.

I put a hand on Rose's arm. "Let's take this down a notch. Maybe go inside and have another drink."

She jerked her arm free and turned to me. "Don't you touch me. You don't get to do that anymore."

The mother stepped back, hands raised, as her second child started to cry.

Rose took a deep breath, tried to regain her composure. She gave the mother a wan smile. "I'm sorry. I haven't been sleeping very well lately."

The mother nodded and scurried back to the other end of the pool, where a man in a white polo shirt with a name tag on the lapel, a manager type, was watching us.

Rose glanced at the man in the white polo shirt. "I need to show you where the body was found," she said. "We don't have much time."

CHAPTER THREE

The hotel sat atop a hill overlooking a creek. The creek, lined with willows, was a ribbon of water that cut through the ritzy part of Dallas, an area dotted with high-rises just north of downtown.

Rose beelined down the manicured lawn to a gazebo by the water. I followed.

The gazebo was only a few feet from the creek's bank, sitting under a cottonwood tree so old that it looked like it might have been planted during the First World War. A footbridge led across the creek to a heavily wooded tract of land on the other side. The bridge appeared to be secured by a locked gate.

"Hotel guests come here to smoke," Rose said.

There were three lawn chairs under the gazebo. An ashtray sat on a wood floor that looked like it had been freshly painted.

"The body was found forty-eight hours ago," she said. "And they've already got it all cleaned up."

"This is a fancy hotel. Violent death can't be a good marketing tool."

"It's a crime scene, Dylan."

I decided not to mention that the crime was most likely a suicide. "You want to fill me in on what happened back there with the beach ball?" I asked.

She walked to the edge of the water. Arms crossed, she stared at the plot of land on the other side of the creek.

"What aren't you telling me, Rose? Why are you holding back?"

She turned around to face me. "I know how you are with me and my hunches, but this is not a suicide." She took a deep breath. "I'm off the case. I want you to find the killer."

I wondered why she wasn't working the case anymore, but I didn't particularly want to ask. I also didn't want to disappoint her, so I didn't say anything.

No way could I take an assignment like this. Private investigators depended on having a good relationship with the police, especially PIs who used to be cops themselves. Nothing could mess that up faster than getting involved in a case where the resolution was already obvious, and the police brass had made the decision to move on.

"I'll pay you," she said. "I'm not looking for a freebie."

I stepped out of the gazebo and wandered to the creek bank. I stood next to her, stared at the woods on the other side. Neither of us spoke for a few moments.

"I'm sorry, Dylan. It couldn't have been easy being married to me."

"You really want to go down that road right now?"

Her decision to separate had come out of nowhere, a locomotive streaking down the dark but comfortable tunnel that was our marriage.

As a follow-up, she'd served divorce papers while I was working internal affairs, interrogating a narcotics officer accused of taking bribes from a drug dealer, the payoffs coming in the form of underage girls who the officer sold to a brothel.

My head was in a pretty dark place, and then the process server showed up while I was talking to the crooked narc, delivering the message that my wife wanted to end our marriage.

"Wish I could have explained better." She rubbed her eyes. "I didn't mean to hurt you."

I wanted to get mad at her, but too much time had gone by. Despite the circumstances of our reunion and the pain she'd caused me, I found myself enjoying being around her, slipping into the routine of discussing a case, the easy familiarity that came from like minds working in tandem.

We were good together, until we weren't, and I realized how much I missed her company.

From the pool area came the metallic clang of a wrought-iron door slamming. I looked up the hill.

The manager in the white polo shirt and a beefy guy in an ill-fitting suit marched toward us, the latter obviously hotel security.

I said, "What's going on, Rose?"

She didn't answer.

The two men glanced at me as they approached but were clearly focused on Rose. They stopped a few feet away from us, out of arm's reach.

The manager's name tag read OWENS. He was in his forties with the mustache of an adolescent, a thin wisp of hair on his upper lip.

"I thought we made ourselves clear yesterday," Owens said. "You shouldn't be on the property anymore."

She put her hands on her hips. "I'm investigating a crime."

The movement opened her blazer enough to display the gun and badge on her belt.

Owens shook his head, expression weary.

"Ma'am, you need to leave," the security guy said.

"Why'd you paint so soon?" She pointed to the gazebo.

The men gave each other a what-the-hell-do-we-do-now look. Rose might have been off the case, and told not to come back, but she was still a police officer.

"Rose, let's bounce," I said. "We'll find a coffee shop and keep talking."

She ignored me, jabbed a finger at Owens. "What are you hiding?"

He turned to the security guy. "Get her out of here, will ya?"

The security guy advanced toward her, arms out.

"You touch me," she said, "I'll have you in lockup so fast— "

I stepped between her and the two men, my hands raised. "It's all good. We're leaving."

The security guy stopped, glanced at Owens. Neither spoke.

I turned to Rose. "Isn't that right? We won't go inside. We'll head around the back of the hotel to the valet stand. Then we're out of here."

"Screw you, Dylan. Screw all of you." She stalked off across the lawn.

CHAPTER FOUR

After Rose was out of earshot, Owens said to me, "You friends with her?"

"More like acquaintances. The day that the guy died, what'd the video show?"

"No coverage down here." He shook his head. "We're fixing that, believe me."

"What about the cameras by the hotel? Did anybody follow him to the gazebo?"

"Are you a cop?" the security guy asked.

"Back when, yeah. You?"

"State trooper, a long time ago."

"Mr. Gannon came down here alone," Owens said. "Nobody followed him either."

"What about the gate across the creek?"

"It was locked," Owens said.

"So, it's a suicide," I said.

"The simplest explanation is usually the right one." The security guy crossed his arms. "If you have any stroke with that woman, you need to tell her to stay away."

Owens nodded. "If she comes back, we'll have to escalate. Nobody wins then."

"I'll do what I can," I said. "But Sergeant Rose Doucette doesn't take well to people telling her what to do."

"Don't I know it." Owens shook his head wearily. He and the security guy trudged back to the pool area.

The lawn between the hotel's valet stand where Rose was headed and the gazebo was huge, two or three football fields at least.

She was halfway across the expanse of grass when I started after her, following from a distance.

I thought about jogging to catch up, but I wasn't sure what I was going to say that would stop her from following whatever course she was on. Once Rose took hold of something, she had a hard time letting go. Unless it was something minor, like a marriage.

She ignored the valet stand at the front of the hotel and the rows of expensive automobiles, gleaming metal skins shaded by the live oaks that ringed the parking area. Walking down the driveway, she exited the property, turning left. She had obviously parked off the hotel grounds, as had I.

When I reached the end of the driveway, she was almost a block ahead, moving briskly like she was eager to get to her next destination. My pickup was in the same direction, so I continued to follow her.

The street was lined with small but expensive apartment buildings and old houses that had been converted into offices, the typical occupant being a plastic surgeon or an investment firm specializing in wealth management. Parked cars crowded the street, most of them high-end as befitting the neighborhood.

In the middle of the second block, Rose got into a small hunter-green SUV, obviously her personal car. She pulled away from the curb.

A few yards in front of me, a ten-year-old Toyota Camry pulled away from the curb too.

The Toyota was dark gray, with dealer plates, deeply tinted windows, and brand-new tires.

Funny, the details that register with an ex-cop.

The Camry matched Rose's speed, following her to a cross street in the distance.

The extra layer of awareness that cops and soldiers develop is not something that can be easily explained. A dark crevice of the brain takes sights and sounds, even smells, and processes them into something more than just the realities of the physical world. It's something you feel deep inside.

Right now, I had a feeling that whoever was in that Toyota meant harm to Rose Doucette. I hoped I was wrong, but I decided to follow Rose's SUV for a while just for the heck of it.

My pickup was a few spaces in front of where the Camry had been parked.

I got in. Cranked the engine, turned on the AC.

Ninety seconds later, I was stopped at the light at a major intersection a few blocks from the hotel. The Camry was in the middle lane, three cars behind Rose. I was three cars behind the Camry. At the next intersection, Rose turned right. So did the Camry.

I trailed them both, keeping several cars back.

When the Camry followed her SUV onto Central Expressway, a highway in the middle part of town, I dialed Rose's cell.

The call went to voicemail after a few rings.

Ten minutes later, Rose exited the expressway and headed east, the Camry a half-dozen cars behind. I dialed her again. No answer. A tendril of fear crept up my spine.

Rose was now on a major thoroughfare looping the entire city—Northwest Highway—and the Camry could have been going to any number of places not connected to her. Maybe my extra layer of awareness was having an off day.

I didn't think so.

A Dallas police substation was a couple miles ahead, just past a park at the north end of White Rock Lake, and I figured that was Rose's destination.

I relaxed slightly. Only so much harm could come to someone in the secured parking area of a police station.

She turned into the park on a side street and headed north, the Camry following closer now. My mouth grew dry, adrenaline spiking in my system.

I called again. Same result. I made the turn and stopped in the middle of the street long enough to send her a text—*911! CHECK UR 6.*

Then I sped up to catch the Camry.

The park was heavily wooded, split by a creek that fed into the lake. It was early afternoon, but the canopy of trees made the light dim.

Around a bend, the Camry turned into the entrance to a parking area.

I stopped on the opposite side of the road, on the shoulder in front of a stable. A half dozen horses milled around a paddock, swatting flies with their tails.

The tree growth was so heavy across the street, the parking area wasn't visible from the road. I couldn't see any sign of Rose's SUV.

I got out. The air was still and humid, thick with the smell of stagnant water, hay, and manure. Sweat began dripping down my forehead.

I dashed across the street, jogging down the narrow blacktop the Camry had taken. After about twenty yards, I heard a female voice shouting. I sprinted toward the sound.

Rose's SUV was parked at the far end of the lot, maybe fifty yards away, the gray Toyota Camry at an angle behind her vehicle, the driver's side facing her.

She stood by the SUV, clawing at her hip.

I grabbed my pistol and ran faster, sweat stinging my eyes.

BAM-BAM.

Rose fell.

SCREECH.

The Camry peeled away, barreling across the lot. Headed toward the exit. Toward me.

I aimed just above the steering wheel, squeezed the trigger. My foot stepped on an uneven spot, and I staggered as the pistol fired. The shot missed.

The Camry accelerated, close enough to see that the driver was a man wearing gloves and a ball cap pulled low.

Two choices. Shoot again or jump out of the way, the time to decide measured in milliseconds.

I jumped but not fast enough.

The Camry sideswiped my right side, throwing me against a tree. I bounced like a pinball, landing on the gravel drive with a thud, all the air gone from my lungs.

Vision blurry, hands empty. Where was my gun?

Feet crunched on gravel. I struggled for air, patted the ground, searching for my pistol. Then, an explosion of pain on the back of my head as something struck me.

CHAPTER FIVE

My eyes opened. I was on the gravel drive leading to the parking area a few feet from the tree I'd hit when the Toyota sideswiped me.

Everything hurt, but I could breathe again. Barely.

Rose's SUV was still on the other side off the lot. A figure lay on the ground. No sign of the Camry.

I pushed myself to my knees. My gun lay a couple feet away. I grabbed it and staggered toward the vehicle, ignoring the pain in my back and head.

They say that when you're about to die, your life flashes before your eyes.

Despite the various pains in my body, I started walking faster toward Rose's SUV.

What nobody ever talks about is what happens when someone else is dying—someone you're close to—how your life together flickers across the high-def screen in your mind.

My walk turned into a jog. Then a dash.

I skidded to a stop by Rose's prone body. She wasn't moving. Her head was turned to one side, hair in her face.

The bullet had hit just above her collarbone. Just above the protective vest she wore. A dark hole pumping blood.

I pressed down on the wound with one hand, fumbled for my cell with the other. "Stay with me, Rose."

We had met in our twenties, at a bar frequented by cops, a place with sawdust on the floor and Merle Haggard on the jukebox. Post Y2K, pre-September 11, when the new millennium still held promise, especially for a pair of young officers looking to make their mark.

Blood seeped between my fingers.

"It's all good, Rose. You're going to be fine." I managed to get the phone out of my jeans and punch in 911.

That first night at the bar she'd strolled over to the pool table where I had been playing eight ball with my partner. She'd placed a pair of quarters on the table, challenging the winner to a game. The way she looked at me when she slapped the quarters down—those mahogany eyes shimmering in the dim light, a sardonic smile on her lips—I felt my pulse beat a notch faster.

My partner, sensing the attraction, scratched twice in a row, allowing me to win.

Rose and I had played for the next hour, each winning as much as losing. She shot pool like she investigated a crime, methodically, with a single-mindedness that bordered on obsessive, occasionally taking a risky shot. Working on a hunch, she'd told me with a grin. Just felt like that ball belonged in that pocket.

"D-Dylan."

Her voice was weak and raspy, something rattling deep inside, skin a waxy gray.

That first night, after we were tired of playing pool, we'd gone across the street for burgers. We'd talked for hours, both of us surprised at how well we got along.

I blinked sweat out of my eyes. There was more blood on my hands. A commotion nearby. Voices, the squawk of a radio.

A uniformed police officer appeared in front of me, a woman in her twenties, gun drawn.

Behind her was another officer, a man about the same age, pistol in his hand.

"Call an ambulance." I dropped my cell, used both hands on the wound. "She's in shock, lost a lot of blood."

"Step away from the body," the officer said.

"What?" I didn't move. My skin felt clammy.

"Sir, move away from the body."

"Get an EMT, dammit." I looked down at Rose. "She nee—"

The blood had stopped flowing from the wound by her collarbone.

I touched her chin, eased her head so she was looking up, her hair falling away from her face. One eye was open. The other was missing because that was where the second bullet had hit.

"R-Rose?" I struggled to catch my breath.

She must have died instantly, which made no sense because I had heard her call my name. Or thought I had.

The officer pointed to a spot a few feet away.

A revolver I'd never seen lay in the dust.

"Is that your gun?" she asked.

CHAPTER SIX

The officer's name was Hernandez, a corporal according to the name tag on her uniform. She had dark hair; the temples flecked with gray despite her age.

She hustled me away from Rose while her partner called it in, initiating the organized chaos that was a murder investigation. The coroner and the crime scene techs, various investigators, and at least one media liaison officer.

I told Corporal Hernandez that I used to be a Dallas cop and that wasn't my revolver.

Then I gave her a quick summary of what had happened.

She jotted everything down on a notepad as I told her about meeting Rose at the hotel, seeing the Camry follow her when she left, how I'd trailed both vehicles. I described the shooter as best I could, a white male between the ages of twenty and sixty, which was better than nothing but not by much.

"I recognize the victim," Hernandez said. "Sergeant Doucette. She spoke to my class at the academy."

Another unit peeled into the parking area, stopping by the first squad car. An officer got out and began unspooling yellow crime scene tape.

"What's your connection to Doucette?" Hernandez asked.

"Ex-husband. We were married for fifteen years."

I didn't know why I mentioned the last part. What bearing did that have on anything? I glanced at the body, and then looked away. Nothing seemed right. The sky looked brittle, and I could feel every pebble on the ground through the soles of my shoes. Rose was dead?

"So, you followed your ex-wife." Hernandez paused. "To a deserted parking lot."

"I followed a Camry that was following her."

She scanned her notes. "A Camry with paper plates. Right?"

"Yeah."

"Are you armed?"

I nodded, told her where on my person the firearm was located.

She looked at Rose's body. Then at me. She read her notes one more time, tapped the pad with her pen.

"I'm gonna need to take your weapon," she said.

"How about I pull up my shirt and you remove it from the holster?"

"That'll work." She put the notepad in her pocket and slid on a pair of latex gloves.

I raised my shirt. and she pulled the pistol free.

She examined the gun, sniffed the barrel. "Have you fired this weapon recently?"

I realized it wasn't going to help much if I lied. So, I explained about shooting at the Camry as the driver tried to run me over.

She told me to stay where I was. Then she called her partner over and they held a whispered conversation on the other side of their squad car, glancing at me every so often.

The partner made a call on his cellphone. After a minute or so, he hung up and spoke again to Corporal Hernandez. She nodded once and walked over to where I was standing, pulling her hand-cuffs off of her belt as she came.

"We have to take you into custody," she said. "Homicide's decision."

I took a step back, an involuntary movement, but stopped, look-ing at the situation from their perspective.

A decorated police investigator had been killed. The responding officers discovered her ex-husband by the still-warm body, along with what appeared to be the murder weapon, talking about a mysterious shooter in a nondescript car.

"I understand," I said. "But I didn't kill her."

Hernandez patted me down, removing my cellphone, wallet, and keys, as well as the small folding knife I kept in my waistband at the small of my back. Then she cuffed my hands, led me to her squad car, and slid me in the back. She got in the front and turned on the AC so neither of us would die from heatstroke.

She punched in data on a mobile computer terminal.

Every file started somewhere, and this was how the one for the death of Rose Doucette began.

She peered at me through the cage separating the front from the back. "What's your date of birth?"

I told her.

"Sergeant Doucette," she said. "A lot of women on the force looked up to her. She was a real inspiration."

I nodded. "Rose is . . . was a hell of a cop."

She entered my information into the terminal. "Whoever killed her, I hope they get the needle."

CHAPTER SEVEN

The homicide detective who drew the case was named Lutz.

Six months before I'd left the force, when I was an internal affairs officer, I'd had Lutz's partner fired for working security at an illegal casino in the Fair Park section of Dallas.

Lutz was involved, too, taking a slice off the casino's bank in exchange for providing notice if vice was planning a raid. Unfortunately, there wasn't enough evidence to warrant his termination and then pass muster with the civil service board. So, Lutz remained a cop, but one with very little chance for career advancement.

Now we were sitting across a table from each other in an interview room at police headquarters, a sleek, six-story building just south of downtown. They'd already processed me at the jail, the sheriff's deputies silent as they took my mug shots and fingerprints. Nobody liked a cop killer.

The room looked like an insurance adjuster's office. Tile floor, white walls, acoustic drop ceilings, everything brightly lit by the overhead fluorescents.

The main differences: the video camera in the corner recording everything and my cuffed hands, Rose's blood still on my skin despite the samples taken by the crime scene techs and the finger-printing at the jail.

Lutz was in his fifties, but he dressed like a Dallas cop from a generation ago. He wore a pale green jacket with a western yoke, beige polyester pants, brown cowboy boots, and a smirk on his face, the latter no doubt because I was now in his crosshairs as a suspect.

He pulled a card from his pocket and read me the Miranda warning, his voice monotone.

When he was finished, he said, "I never figured you for a killer."

I desperately wanted to tell him what had happened, the same facts that I'd related to Corporal Hernandez. I wanted to get them started looking for the Toyota Camry, but I'd been on the other side of the table enough to know what the proper response was.

"I want my lawyer."

He put the card away. "I know Rose dumped your sorry ass, but that was a long time ago. Can't believe you waited this long to pop her."

I didn't speak.

"People around here, they still remember when you two got into that screaming match in the parking lot. You threw a walkie-talkie at her, right?"

I tried to keep my face blank. Tried not to think of Rose's gray skin as she lay dead.

"And now we got a witness who saw you two scuffling," he said. "Thirty minutes before you shot her."

The woman at the pool. Rose jerking her arm free from my hand.

"I thought you were smarter than that, Dylan."

"My lawyer needs to be here. Even a bent cop like you has to follow the rules on occasion."

He chuckled. "A case like this, don't count on making bail. I'll make sure you're not in protective custody. Should be a fun time."

*   *   *

Lutz left, and I remembered the first real argument Rose and I had, not long after we were married.

She'd been working for the sexual assaults unit, investigating a string of rapes, college girls who were followed home from a series of three bars in the same block near the university.

The attacks were violent; four of the victims ended up in the hospital for periods of time. But the rapist wore a condom so there was no DNA evidence.

Rose had started with the obvious—boyfriends and ex-boyfriends, online acquaintances, people in the area with a record of similar crimes. She came up with nothing.

From there she progressed to employees at the bars—waitstaff, bartenders, even busboys.

She'd found a valet who'd been arrested ten years earlier for aggravated assault, no conviction, and thought maybe she'd gotten lucky. But the valet, a small Latino in his late twenties, had an unshakeable alibi for two of the attacks, and his physical appearance was at odds with the victims' descriptions—a tall, heavyset man, middle-aged, most likely an Anglo.

Rose dug deeper, as was her way. She investigated the owners of the bars, clearing each one, before turning to the building where the three establishments were located.

There, she hit pay dirt.

The owner of the building was a Caucasian in his forties, six-three, 240 pounds. A dropout from the university, he'd been

arrested or detained on campus a half-dozen times in the past
decade for a variety of offenses, all involving female students.

Harassment, lewd behavior. Sexual battery.

He'd come from a family of influence—a grandfather had been
mayor at one point—so the cases were never investigated as vigor-
ously as they might have been otherwise.

Tucked in one of the files was a handwritten note from an
arresting officer—*The vic says the perp took her sorority pin.*

From a photo array, two of the seven women identified him
as their rapist. One thought he was responsible but couldn't be
sure. The last four, the ones who'd been hospitalized, IDed other
people.

Rose arrested the man at his high-rise apartment, and a team
of investigators searched the premises, uncovering a treasure trove
of items belonging to female college students—clothing branded
with the school's mascot, notebooks and key rings, half-used tubes
of lipstick, and dozens of pieces of jewelry.

And seven sorority pins.

Unfortunately for Rose's case, the seven pins didn't belong to
her victims. They were either for different sororities or of an older
style.

Even worse for the case were the man's lawyers, who threatened
to sue the city for malicious arrest. Their client was an upstanding
member of the community, they said, one who'd be able to provide
airtight alibis for all the assaults.

The man bonded out within hours, and Rose did what frus-
trated cops sometimes do but never talked about. She decided to
get him off the street by whatever means she could. So, she called
in a favor with a narcotics officer, who pulled over the alleged rapist

for a busted taillight and just happened to discover an eight-ball of coke on his floorboard in plain view.

The drugs violated the terms of his bond for the rape charge, so he was sent back to jail, out of circulation at least for a while.

And that had led to our disagreement.

"What was the point?" I'd asked. "You planted evidence to lock up a guy with a clean record—other than the campus arrests."

She'd shrugged. "He's off the street. That counts for something."

"He's got good lawyers," I'd said. "He'll be out in no time. Better to concentrate on the rape investigation, work on breaking the guy's alibis. Look at him for past offenses. Try to find who those other pins belong to."

"Every day he's in lockup is a day he's not hurting some innocent person," she'd said. "You take a win where you can get it."

"That's one way to look at it," I'd said, trying not to get angry. "But is it worth committing a felony?"

She left the room in a huff and we never talked about what she'd done again.

I wish the story had a clean ending, but like many things in life, it did not. The accused, an arrogant loudmouth who'd gotten into a number of fights with other inmates, slipped and fell in the jail shower, hitting his head, resulting in his demise. He was alone at the time, and his death was termed accidental. No water was running and there wasn't any soap on the floor, but nobody much cared about the details, not even his family, who almost seemed relieved.

One footnote to the case: the only alibi his attorneys could provide appeared solid. The accused had hotel receipts for an out-of-town trip when the third woman was assaulted.

So, was he the guy responsible? Who knows? The rapes did stop after he was off the street. Maybe that was just a coincidence. Maybe Rose's actions had achieved some form of justice.

Lutz entered the interview room.

"Your attorney is here." He leaned over the table so our faces were only inches apart. "You killed one of our own. My mission in life is to see you on a one-way bus to Huntsville."

CHAPTER EIGHT

I had a number of clients—insurance companies, banks, CEOs of major corporations, a billionaire with a sex addiction—but most of my work came from one person.

Attorney Mia Kapoor.

Mia specialized in divorces and child custody, practice areas not for the emotionally faint of heart, but she also handled criminal cases, a natural for her since she'd started at the DA's office when she'd graduated from law school fifteen years before.

I'd helped her with a number of cases over the past two years—mostly divorce work—and we'd become good friends.

Mia was five foot two inches tall and soft spoken, affecting a southern lilt when it suited her, despite the fact that her parents were first-generation immigrants from a village in the Punjab region of northern India. She was the smartest person I had ever encountered and the most ruthless. I'd once watched her make a linebacker for the Dallas Cowboys cry during a deposition.

She breezed into the interview room and asked, "Why is my client in handcuffs?"

"Because he killed his ex-wife?" Lutz said. "Or is this a multiple-choice question?"

Mia was dressed like a soccer mom, wearing a pair of yoga pants and an Adidas warm-up jacket over a T-shirt, her usual attire if a court appearance wasn't on the day's calendar. Her skin was sepia colored, a rich reddish brown. Perspiration dotted her forehead like she'd just run up the stairs.

She smiled at Lutz. "Oh, look. We have a comedian." Her voice sounded like Scarlett O'Hara's.

"You can have five minutes." Lutz tapped his watch. "Then schedule a meeting at jail."

"We have a bail hearing in an hour," she said. "I think it would be entirely appropriate to hold my client here until then."

Lutz shrugged. "You got me mistaken for someone who gives a damn what you think."

Mia's eyes narrowed into slits, which I knew was a bad sign for whoever was in her way.

I said, "Give us thirty minutes, Lutz. That's not going to hurt anything."

"Don't tell me what to do, Dylan." He shook his head. "You're lucky—"

Mia snapped her fingers and Lutz stopped talking.

"When I was a prosecutor," she said, "I handled an indecent exposure case, a guy about your age, Sargent Lutz. He used to drop his pants and moon people. Really gave 'em a show."

Lutz stared at her, expression deadpan.

"The case was a slam dunk. We had video of him pulling his butt cheeks apart." She paused. "For some reason, you really remind me of that man's anus."

Lutz gulped, face reddening.

"The video recorder," Mia said. "Unplug it on your way out."

*   *   *

Thirty seconds later we were alone, the recorder disabled.

Mia asked, "What happened?"

I told her, leaving nothing out. She was my attorney, after all, as well as my friend and biggest client.

I began with the out-of-the-blue email from Rose, asking for a meeting, then the story about Josh Gannon, the ex-con who died from a GSW on the hotel grounds. I related how I tailed the Toyota Camry that was following Rose and how we all ended up in the park just north of White Rock Lake.

I said I had fired my pistol at the Camry as it tried to run me over, which meant that the gun shot residue test they performed at the jail would probably come back as positive. I ended with the mysterious revolver lying a few feet away from Rose's body.

"I've already talked to a source at the police," she said. "Your prints are on the revolver."

That was bad news.

"The driver got out of the car." I rubbed my face, trying not to let the panic overcome me. "He must have hit me on the head, and then stuck the gun in my hand."

"Lord have mercy. What have you gotten yourself into?"

Neither of us spoke for a moment.

"The blood." She pointed to my hands. "Mind telling me how that got there?"

"Rose had a wound in her torso. I tried to stop the bleeding."

"She was shot in the face too."

I didn't reply.

"You didn't see that?" Mia raised one eyebrow, her tone edging close to incredulous.

"I was a tad bit disoriented at that point, what with the car almost running me over and somebody nailing me on the skull."

What I didn't say was that maybe I didn't want to see that second wound. Maybe I couldn't get my mind around the fact that a woman I had once been married to—had loved—was dead.

"How's your head?" she asked.

"The paramedics said I was in good shape. Maybe a minor concussion. Take it easy, yadda yadda."

"Well, at least it's minor," she said sarcastically as she stuck her head outside and called for Lutz.

Three minutes later, he entered the room and under Mia's careful supervision, I told my side of the story again, concentrating on the Toyota Camry and the driver.

"A dark gray Camry," Lutz said. "With dealer tags."

I nodded.

"The most nondescript car there is. No plates. How convenient."

Mia leaned across the table. "Detective Lutz, my client is a highly respected former police officer. Might I suggest you dial back the sarcasm and attitude?"

"See you two in court." He grinned like he was enjoying himself before he closed his notebook and left.

When he was gone, Mia said, "Did you tell Rose that you'd take the case? This GSW that she thought was a murder?"

I shook my head.

Mia looked at her watch. "We're in front of a judge soon. I need to change."

"You think you can get me bail?"

"Let's hope so." She smiled and patted my cheek. "You're too pretty for jail."

CHAPTER NINE

For my bail hearing, Mia and I sat in the first row, just behind the defendant's table. Mia was now wearing a tailored blue suit and a white blouse, the latter highlighting the mocha tones in her skin. Detective Lutz sat across the aisle behind the prosecutor.

The courtroom was in the building next to the county jail, a monolithic structure that looked like it had been designed by a Soviet architect in the 1970s.

The room was all hard surfaces, everything gray or brown. Uncomfortable wooden benches, laminate flooring, metal tables for the prosecution and the defense. The only brightness came from an American flag behind the bench. The air smelled like sweat and french fries.

Judge Olive Ramirez was in charge of the proceedings. She had grown up in the barrios of West Dallas, not far from where Bonnie and Clyde had been raised, and she wore her progressive politics like a badge of honor, well known for having served as an advisor for the Innocence Project. She suffered no love lost for the district attorney's office or the Dallas Police Department—a feeling that was mutual.

She and I had a history, too. Ten years earlier, she'd threatened to hold me in contempt because I wouldn't reveal the name of a confidential informant. The CI died soon after during a drive-by shooting so the point became moot.

Several years after that, I made the decision not to arrest a home-less young woman caught up in a narcotics sweep outside a drug house. The woman, clearly an addict, wasn't actually in possession of a controlled substance, so it was up to the discretion of the super-vising officer (me) as to whether she would make the ride downtown.

I saw no benefit to locking up someone who was dope sick, so I arranged for her to be taken to a shelter specializing in addicts.

The young woman was Judge Ramirez's niece.

The judge and I had not spoken since then, and I wondered how she would react to a bail request regarding the State of Texas versus Dylan Fisher on a charge of capital murder.

The assistant DA handling the case was an ambitious man in his late thirties named Garofalo, rumored to be considering a run for Congress.

ADA Garofalo had a tennis court tan and chestnut-colored hair coiffed in a style that could best be described as post-modern tel-evangelist. High and long on the top, wavy on the sides and back. He wore a three-piece blue pinstripe suit and black double-monk shoes.

Judge Ramirez slid on a pair of reading glasses as she picked up a file and called for my case.

Mia and I made our way to the defendant's table.

The judge said, "How does the defendant plead?"

"Not guilty, Your Honor." Mia's voice was loud and clear.

"Does the state wish to make a bail recommendation?" Ramirez asked, scribbling some notes.

Garofalo stood, thumbs hooked in his waistband. "This is a very serious case, Your Honor. The state asks that the defendant be remanded until trial."

Judge Ramirez looked up.

"Mr. Fisher is accused of killing a police officer," Garofalo said. "His ex-wife."

Mia said, "Your Honor, my client is a well-regarded former law enforcement officer with no criminal record."

"He has a history of violence in regard to the victim." Garofalo scowled in my direction.

"Really?" Mia arched an eyebrow. "Do tell."

Garofalo didn't reply, rummaging through his files like he was stalling for time, looking for evidence he knew didn't exist.

Judge Ramirez said, "Has the defendant ever been arrested for domestic violence?"

"Uh, no, Your Honor." Garofalo paused. "Not in the state of Texas anyway."

"Has he ever been arrested for anything?" the judge asked.

Garofalo didn't reply so Mia said, "He has not, Your Honor."

"So what proof of this history of violence can you offer?" the judge asked the ADA.

"His behavior was well known within the police department." Garofalo shrugged.

Mia took a deep breath, fists clenched, her expression indicating she was either going to object or scratch the ADA's eyes out.

"Easy, Ms. Kapoor," the judge said. "I'll take care of this." To Garofalo, she said, "In my court, that doesn't count as proof. Are we clear on that?"

Garofalo nodded. "Yes, Your Honor."

"Anything else?" the judge asked.

Mia Kapoor slid a sheet of paper from her briefcase. "Your Honor, I'd like to call your attention to a statement made by my client about a vehicle he saw at the scene of the crime, a dark gray

Toyota, which was spotted on a traffic camera entering the park right before the murder."

The traffic cam comment set off a whispered conversation between the assistant DA and Detective Lutz, the latter glaring at me every few seconds.

The judge shuffled through her papers until she found what she was looking for. She read silently for a few moments. Then she looked at Garofalo expectantly.

I leaned over to Mia and whispered, "How did you know about the video of the Camry?"

"Same guy who told me about your fingerprints on the murder weapon."

The confab between ADA Garofalo and Lutz went on for a long time, so long that Judge Ramirez cleared her throat and asked, "Does the state wish to comment on this information?"

Lutz held up a finger at the judge.

Garofalo stared at the finger, his eyes wide.

Lutz realized his error and jerked his hand down.

The judge smiled sweetly. "Detective Lutz. Would you please stand?"

Lutz gulped and did so.

"Was there something on the ceiling to which you were pointing?" the judge asked, one eyebrow raised.

"Uh, no, Your Honor."

"Were you testing the wind in the courtroom?"

Lutz licked his lips. "No, Your Honor."

Judge Ramirez rubbed her chin. "Surely, you weren't requesting more time, something that Mr. Garofalo is perfectly capable of handling himself?"

Lutz didn't speak.

Garofalo stood. "Your Honor, may it please the court, I'd like to ask opposing counsel about the source of her information."

"Is it true?" the judge asked. "A car similar to the one in his statement was seen entering the park?"

Garofalo glowered at Lutz for a moment before addressing Judge Ramirez.

"Yes, your Honor," he said. "But that doesn't negate the fact that the accused's fingerprints are on the murder weapon."

The judge rifled through her papers. "The deceased, Sergeant Rose Doucette. Was she working a case?"

Garofalo and Lutz glanced at each other. Neither spoke.

"Was she on the clock?" the judge asked. "Is this a line of duty death?"

Garofalo shook his head. "No, Your Honor. She was not."

"She was off duty?"

"In a manner of speaking." The ADA paused. "Sergeant Doucette had been temporarily suspended from the force at the time of her death."

Mia Kapoor cut a look my way, eyebrows raised.

I didn't say anything, shock tingling up my spine. Rose had told me she was off the case, not off the force—a fairly significant difference. I couldn't imagine what she had done to warrant a suspension. Or why she had lied to me about her status.

Rose Doucette was a cop's cop. Despite being headstrong, she was well liked within the force, respected for her skills and dedication. I wondered if this was related to Josh Gannon's death.

Judge Ramirez nodded and stared at me; eyes half closed. She tapped her pen on the desktop for a few moments, and then set bail at two million dollars. A deposit of 10 percent would be needed to secure my release.

Two hundred thousand dollars. Money I did not have.

Mia let out a breath, either surprised or grateful that bail was an option, no matter the amount. She told the judge that we were prepared to post the bond immediately.

I wondered how but didn't ask. I let myself feel a small sense of relief.

Garofalo looked angry enough to commit murder himself while Lutz tapped furiously on his phone.

Judge Ramirez banged her gavel. Then she asked me to stand.

"I remember you from when you were on the force," she said. "As cops go, you weren't a bad sort."

"Thank you, Your Honor."

She tapped a piece of paper. "I see that you are a private investigator now."

"Yes, ma'am."

"You're not to contact witnesses or anyone connected to this case." She peered directly at my eyes. "In other words, don't investigate. Is that understood, Mr. Fisher?"

"Yes, ma'am."

I hoped my face didn't reflect what I was thinking: *There was no way I wasn't investigating what had happened. My freedom if not my life depended on finding out who had killed Rose Doucette.*

The judge told me I was not to leave the county either, and then called for the next item on her docket. Mia and I exited the courtroom, Detective Lutz staring at me with unabashed loathing.

I was safe, but only for a moment.

Every police officer in Dallas wanted my head on a silver platter, and now that I was free on bond, I was an easy target.

CHAPTER TEN

From the passenger seat of Mia's Volvo station wagon, I stared out the window as the city passed by.

Late afternoon. Traffic was heavy, a torrent of cars clogging the freeways.

Downtown looked like a cluster of glass mountains jutting up from the prairie, multistory totems reaching toward a cloudless, pewter sky, offerings to the gods of commercial real estate and phallic architecture.

Lutz had impounded my pickup as part of the investigation, the search warrant requesting permission to locate "additional ammunition for murder weapon." I would need to arrange alternative transportation since I didn't see the Dallas Police rushing to release the vehicle.

Mia and I hadn't spoken since leaving the courthouse. She made several calls as she drove, rescheduling meetings, getting back to clients who'd called, lawyer stuff.

Her office, a brick bungalow from the 1920s, was nestled under a canopy of sycamore trees only a few blocks from the hotel where Rose and I had met earlier in the day. Mia ended her last call and parked in the driveway but didn't turn off the engine.

"I'm sorry," she said.

"For what?"

"Rose's death."

I nodded, swallowing a lump of emotion rising in my throat.

"I know she was your ex-wife," Mia said, "But it's a big loss. Gotta sting a little."

A loss that I was still processing, my mind more than a little numb from what had transpired.

"The judge gave you good advice. Don't get tangled up in the investigation."

"A little late for that, don't you think?"

She sighed. "You know what I mean."

"Where'd you get the money for my bail?"

Mia was a successful attorney but a sole practitioner. Two hundred thousand was a lot of liquidity to just have lying around.

"Line of credit on the office building," she said. "Sometimes you need to be able to move quickly in situations like these."

I smiled at her. "Like when your favorite PI is arrested?"

"Seriously, Dylan. Don't get involved in the investigation. Ramirez'll be madder than a wet hen."

"Thanks for posting my bond. I promise not to be a flight risk."

We exited the Volvo and entered the office through the back door into the kitchen, an area that looked like a showroom for expensive stainless-steel appliances and marble countertops.

The building had been redone by the previous owner. The hardwood floors were the color of coffee, polished to a high gloss, a nice contrast with the bone-white plaster walls.

Mia's personal office was in the old dining room toward the front of the house. Her assistant, Archie, sat at a desk in the foyer.

Archie was in his mid-twenties but barely looked old enough to drive, despite the gray herringbone suit he wore. He had a thick head of curly auburn hair and a swath of freckles across his cheeks.

Without looking up from his computer, he handed Mia a stack of message slips. Before he could say anything, his desk phone rang.

As he answered, Mia and I tiptoed down the hall toward the back bedroom, which had been turned into a nursery for Mia's eleven-month-old son, Caleb.

The nanny, a Honduran woman named Luna, sat in an easy chair, watching a video on her phone. She looked up when we entered and pointed to the crib where Caleb was snoring.

Mia and Luna had a whispered conversation in Spanish. Feeding times and naps and the diaper situation. Caleb burned through diapers like a frat boy through a case of beer.

Luna smiled at me and tried to bring me into the discussion. I smiled back and thought about explaining to her once again that I wasn't the father nor were Mia and I romantically involved. I doubted she'd believe me, as we'd had the same conversation a number of times.

Senorita Mia. She's a pretty lady. Why don't you like her?

Because we're just friends, Luna. And we work together. That's why.

Like many successful, driven people, Mia didn't have time to date. Plus, much of her caseload consisted of clients eager to dump salt into whatever raw wound they could find on their soon-to-be ex-spouse, which didn't exactly foster a healthy view of family life.

On Mia's thirty-ninth birthday, I'd driven her to a fertility specialist who inseminated her using material from a sperm bank. Nine months later, Caleb Kapoor entered the world to the delight of his mother. And, truth be told, his occasional uncle, yours truly.

I slipped out of the nursery, padded down the hall to the vacant office I used on occasion. There, I sat behind the desk, flicked on the computer, and logged on to the most comprehensive database available to licensed investigators, one that was tied into multiple credit agencies, law enforcement records, and various social media platforms.

Moments later, a relatively complete and accurate portrait of Josh Gannon appeared, a forty-one-year-old white male whose life appeared to have gone off the rails sometime in his late teens, based on the arrest records.

A sad, but unremarkable existence forever damaged by addiction. Nothing unexpected.

Until I clicked on the social media tab and saw the picture of a teenage Josh Gannon standing arm-in-arm with my former wife, Rose Doucette.

1996. A high school football game.

"What are you looking at?" Mia appeared in the doorway.

"Rose and the GSW guy," I said. "They went to school together."

"So, you're all up in it. Like the judge said not to do."

I didn't reply, trying to figure out under what possible scenario Rose would think this information was not important to reveal to me.

Mia Kapoor swore, marched off down the hall.

CHAPTER ELEVEN

Josh had been killed at the hotel; Rose followed from the same place by her assailant. What were the odds of two people who went to high school together being randomly murdered two days apart, twenty-some-odd years after graduation, both killings connected to the same location?

On par with finding a virgin in a whorehouse? The same as being struck by lightning on Friday the 13th? A connection had to exist between Rose and Josh, other than just being old school buddies.

Mia and the judge were right; I should just let this go, let the police do their job. Only problem with that was the police thought I was the killer, and they were planning to go all in toward proving that point. Plus, Rose had asked me to investigate the case, right before she'd been gunned down. I owed her.

To clear my name, not to mention find out who killed Rose, I needed to learn as much as I could about Josh Gannon. Searching online was fine, up to a point. After that, the situation required a boots-on-the-ground-approach, chasing down next of kin and known acquaintances, knocking on doors, knocking on heads if need be.

It was half past seven in the evening, the longest day of my life, and I needed a shower, clean clothes, and some rest before beginning a deep dive on Mr. Gannon.

Mia stalked out of her office without so much as a word of good-bye, Caleb in his car seat.

Guess she was still miffed at me.

I ordered a ride-share and had the driver drop me off on Jefferson Boulevard south of downtown, at a used furniture store.

The furniture store was three blocks from the office where I got my mail, a narrow storefront next to the Texas Theater, the place where Lee Harvey Oswald was arrested after killing President Kennedy and a police officer named J. D. Tippit.

Jefferson was once the main drag for a town called Oak Cliff, a white bread slice of Norman Rockwell's America back in the day, long since annexed by its larger sibling, Dallas.

Now the street looked like a cross between the market in Nuevo Laredo and a hipster neighborhood in Austin—Mexican grocery stores and places selling *quinceañera* dresses interspersed with the occasional shop specializing in artisanal coffee beans and CBD oil.

I fell in walking behind a family of four—a father carrying a toddler and a mother pushing an infant in a stroller. They meandered down the sidewalk, chattering about the day's events in Spanish, munching on ice cream cones.

My official residence was a condo in North Dallas, but there was an upstairs apartment at the office where I spent most nights, preferring this part of town to the antiseptic coldness of my complex.

I followed a few yards behind the family, window-shopping, until we got to the corner of my block. Then I stopped in front of a store that sold folk remedies and religious statues, a *botanica*. I scanned the street, feigning interest in the window display, a plaster rendition of Our Lady of Guadalupe.

I'd been in this office for a year, paying reduced rent because I'd helped the landlord enforce a restraining order against her ex-boyfriend. I was familiar with the rhythms of the neighborhood. Who belonged where. What car was usually parked in which space. That sort of thing.

Everything looked normal at first glance. People similar to the family I'd been behind.

Lots of work trucks and chromed-out SUVs.

The two late model Chevrolet Tahoes backed into spaces across the street from my office stood out in their drabness. They were black with heavily tinted windows and plain rims, and too far away to make out their license plates. They looked like unmarked police cars, except that the Dallas PD's Tahoes were usually white or gray.

I didn't know if the Tahoes were with a federal or state agency or even if they were interested in me at all. But I hadn't made it this far in life by taking chances, so instead of walking in the front door of my office, I headed down the cross street and ducked in the alley.

Thirty seconds later, I stopped by the rear entrance of my office, a metal door usually secured by a dead bolt.

The door was ajar.

I reached for the pistol that was usually on my hip. Remembered it was in police custody. From inside came a rustling noise followed by the sound of footsteps getting louder.

A brick lay on the ground near my feet next to an empty wine bottle.

I grabbed the brick as a man in gray jeans and a black T-shirt stepped outside, his hands clad in latex gloves.

He was fit like an athlete, with close-cropped red hair. As soon as he saw me, his eyes went wide and he reached for his back pocket.

I punched him in the nose with the brick. He fell backwards. I followed him inside.

I was angry. Getting nearly run over, falsely accused of murdering your ex-wife, and then finding someone breaking into your place of business will do that to a person.

Unfortunately for me, he wasn't alone.

The back of the office was a storeroom. After coming inside from the light of a summer evening, it was hard to see, but I could discern the shapes of two others a few feet away.

I swung the brick at the closest one, hitting him on the shoulder.

He rocked backwards as the other guy punched me in the gut. I doubled over. Someone sweep-kicked my leg, and I fell to the floor.

One of them jumped on top of me and began flailing at my head, angry strikes, not doing much damage, but not much fun either.

A voice said, "Stop."

The blows ceased. The man got off me, breathing hard. Probably the guy I'd pissed off by slamming him in the nose with the brick.

I tried to stand but another punch hit my stomach. I curled in the fetal position, struggling for air.

Shoes scuffled on the floor. Then silence.

I pushed myself to my knees, now able to see in the gloom.

The storeroom was empty, all three men gone.

I glanced at my small safe that sat in the corner, bolted to the concrete floor. Scrambling across the room, I opened the safe. Pulled out a pistol. Headed to the front room.

The office area was simple and small, the space only about twelve feet wide, the walls unfinished brick. Curtains hung over the front window and door, blocking people from looking in. A desk from the store down the street sat in the middle facing a sofa and a coffee table.

The room was empty.

I strode to the front window, yanked aside the curtain.

The Tahoes were gone. The front door was unlocked but not damaged, meaning the three thugs had most likely used a lock pick to enter through the rear, and then made a hasty exit out the front.

I secured both doors and surveyed my office, wondering who those guys were and what they were after.

Desk drawers were open, papers scattered about, but nothing appeared to be missing.

My laptop was in a locked drawer that hadn't been opened. Even if they'd managed to gain access to the computer, there wouldn't be much for them to see. In addition to being password protected, I kept the device pristine, clearing search history, cookies, and the cache after every use. No lists of passwords anywhere or secret phrases. No client materials.

I headed upstairs.

The door to the apartment was still locked. The living quarters were simple too. A bedroom and a bath, a living area with a kitchenette in one corner. I didn't sense anything out of place.

Just about every part of my body ached, so I swallowed a couple of aspirin and threw some clothes in a duffel bag, enough for two or three days. This location was compromised, so it was a safe bet my condo was too. I trotted downstairs, opening the ride-share app on my phone as I went.

I headed to the front door, intending to wait for the car by the Texas Theater, and reached for the dead bolt.

A man in his early fifties loomed on the other side of the glass. He wore a pair of Wrangler jeans, a starched khaki shirt, and a straw cowboy hat.

His eyes were cold and empty. He pulled a gun from his waistband and aimed at my face through the glass door.

Rose's husband had found me.

CHAPTER TWELVE

Tito Mullins had married Rose Doucette right after our divorce was final. Minutes after.

He was a criminal defense attorney of some renown, familiar to anyone who spent much time in the trenches of the Dallas County judicial system.

Despite residing on opposite sides of Lady Justice's scales, Tito and Rose had struck up a friendship, often bumping into each other because they used to get coffee from the same place near the courthouse. The friendship had apparently turned into something more while I was serving as an internal affairs officer, wallowing in the gutter with bent cops.

I flipped the dead bolt, opened the door.

Tito's fingers were white on the grip of the gun. His nostrils flared with each breath.

"If you're going to shoot me," I said, "come inside so you don't bother the neighbors."

Tito was a fearsome attorney, a gladiator in the courtroom. He waged war using motions and briefs, expert witnesses, surprise testimony, each tool as effective in his hands as a blade or a bullet.

His prowess as a gladiator on the street was a different story. Actual violence was not something with which he was familiar.

"You killed her." He stepped inside.

His nose was wide and flat, his jaw thick like a chunk of ham. Both body parts seemed like they were in a turf war for control of his mouth.

"Put the gun down before you hurt yourself," I said, pondering once again why Rose had left me for him.

He made a lot of money but that was never a motivator for her. I wondered what he had that I didn't, what need he filled that I couldn't.

Tears welled in his eyes as his arm began to shake.

I realized he loved her as much as I had. Rose was smart and tough and not afraid to speak her mind, qualities valued by men who wanted a partner instead of arm candy. Now she was gone, and a little piece of Tito Mullins had disappeared too.

"Say your prayers." He cocked the hammer. "You got about two seconds before I plug you."

"You're not going to kill me." I reached out, took the gun from his hand.

He offered no resistance.

Tito—who'd grown up in a suburban tract house in Plano, Texas—fancied himself a cowboy. He owned a gentleman's ranch south of town where a hired hand cared for a couple longhorn steers while Tito rode around in a pickup, dipping snuff and talking about the price of cattle feed.

The gun and the hat and the boots, those were part of the Tito Mullins show. *Look at me, I'm a modern-day John Wayne.* Totally believable, too, if the Duke had been reincarnated as a five-foot-six attorney who made a living setting murderers free.

"You may defend killers," I said. "But you're not one."

He rubbed his nose as tears streamed down his face.

"I didn't murder Rose," I said.

"You're lying."

"An adulterer like you, I guess you have a problem recognizing honesty."

Anger flared in his eyes. He balled his hand into a fist.

"Rose reached out to me about a case," I said. "Did she ever mention a guy named Josh Gannon?"

"The cops and the DA's office . . . they're going full tilt on putting you away."

"Tell me something I don't know. Gannon went to high school with Rose. Does that name ring a bell?"

I thought he was going to reply, but instead he surprised us both by punching me in the chin.

He was a small man, his fingers thin and delicate. He didn't pack much of a wallop, but the scope of his anger and sadness was a force unto itself.

I rocked backward, his gun falling from my grasp.

He scooped up the weapon and stuck it in his waistband.

"I'll be in the front row every day for your trial." He raised his fist like he was going to strike again. "And then I'm gonna throw one hell of a party when you get convicted."

I rubbed my jaw. "You hit me again, Tito, I'll break your arm."

He lowered his hand and stepped back like he just realized he'd started a fight with a guy who had a good six inches and fifty pounds on him.

"Tell me about her suspension," I said. "What happened?"

"What the hell are you talking about? She was up for a promotion, getting ready to take the lieutenant's exam. She wasn't s-suspended."

Tears filled his eyes again. He blinked and sniffled, trying to tamp down the emotion.

If he hadn't helped break up my marriage, I might have offered my condolences. But I could carry a grudge to hell and back, so I stayed silent.

He cried softly for a moment and then wiped his cheeks.

"She was going to leave me," he said. "I could see it coming. She'd grown—I don't know—distant, like a different person almost."

An apt description of the last few months of our marriage as well. Rose had changed.

"Forgive me if I'm unable to muster up any sympathy for your marital woes."

"Making jokes now?" he asked. "You think it's funny that you saved me a divorce?"

"There's nothing funny about any of this," I said.

"Everything I've got, whatever the police need. Anything to get your ass nailed for killing my wife." He turned and left, striding down the street.

I stepped outside and watched him drive away in a dual axle, extended cab pickup, the diesel exhaust belching black smoke. The truck was fire engine red with a massive winch on the front grille and extra-large, knobby tires suitable for off-roading in the Moab desert. After he was gone, I locked up and called for a car. I had the driver drop me off at a hotel downtown where the manager owed me several large favors.

The manager was named Eagan and he was eager to help, comping me a suite on the twentieth floor. He registered me under a different name and directed room service to send up dinner. At ten o'clock, I was showered and fed and staring out the window at the city.

I opened the pictures on my phone, scrolled through some old shots.

Our wedding day, June 2003. Rose was radiant in a dress the color of eggshells. I, on the other hand, looked ridiculous in a rented tux, an expression on my face like a small animal about to be run over by an approaching vehicle.

I wondered what had happened to us, how we'd let our marriage go astray. Then I thought about what Tito Mullins had told me and I realized perhaps the better question was what had happened to Rose. And what role had Josh Gannon played in any of that?

I stared at the lights of Dallas.

They grew hazy and indistinct, tears filling my eyes as a deep sadness overcame me, a mourning for the loss of Rose Doucette and all that was never to be.

CHAPTER THIRTEEN

The hotel hooked me up with a rental car the next morning, the only one available on short notice being an ivory-colored Cadillac Escalade with 22-inch chrome rims. Not exactly nondescript, but Eagan my manager friend got me the employee discount, so who was I to complain?

I needed to canvass the area where Rose had been killed—the park and whatever was nearby—but since that was an active crime scene, and I was the number one suspect, I thought that might wait for a day or two. Instead, I decided to concentrate on Josh Gannon.

According to the database results from yesterday, Gannon's last address before he went to the penitentiary was in East Dallas. An internet search of the address turned up a place called the Lifeline House, a residential facility for people with substance abuse issues.

I left the hotel and headed east. Fifteen minutes later, I parked the Escalade across the street from a large ramshackle structure that looked as if it had started life as a mansion at the turn of the last century, its white columns picketing a wraparound porch.

Maybe it had been the home of a doctor or a banker, someone who appreciated the finer things in life. Now it was a dilapidated dowager in a neighborhood the original owner wouldn't recognize, sitting between a pawnshop and a KFC.

A skinny white guy in a sleeveless undershirt and cutoffs sat on the front steps, drinking coffee and smoking. His age was difficult to determine, somewhere between forty and sixty, all of those years hard ones.

I exited the SUV, chirped the locks.

He glanced at the Escalade as I approached. "If you're slinging dope, go somewhere else."

"I'm in a different line of work. You the manager?"

"Who wants to know?" He stubbed out the cigarette. The old needle scars on his arms looked like earthworms—gray, the color of decay—stark against pale skin.

I pulled a twenty from my wallet. "Not looking to jam anybody up."

"My official title is house supervisor." He took the bill.

"How long you been here?"

"Five years." He lit another cigarette. "Right after I got clean."

"There was a guy who lived here a while back. Josh Gannon. You remember him?"

A moment passed as he smoked, his gaze alternating between me and the Cadillac.

"People start coming around here asking about a dude like Josh, one of 'em in a gangster mobile . . . makes me nervous."

"Who else has been asking?"

He looked at the twenty in his hand, and then at me. I handed him two more. He stuffed the money in his wallet and said, "Josh was a resident here for a while. Not long."

"Why'd he leave?"

"This place is the rock bottom of the rock bottom," he said. "If you end up here, you're working on your last chance. Most people understand that. A few don't."

"For sixty bucks, I need you to flesh out the details a little."

"Some people can't get past themselves," he said. "You gotta let go, so the program can work. Whatever Josh was holding onto, it was eating him up."

"Any idea what that was?"

"If I knew—and I don't—I wouldn't tell you."

"Gotcha. The anonymous part."

He nodded as a Dallas County sheriff's squad car pulled up behind the Escalade. Two deputies in the front, a third guy in the back.

My heart rate cranked up a notch. The Dallas Police and the sheriff's department weren't exactly besties, but blue backs blue, especially when a fellow officer's been killed. Had they followed me? Was this the beginning of a harassment campaign orchestrated by Lutz?

"Not a fan of the five-O?" The house supervisor must have noticed my expression.

Before I could reply, the deputy behind the wheel got out and marched across the street and up the sidewalk.

I tried to keep my face blank. After all, I wasn't breaking any laws, just explicit instructions from a judge who could revoke my bail at any time. No need to panic. Yet.

The deputy ignored me and spoke to the house supervisor.

"Any rooms open?"

The supervisor shrugged. "What do you got?"

"My wife's cousin. He stole a gurney and a bunch of Oxys from an ambulance. I ought to take him downtown, but my in-laws hate me enough already."

The house supervisor said, "Bring him in."

"Thanks. I owe you." The deputy glanced at me and then headed back to his car.

When he was out of earshot, the house supervisor said, "You look like a cop, but you're scared of them. That's gonna keep me up tonight."

I pulled a fifty from my wallet, my last cash other than a few fives and ones.

"Find something else to ponder." I held the bill out of reach. "Tell me who else has been asking about Josh Gannon."

He slid a business card from his pocket and held it out, offering the card in exchange for the fifty. I nodded and we made our trade. The card was for a reporter at an alternative news outlet, one of those places that had a lot of ads for escorts and clean urine, a small but influential weekly publication that broke big stories, both online and in print.

"You know what else is gonna keep me up tonight?" he asked. "Wondering why everyone's so interested all of a sudden in one little bitch-ass junkie."

I headed back to the Escalade, wondering the same thing.

CHAPTER FOURTEEN

I left the Lifeline House and stopped a few blocks later, idling in front of a convenience store, away from the deputy sheriff and his addict cousin-in-law. There, I googled the reporter's name on my phone.

Madge Boatwright had written a number of high-profile stories, including an exposé about a sex ring operating out of the local office of a defense contractor and another about the president of a major bank who had ties to the Aryan Brotherhood. As far as I could tell, her stories had no common theme except for their ability to generate attention-grabbing headlines.

I searched her name in conjunction with Rose Doucette and Josh Gannon, together and separately. Nothing. Her name and variations on drugs and addiction yielded too many hits to sift through.

I could call or email her, but one thing cops learned early on was to have a healthy wariness when it came to reporters. Off-the-record could be a fluid concept and one I didn't want to explore right now while under strict orders to stay the hell off the case.

Josh Gannon's address prior to the Lifeline House was on the opposite side of town, Lively Lane in northwest Dallas, the same street where Rose had grown up, most likely his parents' place.

The neighborhood used to be blue-collar, small homes constructed in the fifties for working-class families. In the 1990s, much of the area turned Hispanic, first- and second-generation immigrants freshening the elderly houses.

Now, the lots were worth so much that developers were eating their way down the streets like platoons of Pac-Men, demolishing the wood-framed structures and replacing them with houses quadruple the size, dwellings with modernistic masonry facades and xeriscape yards.

Maybe three-quarters of the lots on Gannon's old block had been redeveloped, giving the street an uneven feel, the old one-stories at odds with the new, taller houses.

The original home at Josh Gannon's address had been demolished. The replacement was a mishmash of glass and stone, all angles and hard lines, like the guesthouse at a Bond villain's lair. A builder's FOR SALE sign was in the front yard.

Across the street was one of the older places, a small but tidy house with a fresh coat of white paint and an American flag hanging from a pole by the front door.

A man in his seventies was in the yard, raking a lawn so green that it looked like something out of a fertilizer ad. He resembled the rake, tall and thin, except for the liver spots and red blotches dotting his pale skin.

I parked, exited the SUV, and approached him.

The man stopped raking and stared at the Escalade.

"Morning," I said.

He wore a Vietnam veteran ball cap. He removed the cap, fanned himself. "Let me save you some time. I'm not interested in selling."

"Uh, okay."

"I know you realtor types in your fancy cars," he said.

Note to self: find new transportation as soon as possible.

"You're here to smooth-talk an old man into moving from his home of forty years." He put the cap back on. "Not gonna happen."

"You get bothered a lot by realtors?"

"Every week seems like. This is my home, fellow. Only way I'll leave is feetfirst."

I pointed to his hat. "Thanks for your service."

He frowned, obviously not sure how to respond.

"Where were you during the war?" I asked.

"Loc Ninh. Near Cambodia." He paused. "I was there in January of '68. The Tet Offensive."

"When I was a cop, I worked with a guy who was there at the same time," I said. "He told me the VC poured over the wire like water."

The old man nodded. "I can still hear 'em. When they rushed us, before the shooting started, the slap of their sandals. There were so damn many."

It was hot and humid. His skin had grown paler.

"You okay?" I asked.

He blinked like he was shaking off a bad dream. Then nodded.

"I'm a private investigator, not a realtor," I said. "You remember the family who used to live across the street? The Gannons?"

"They moved to Houston a couple years back. They got a daughter down there."

"You remember their son, Josh?"

"What exactly are you investigating?"

"Josh Gannon died several days ago. I'm looking into the circumstances of his death."

He shook his head warily. "Drugs?"

"I don't know. Maybe. Was that an issue with him when he was younger?"

"That boy was a troublemaker from the get-go. Ten years old, he and his buddy from down the street almost got arrested for throwing rocks at cars."

"Who was the buddy?"

"Another punk. Boyd."

Rose's younger brother was named Boyd.

"Punk" wasn't a word I'd use to describe my former brother-in-law. Loser seemed more fitting. Boyd was a nice guy but a doormat. Rose, who was a good sister, used to say things like "he has a lot of unfulfilled potential" or "he's just having trouble finding himself." He also had trouble with getting to work on time more than one day in a row and not screwing up the simplest of tasks.

"Boyd Doucette?" I said. "He was Josh's buddy?"

"That's the one. They were thick as thieves. Hell, they were thieves. Stole my inflatable Santa one year."

"Do you remember Boyd's sister?" I asked. "Her name was Rose."

He nodded. "That poor girl. She carried the weight of the world on her shoulders."

The image of Rose as a child caused a knot to form in my throat. Riding her bike down the sidewalk. Playing with her friends. Being a kid.

"She was just a kid," he said. "The only functional human in that house, let me tell you. Stepfather drunk, mother running around with all kinds of men."

That was a tidbit she'd never mentioned, her mother's affairs.

"The mother really went off the deep end after that one summer," he said. "Guess they all did."

"Which summer would that be?"

He gave me a suspicious look, squinting, lips pressed together.

"Time for my blood pressure medicine." He picked up the rake.

"Just a couple more questions. I'll be quick."

"All that was a long time ago," he said. "Besides, the police told us not to talk about it."

CHAPTER FIFTEEN

For an old guy he moved pretty quickly.

Before I could press him on what he wasn't supposed to talk about, he darted inside, leaving the rake against the side of the house. A second later came the metallic click of the dead bolt locking.

I got back in the Escalade, turned on the AC, pecked out some notes on my phone. Date, location, address, and description of the interviewee followed by a brief summary of what we'd discussed. I highlighted the most important points.

What summer / what happened?? Boyd Doucette & Josh Gannon buddies. Then and now?

Rose's mother—WTF? Find Boyd!

I put the phone down and drove the half-block to where Rose and her family had lived. The house was still there, a sad little place that was years past needing a new coat of paint, the wood siding rotten in places, the yard mostly weeds and dirt.

I looked up the address on the county website, saw that it had sold at least a half-dozen times in the past decade, so there was little chance that whoever lived there now would know anything about the Doucette siblings.

Rose and I had been married for a long time and she'd only shown me her old house once, a Christmas Eve when neither of us had to work. When I asked her to drive me by her childhood home, she'd done so reluctantly, her silence speaking volumes. There'd been no stories about the tire swing hanging from the old oak tree or the keepsake ornaments on the Christmas tree.

When I pressed her, she slipped her hand into mine and said, "Why go back to all that?"

I stared at the house for a while, wondering what it had been like growing up within those walls.

And what had happened during that unknown summer.

*   *   *

The last time I'd seen Rose's brother was eight years ago when he had been working at a bowling alley in Irving, one of the small cities between Dallas and Fort Worth. The bowling alley was old school, a throwback to a simpler time when beehive hairdos were fashionable and cigarettes were considered an essential food group.

Boyd was the assistant mechanic, in charge of the machines that set the pins. He'd always excelled at two things—taking care of animals and working with his hands, so the job was a good fit, at least in terms of the latter.

Rose had made the homicide squad by that point, and I was two years into a stint with the Criminal Intelligence Unit, a prestige assignment that put me in regular contact with officers at various departments in the area.

So, it was normal that a shift commander from the Irving PD would call me. What wasn't normal was the reason for his call.

Boyd Doucette had locked himself in a storeroom at the bowling alley with another employee, a teenaged boy with Down syndrome, and was refusing to come out. He was asking for his sister, Rose, a Dallas cop, who the Irving shift commander knew to be my wife.

Complicating the situation was the fact that Boyd had taken a butcher knife from the kitchen and was threatening anyone who came after him.

I called Rose and we arranged to meet at the bowling alley as soon as possible. As I drove, I tried to figure out what could have set off Boyd. My brother-in-law didn't threaten people. He barely had the wherewithal to complain about his order at a restaurant, much less hold someone hostage.

The bowling alley smelled like stale beer and fried onions. Most of the lanes were occupied even though it was the middle of the day, and a number of police officers were clustered around a door by the restrooms marked EMPLOYEES ONLY.

The Irving cop in charge, a Vietnamese woman in her forties named Tran, pointed to a man in a booth holding an ice pack against his face.

"Before he locked himself in the storeroom," she said, "your brother-in-law punched a customer."

"Any idea why?" I asked.

"Who knows? According to the manager, he's been hinky all day."

Boyd Doucette suffered from bouts of anxiety. He was a worrier, obsessing over the smallest of things. Sometimes medication eased his symptoms, sometimes not.

I approached the customer, a slim man in his thirties wearing a pair of khakis and a navy-blue polo shirt. The guy was about as threatening as a piece of spaghetti.

"You all right?" I asked.

He lowered the ice pack and shrugged. He had blond hair and fair skin, and the shiner forming under his eye promised to be a doozy.

"What's your name?" I slid into the other side of the booth.

"Max."

"Hi, Max. My name is Dylan. Can you tell me what happened?"

"I was just waiting for a friend of mine." Max was shaky from adrenaline, words spilling out. "Then this guy showed up and hit me."

"The guy that hit you. Do you know him?"

"Never seen him before."

"Did you speak to him beforehand?"

He shook his head.

"Did he speak to you?"

Max nodded. "'Stay away.' That's what he said right before he hit me."

I was about to ask if he had any idea what that meant, other than the obvious, when Rose arrived.

She looked at Max and his ice pack, her lips pressed together. I filled her in on what had happened. She asked a couple of questions and continued to stare at the man and his blackening eye. Max stared back.

"What's going on?" he asked. "You know that guy or what?"

"You need to get the hell out of here," Rose said to Max. "He won't come out if you're around."

I winced. When she was stressed, my wife could be a tad abrupt.

Max was starting to piece things together. The Irving Police had responded to the call. Then a guy in a Dallas PD uniform showed up and started asking him questions. Then another cop, a woman who was obviously connected to the guy who hit him, arrived.

"What the hell is this about?" he asked. "You're telling me to get out of here like it's my fault or something?"

"He didn't mean to hit you," Rose said. "You don't understand."

I didn't understand either, but one thing cops never did was let on to a civilian that they weren't up to speed on whatever was happening.

"He punched me in the face." Max jumped to his feet. "What's there to understand?"

Rose's lips compressed into a thin line. Before she could reply, I told Max to sit tight; I'd be right back. I pulled Rose off to one side.

"You need to tiptoe on this one," I said. "Let's see if we can keep Boyd from getting an assault on his record."

Officer Tran had followed us. "You the sister?" she said to Rose. "There's a bunch of witnesses. If that guy wants to press charges, we're going to have to let him."

Rose rubbed her forehead, looking tired all of a sudden.

"We'll take him to the station," Tran said. "Hold him out of booking. Maybe the vic'll decide not to go forward."

"I appreciate anything you can do," Rose said. "My brother's not a violent guy."

Officer Tran and I looked at each other, both of us confused at what constituted "not violent" in this situation.

I pulled a business card from my wallet and approached Max. "This has my cell number. If you ever need help from the police, give me a call."

He took the card and stared at it.

"I'd be angry in your situation too. But if you could see your way to not pressing charges, I'd really appreciate it."

He grumbled for a moment. Then he nodded and stalked out of the bowling alley.

When he'd left the premises, I found Rose by the storeroom, talking to her brother through the door. "He's gone, Boyd. I promise."

Tran and I glanced at each other, neither of us sure what was going on.

"Whoever's in there with you," Rose said. "They're safe too."

"I just wanted him to stay away," Boyd said. "Stay-away-stay-away-stay-away."

Even muffled by the door, his voice was loud, tinged with hysteria.

"Shh, calm down," Rose said. "Just come out and everything will be okay."

Silence.

I whispered to Rose, "What's going on?"

She didn't answer.

"Who's he afraid of?" I asked.

She sighed, covered one eye with her hand like she had a headache. "Nobody. He just gets . . . confused."

I realized with a start that she wasn't being truthful. Her tone of voice, her body language, everything indicated she was hiding something. The strange part was I didn't know if she even realized it.

After a moment, the door opened. The Irving officers moved closer, pistols drawn.

"He doesn't have a gun," Rose said. "Please. Let me take care of this."

The lead cop hesitated, and then nodded, and they all lowered their weapons. Boyd stepped out, his hands up. His hair was mussed, lips trembling with emotion.

I darted inside, found the other employee, a young man sitting on the floor playing a game on his phone, oblivious to what was happening. I hustled him away, handing him off to the manager in the restaurant area.

When I got back to the storeroom, Rose was holding her brother in her arms, telling him that everything was all right.

She almost sounded like she meant it.

CHAPTER SIXTEEN

There wasn't much more for me to learn on Lively Lane. The longer I stared at Rose's old house, the sadder the structure appeared, almost like it was getting smaller and less distinct among the newer, larger homes, a shadow fading as the light grew stronger.

I put the Escalade in gear and tapped my finger on the wheel, debating my next move.

When I'd left the hotel that morning, I had checked several news outlets for reports of Rose's death. Only one had picked up the story, the local paper, a mention in the metro crime section about an off-duty Dallas officer who had died from a gunshot wound near White Rock Lake. No name was released, pending next-of-kin notification.

Rose didn't have a big family, a few cousins here and there, and an uncle who lived in Denver. Rose's next of kin were her husband, Tito Mullins; her brother, Boyd, whereabouts unknown; and her mother, currently living in the memory care unit of a local nursing home. The stepfather had died not long after Rose graduated from high school.

Tito had obviously been notified, so I wondered why the police were trying to sit on the story. Was it an image thing? *Drama at the DPD! Former internal affairs officer accused of murdering his ex-wife.* Or was something else at play?

In any event, the news blackout wouldn't last forever. To prove that point, a reporter acquaintance at the paper texted me, looking for a comment (i.e., information) on Rose's death.

I ignored the message and drove away from the shabby little house on Lively Lane, my ultimate destination Mia Kapoor's office. I hadn't spoken to Mia since the previous evening, and I imagined she was still angry.

Time to make amends. Also, searching for Boyd Doucette would be easier in an office environment on a computer instead of a phone. Perhaps I wouldn't mention that to her.

Before beginning my search, I made a quick stop at an independent bookstore near Inwood Road, a charming little place called Interabang. Even though he wasn't a year old yet, Caleb Kapoor loved books, a passion I liked to encourage by reading to him as much as possible. We were currently working our way through a series about a caterpillar who wore a red hat, a character who Caleb found hysterical. I bought the next three titles and then headed to Mia's.

The street was crowded. A white service van was directly in front of the office, so I parked in the driveway. Luna's car and the one belonging to Mia's assistant were in the back. Mia's Volvo was nowhere to be seen.

I entered through the front door.

Mia's assistant, Archie, was at his desk in the foyer, tapping on his phone. He spoke without looking up. "Internet's down again."

Despite having been remodeled only a few years before, the building was old and had constant problems with its internet and phone service.

So much for searching on the big computer. I headed toward my office anyway.

"Glad Mia called somebody new," he said. "That guy who used to come out could never get everything working at the same time."

I stopped. "Somebody new?"

"The dude in the back. He said Mia called."

Mia Kapoor was frugal like a Depression-era farmer or whatever the Indian equivalent was, taking after her parents who had struggled financially during their early years in this country. The regular IT person owed her money for legal services. There was no way she would have brought in someone new if it meant she'd have to write a check.

I slid my pistol from its holster, kept my voice low. "Where's Caleb?"

The sight of the gun made Archie go pale. "Uh-uh-uh, in th-the nursery."

"Mia?"

"C-c-court." His teeth chattered.

"Go outside." I pointed to the front door. "Stay there until I come and get you."

He darted to the exit as I headed toward the back of the building.

A closet in the hallway served as the mechanical room where the server and phone equipment were kept. The door was open, blocking my view of the back half of the hall.

I ducked inside Mia's office, the one closest to the front. It was empty.

A few seconds later came the heavy clod of footsteps in the hallway. The noise got louder, and then softer. Finally, silence.

I needed to get to Caleb. I stuck my head out of the office, peered down the hall.

The door to the mechanical room was shut.

A man in coveralls and a brown cap was at the end of the hall-way by the entrance to the kitchen. He had a small backpack over one shoulder, a phone in his hand. He moved the phone around like he was looking for a signal of some sort.

A tiny bit of red hair was visible below the edge of his cap. He turned enough for me to see the bandage on his nose from where I had hit him with a brick yesterday. He turned some more, moving the phone this way and that, still searching.

Then he saw me.

The worst-case scenario played out in my mind. He would draw a weapon and start shooting with an infant in a room only a few feet away.

I couldn't let that happen. I holstered my gun and charged after him, my only thought to protect Caleb no matter what.

He dashed away, disappearing into the kitchen.

The hallway was short, and I got there only a couple seconds later, but he was gone, the back door wide open.

I didn't pursue him though I dearly wanted to. Instead, I ran to the nursery, heart pounding, and slung open the door.

Luna was in the easy chair, reading a magazine, Caleb in his crib sleeping.

"*Hola*," Luna said.

"Hi. Everything all right?" I tried to keep my voice soft and normal sounding. She frowned.

Maybe I wasn't as normal sounding as I thought.

She nodded.

I left the nursery. Went outside.

The white van was gone.

Archie stood on the porch, taking deep breaths. He pointed to the spot where the van had been. "The IT guy just ran outside and drove off."

"Did he see you?"

Archie blinked several times, no doubt pondering if he was in any danger. He said, "I don't know." A few seconds passed. "I don't think so. He was in real hurry."

"Stay here." I went back inside and searched the entire house, every closet and cubbyhole. It was empty, except for those of us who belonged. But that didn't mean it was clean.

I called a friend who specialized in electronic eavesdropping and computer security. He said he could be there within a half hour.

I opened the front door and told Archie he could come back inside but to stay off his computer. Then, I went to the nursery and picked up Caleb, holding him tight. He smelled like talcum powder and warm milk. Like innocence.

Breath caught in my throat as I let myself think about how close to danger he'd been because of me.

I squeezed him tighter, not wanting to let go.

*   *   *

My tech friend was true to his word, arriving thirty minutes later with a duffel bag full of equipment—scanners and laptops and strange devices with a multitude of screens and dials. He inserted thumb drives into all the computers and let the software do its thing while he scanned each room for eavesdropping devices, both audio and video.

Forty-five minutes later, he found me in the nursery, bouncing Caleb on my knee. I told Luna to take a break, and she left the room.

After she'd gone, my tech friend said, "This place was filthy. Spyware on all the machines, cameras everywhere, phones tapped."

"Are we clean now?"

He nodded. "This was some high-end stuff. Not the run-of-the-mill nanny cam crap you buy on Amazon."

From the nursery, I heard the back door open and the sound of high heels clicking on the kitchen floor. Mia had returned from court.

My tech friend said, "Whatever you've gotten yourself into is big-time. Watch your back."

CHAPTER SEVENTEEN

He left and a few moments later, Mia stepped into the nursery, leather briefcase slung over one shoulder. She was dressed for battle in a black blazer and matching skirt over a light blue blouse.

"How was court?" I asked.

She walked across the nursery and picked up her son, kissing him on the forehead.

"I had an interesting day," I said.

She fussed over Caleb, tugging on his onesie, pointedly not speaking to me.

"You're going to have to talk to me eventually," I said.

"Is that written down somewhere?" she asked. "Some codicil of man-law I don't know about?"

"C'mon. Don't be lawyery."

She rolled her eyes, an exasperated look on her face.

"Court was awesome," she said. "A public defender OD'ed in the men's room on the second floor, and I'm pretty sure my judge was hungover. Who was the guy with the backpack?"

I searched for the right words, finally settling on: "He swept the office for bugs."

She stopped fussing with Caleb and stared at me, eyes wide.

"We need to talk," I said.

Her brow knitted, the look people get when they know bad news is coming but they don't know what it is or how bad it might be.

She sat in the easy chair, Caleb in her lap, while I explained what had happened during the last eighteen hours.

I told her about the Chevy Tahoe guys searching my other office the night before. I described the one with red hair that I'd clocked with a brick who turned up this morning to work on the network, supposedly at her request.

Then I recounted the meeting at the Lifeline House followed by the interview with the old neighbor when I learned something happened with Josh and Boyd one summer, something that the police didn't want people to talk about.

She held Caleb close throughout.

When I was finished, I said, "And now this has ended up on your doorstep."

"Where my child is." She stroked her son's head, staring into the distance.

Her expression was blank, but I imagined she felt the same way I did. Angry and fearful.

The child was everything. For her and for me.

"It's not your fault," she said.

Intellectually, I knew that was right. The Tahoe squad hadn't broken into my office or wiretapped Mia's place because I'd done a database search for Josh Gannon. They had appeared because of my past connection to Rose.

However, I was still more than a little shaky that the bad guys had only been a few feet from Caleb.

Neither of us spoke for a while, lost in thought.

"You're an investigator," Mia said. "Walk me through what all this means."

I tried to organize the details in my mind, but there were too many unconnected pieces. Instead, I started at a more basic level. "Tell me why you would kill someone."

She raised her eyebrows but didn't speak.

I counted off motives on my fingers. "Revenge, right? Or jealousy. Or maybe a crime of passion—"

"To stop somebody from talking."

She was right. The other motives didn't quite fit this scenario. What made more sense, at least at this point, was someone wanted to silence Josh Gannon and Rose Doucette.

"Talking about what?" I asked.

"That's the question, isn't it?" She put Caleb in his crib. "What do you know about that summer?"

I shook my head. "Nothing. Don't even have a clue what year it was."

"How long were you two together?"

"Over fifteen years. We met when she was twenty-two. Married a year later."

"And she never alluded to an incident that occurred during a summer before you two hooked up? She'd have been young, obviously. Maybe still in high school or before that even."

I remembered talking with Rose about everything and anything, and then some. The early years of a relationship are like that.

Our likes and dislikes. Both of us were die-hard Cowboys fans, despite their lack of success in the post-Aikman era. She liked rom-coms and watching the Oscars nominees every year; I thought that quality filmmaking began and ended with Clint Eastwood westerns.

Starting a family was a major topic. We tried for a while, but after a certain point we both agreed that perhaps it wasn't meant to be. I often wondered if Rose was secretly relieved since our respective careers weren't exactly conducive to a stable home life.

"Nothing comes to mind about a summer," I said. "Rose never talked much about her past, beyond the basics."

"Anybody you could ask?"

"Her current husband?" I told her about my encounter with Tito the night before.

"Anybody but him," she said. "Who else?"

"Rose's mother—but she's got dementia—and Boyd, who's off the grid. Long shots."

Caleb squawked, the sound he made when he was hungry. Mia texted Luna for a bottle.

I stood, prepared to leave.

"You can stay," she said. "You know that."

Being with her and the child for feedings was a strange feeling for me, awkward and comforting at the same time.

I was intruding into something sacred. On the other hand, there was a warmth to being present. No matter what else was going on in the world, some things were constant. Like a baby's hunger. Or a mother's love.

Luna brought a bottle.

Mia took it and nestled Caleb against her breast. "How are you doing with her death?"

"What do you mean?" I stared at the floor, listening to the infant coo.

Sometimes I wondered if the feeling I got when Mia was with her child was a way for me to chase away the ghosts of what might have been with Rose.

Feelings were complicated. That's why I tried to avoid them whenever possible.

She sighed. "Do you miss her?"

I opened my eyes but didn't reply.

"It's okay if you do." Mia stroked the infant's head. "Be careful, Dylan. You're the closest thing to a father my baby has."

I swallowed a lump of emotion and left the room.

CHAPTER EIGHTEEN

On the freshly de-virused computer in Mia's spare office, I searched for Boyd Doucette.

Where Josh Gannon had left a number of footprints in the sands of modern life, Boyd's trail was practically invisible.

Only one hit on the NCIC, the National Crime Information Center database run by the FBI, the bowling alley arrest, which didn't result in charges being filed. A driver's license that had expired seven years ago. No bank accounts. Last credit activity was five years ago. Last known address was from that same credit record, an apartment in North Dallas off Midway Road.

I googled the address and saw the apartment was gone, now just a tract of vacant land.

Something tickled the back of my brain, however, something about that being Boyd's last address.

I stood and paced.

The apartment was his last *official* address, according to the database.

But three years ago, right before Rose and I split, I had driven her to see Boyd at their uncle's house, the man who moved to Denver not long after. Boyd had been living there, as I recalled.

The details were fuzzy. I'd stayed in the car taking a call about a case I'd been working.

I entered a new search and found the uncle's place in the Lake Highlands section of Dallas. The house had sold about the time I remembered him moving out of town. The current owner was a company of some sort, meaning the place was likely a rental. I also discovered that Rose's uncle had died earlier this year, eliminating one more possible information source.

Her uncle's house was in the same part of town as the nursing home where Rose's mother lived.

A twofer. Neither was likely to yield results, but a good investigation meant you followed every lead, no matter how far-fetched they seemed.

I headed toward the front door. Mia was in the foyer.

"When was the last time you ate?" she asked.

Whatever I said was going to be the wrong answer, so I shrugged. She marched me to the kitchen and made me sit while she heated up a plate of her mother's lamb vindaloo.

I had a complicated relationship with both Mia's mother and her vindaloo.

The mother wasn't sure what to make of me, the guy who was always around, but was not romantically involved with her daughter. I think she suspected me of being Caleb's biological father, despite Mia assuring her otherwise. She was an educated woman, recently retired from a prestigious position at a tech firm. But she'd been raised in a different culture, and she'd never quite made peace with the concept of a sperm bank.

Her vindaloo was as hot as the surface of the sun, but once you got past the agony, the flavors were amazing—a melding of cinnamon and cumin and too many other spices to count. Under

Mia's watchful eye, I ate as fast as possible, washing down the fiery chunks of lamb with a glass of milk. Finished, I stepped into the nursery to give Caleb a hug. Then, I headed out to talk to my former mother-in-law.

*   *   *

I once had a partner who called nursing homes "warehouses of death," and I remembered his comment as I entered the Holly Oaks Assisted Living Facility, a low-slung building behind a Motel 6.

A half dozen people in wheelchairs were in the entryway. A couple of them were looking through the glass doors, staring longingly outside. The rest were asleep.

Despite the fact it was August, the temperature inside was kept warm to the point of being uncomfortable, and the air smelled like rubbing alcohol mixed with the faint odor of human waste. *Warehouse of despair* seemed more appropriate.

I used a fake name and signed in with the woman at the front desk. If this had been a facility for children, I would have been required to provide ID and a reason for my visit. But the rules were different for old people, and she barely glanced up as she directed me down a hallway to a set of closed doors where an orderly buzzed me in. The orderly, a heavyset young man who reeked of cigarettes, led me to Gloria Doucette's room, a corner unit.

The room was nice. The walls were a pleasant shade of yellow, pale like a winter sun, the color matching the flowers on the bed's comforter.

A dozen or more pictures were arrayed on the dresser.

The largest had been taken in the mid-1970s, Gloria with her first husband, Rose's father, on their wedding day. Rose's father had sideburns reaching almost to his chin, and he wore a baby blue tuxedo with a ruffled dress shirt.

Gloria was dressed in a similar fashion, but she possessed a timeless quality, the happiness evident in her eyes. She looked a lot like Rose at the same age, petite, her hair thick and dark, a dimple in her chin.

Forty-some-odd years later, my ex-mother-in-law sat in a rocker in the corner of a clean but depressing room, a quilt in her lap, staring out the window at the dumpsters behind the motel across the alley, her hair thin and gray. She turned and saw me. She smiled but didn't speak.

I smiled back. "Hi. You remember me?"

"Billy. Good to see you."

I had no idea who *Billy* was. That wasn't the name of either husband.

"You came to get me," she said. "About time."

"I don't think they're going to let you leave."

She waved her hand dismissively. "Ah, what do you know?"

I peeked again at the pictures on the dresser.

There was one I remembered, a copy that we'd had in our home. Rose, Boyd, and Gloria sat on the front steps of the house on Lively Lane. Rose was maybe twelve or thirteen, Boyd a year younger. They were both all arms and legs, gawky and awkward looking, Boyd wearing big horn-rimmed glasses and high-waisted jeans. No one was smiling.

"You been to the Cockpit Tavern lately?" Gloria asked. "I could do with a burger and a beer. Maybe a little Cutty Sark for dessert."

The Cockpit Tavern was a bar near Love Field that had been popular back in the day. It was a place to drink and make bad decisions, the food an afterthought.

"They're not feeding you well here?" I asked.

She looked out the window again, the tilt of her head and the way she settled back in the chair indicating she'd forgotten about me.

I returned to the pictures.

There was a recent shot of Tito and Rose. Tito was dressed like George Strait. He wore a starched button-down and a belt buckle the size of a dinner plate. Rose wore a sleeveless black dress. She had a smile on her lips, a twinkle in her eyes.

I clenched my fists, the image making me angry. I took a deep breath, tried to stifle the feeling.

"What am I going to do about Phil?" Gloria asked.

Phil was her second husband. Rose's stepfather.

"He got so drunk the other night, he wet the bed." She rubbed her chin.

"What do you want to do?"

"He tried to take the money. I didn't tell you that, did I?"

"What money?"

From what I could gather, the family had been nearly destitute for much of Rose's childhood. Rose let it slip one time that they'd been on food stamps for a short period.

Gloria swiveled her head and looked at me like she was thinking about something, a riddle or nagging question.

"You ever feel bad about what we did?" she said.

I didn't answer, trying to figure out if she meant her relationship with whomever Billy was or something else.

"You were always nice to me." She sounded weepy, eyes filmy with tears.

Tucked among the pictures was one of our wedding day, the same shot I had on my phone. Rose had to have put it there. I wondered why.

"You're a nice person, Gloria." I picked up another photo. "How's Boyd?"

"Who?"

"Your son. Boyd." I examined the picture.

Rose, maybe a year or two after the shot on the front steps of Lively Lane. She was standing next to her brother and another boy about the same age. All three were wearing T-shirts and shorts, the front of the shirts marked with the logo of what looked like a summer camp.

I recognized the third person from the online search yesterday. Josh Gannon.

Outside, a homeless man was rummaging through the dumpster behind the motel. Inside, Gloria watched the man and whimpered.

"Are you okay?" I asked.

"What is he doing?" she whispered.

"I don't know. Trying to survive?"

She pulled the quilt tight around her legs. "Isn't that what we're all trying to do?"

Wisdom came from the unlikeliest of places.

I held up the photo of the three youths. "This is a nice picture."

She looked at the image but didn't respond.

"Is that Josh Gannon, your old neighbor?"

"He and Boyd were such good friends." She paused. "That was the year before."

"Before what?"

Silence. She stared at me with a new expression. Suspicion.

"Looks like they were at summer camp," I said. "Did they go to camp the next year?"

She chewed her lip, clearly agitated. She shook her head.

I tried a new path. "Have you talked to Boyd lately?"

No answer.

"What about Josh?"

"I haven't talked to anybody." She crossed her arms. "About *anything*."

I took a step closer. "Tell me about that summer, Gloria. What happened?"

Footsteps outside the room.

Tito Mullins appeared in the doorway. "What the hell are you doing here?"

CHAPTER NINETEEN

Tito used to advertise on TV, Sunday mornings and late at night when the rates were cheap.

My favorite commercial of his was Tito astride a horse, the Dallas County Jail in the background. He wore a white cowboy hat, a white western-style suit, and a scowl on his face, the latter intended to give him a forceful appearance when in reality it made him look constipated.

A lariat in hand, he glared at the camera and in a twangy accent said, "I promise to lasso justice for the wrongly accused and to put the po-lice in their place."

Not exactly Scorsese but considering the ad ran in the same time slot as a psychic named Madame Harriet, the dialogue wasn't all that bad.

I heard from several people that the commercial had taken all day to film because the horse—a stallion—kept trying to buck him off. According to my sources, a mounted officer who Tito had humiliated in court just happened to bring one of the department's in-season mares to the parking lot across the street.

Tito had the same scowl on his face, but he was dressed more conservatively in a black suit, a Hermès tie, and lizard-skin boots polished to a high gloss.

I tucked the picture of Rose, Boyd, and Josh under my arm and pointed to the hallway. "Let's talk out there."

He strode past me and knelt beside his mother-in-law. "Gloria. Are. You. Okay?" he practically yelled.

I tried not to roll my eyes. She had dementia, not hearing loss.

Her brow furrowed. "Who are you?"

I chuckled.

Gloria turned in my direction. The expression on her face changed once again. She smiled like she was seeing me for the first time. "Dylan! When did you get here?"

"Just came to say hi. Be back in a minute." I looked at Tito and motioned again to the hall.

He followed me out.

"I'm getting a restraining order," he said. "Harassing an old woman like this."

"Ooh, a piece of paper. I'm scared."

"And whatever crap you pulled at my house this morning—"

"What are you talking about?"

He wagged his finger at me. "Don't play dumb."

"Did somebody break into your house?" I asked.

He frowned, a puzzled look in his eyes.

"What'd they take? Do you have video?"

A buzzing sound. Tito pulled a phone from his pocket, looked at the screen. His shoulders slumped, all the aggression draining from his body. He sent the call to voicemail.

"That's the funeral home," he said. "They want to know about caskets and all that."

The aggression drained out of me as well, replaced by sadness.

He peered inside Gloria's room. "And what do I tell her?"

"Anything you want to," I said. "She won't remember more than a few minutes."

He rubbed his eyes. "People are asking about the funeral too. What the hell do I know about funerals?"

I squashed the grief that bubbled up from the pit of my stomach.

"Tell me about the break-in," I said.

"Screw off, Dylan. You're the only suspect in her death. I'm not telling you nothing."

I resisted the urge to grab him by the lapels and throw him across the hall. He must have noticed the look on my face because he took a step back.

"That's right," I said. "Three years after she left me, I decide to kill her. And then stick around long enough for the police to find me. How does that make sense?"

He didn't answer.

"Tell me about your break-in," I said. "I'm betting they didn't take any of the obvious stuff."

After a moment, he nodded.

"That means they were looking for something specific."

No reply.

"Do you have video outside?" I asked.

He frowned for a moment. Then nodded.

"Did you see any vehicles that didn't belong? Maybe a black Tahoe or a white van?"

"There was a dark-colored SUV parked down the street." His voice was soft. "Could have been a Tahoe or a Yukon. How'd you know?"

"I think the same crew broke into my office." I related what had happened the night before, and then today at Mia's office.

"What are you telling me?" Tito asked.

"Gannon allegedly commits suicide. Rose starts digging and gets suspended and then killed." I paused. "Somebody wanted to keep them quiet."

"Quiet about what?"

"I don't know."

Neither of us spoke for a moment.

"Did you ever hear Rose talk about Josh?" I asked.

He shook his head.

"What about an incident that happened during a summer?"

"What summer? What kind of incident? She never talked at all about her past."

A common thread between the two marriages. Secrets from those closest to her.

"Tell me about Boyd," I said. "Do you know where he is?"

"Last I heard he was working at a dog kennel or something. That was a couple years ago. Rose lost touch with him." He hesitated. "Or said she did."

His phone rang again. Tito looked at the screen but didn't take the call. "I gotta go."

"Watch yourself," I said. "The guys in the Tahoes, whoever hired them is playing for keeps."

He strode toward the exit. After a few feet, he stopped and looked back at me.

"Rose had a keepsake box," he said. "Stuff from high school. The guy that broke in, that's what he took."

*   *   *

I stepped back into Gloria's room. She was asleep in her chair. The blanket had fallen to the floor. I picked it up, draped it across her lap, and left.

The uncle's old house was just off Audelia Road, only a few blocks away. The neighborhood was pleasantly middle class, the homes and yards well maintained.

A woman in her twenties was weeding the flower bed in front of the house when I parked the Escalade. She clearly wanted to be helpful, but she had never heard of Boyd or Rose Doucette or their uncle. She rented the place and had only been there about a year. I thanked her for her time and headed back to the SUV.

As soon as I was behind the wheel, my phone dinged, a text message from Mia. A new client was coming in for a meeting, an individual who had need of our services.

The message ended with: *B HERE N 1 HOUR. NO EXCUSES!!!*

I was planning to find a way to dig through Rose's school records, a tall order, but I decided I better head back to Mia's office.

Cash flow was going to be a problem at some point when word got out that I was the chief suspect in my ex-wife's death.

I sped away from the uncle's old house, turning onto Audelia several blocks later. That's when the unmarked squad car pulled me over.

CHAPTER TWENTY

I signaled a turn and eased the Escalade into the parking lot of a grocery store.

The unmarked unit came to a halt a foot behind the Escalade's bumper. A DPD squad car, lights flashing, appeared out of nowhere and slammed on its brakes in front of me, blocking any chance of escape.

The picture from Gloria Doucette's room was on the console, and the lizard part of my brain told me that I might not be in possession of it much longer. Before anyone got out of either car, I slid the photograph from its frame and snapped a shot of the front and back with my phone, sending them to one of my burner email accounts.

A voice on a PA system from the marked unit told me to roll down the window, turn off the ignition, and drop the keys outside.

I did as requested.

The PA voice told me to slowly open the door and step out with my hands over my head. I exited the SUV, arms outstretched. It was early afternoon, and the heat was fierce coming off the asphalt. Sweat dripped into my eyes.

A pair of shoppers making their way across the parking lot stopped pushing their carts and gawked.

Two uniformed officers, guns drawn, jumped out of the marked squad car and approached me like I was Dillinger and I had a machine gun aimed at them. The shoppers scurried off in a different direction.

"There's a pistol on my right hip," I said. "Carry permit's in my wallet."

The closest officer was a burly white guy about the size of a rhinoceros. He holstered his weapon and threw me against the side of the Escalade so hard I thought the sheet metal might dent. He removed my gun and handcuffed me. Then he led me to the unmarked unit and slid me in the back, closing the door.

Detective Lutz was in the front passenger seat. A younger guy in a tacky sport coat was behind the wheel. The car was outfitted for detectives and higher-ups, which meant no recording equipment. The windows were deeply tinted.

"Nice ride." Lutz pointed to the Escalade. "You moonlighting as a rap star these days?"

"Had to get a rental since you won't release my vehicle."

He sighed. "I was supposed to be on vacation this week, me and the wife in Colorado. But here I am, sweating my nuts off in Dallas, all because of you."

"Not to get all legal eagle, but my lawyer should be here for this conversation."

He grabbed what looked to be an electric cattle prod from the floor and jammed the device against my chest.

The interior of the vehicle turned white hot as shards of pain ripped through my body. A minute or so later, I came back around to see Lutz grinning at me.

"Still want your lawyer?" he asked.

I didn't reply, mostly because my mouth and brain didn't seem to be connected.

"You've had a very busy day, Dylan. Unfortunately, it's been stuff the judge warned you not to do."

My tongue decided to function again. "W-what are you talking about?"

"You think I didn't know about you going to the jitter joint this morning?"

The Lifeline House. Maybe the deputy hadn't ignored me as much as I thought.

Lutz seemed to read my mind. "I have a pal or two at the sheriff's office."

I didn't speak.

"Then I get a call from the nursing home that you're talking to Doucette's mother, which is about as low as you can get seeing as how that poor woman's a couple beers short of a six-pack."

One of the uniformed officers rapped on the passenger-side window. Lutz lowered the window and the officer handed him the photo from Gloria Doucette's room, as well as my cell and gun.

"That's all there was," the officer said.

Lutz closed the window and examined the picture. "Where'd you get this?"

"Rose's mother gave it to me."

Not exactly true but who was going to contradict me?

"Criminy, you are a pain in the butt." He tore the photo into pieces. "What else did you get from her?"

My brain was beginning to work more or less normally, but even so the question was puzzling coming from someone who was supposedly convinced that I'd acted alone when I'd killed my ex-wife.

"What do you mean?"

His expression turned dark. "What did the old bitch tell you?"

"Nothing. She's got dementia."

"But she gave you that picture," he said. "Why?"

I realized that he didn't give a damn about Rose's murder. He wanted to know if I'd learned anything about why she'd been killed. He wasn't working for the police right now. He was on someone else's payroll.

"I'm telling you the truth," I said. "She can't communicate."

He held up the cattle prod. "Guess we'll have to go somewhere private and discuss this further."

"I have a meeting with my attorney in forty-five minutes. I don't show up, she's gonna start asking questions. You know how thorough she can be."

He laughed. "Seriously? That's the best you can do? 'I have a meeting with my lawyer'?"

"Check my text messages."

He cocked his head, frowning. I told him the passcode, and he unlocked my phone, swiping this way and that. After a couple of seconds, he swore and exited the car. A moment later, the uniformed officer pulled me from the back and removed the handcuffs.

Lutz stood by the front of the vehicle with the cell jammed against his ear. He ended the call.

"Who were you talking to?" I said.

He glared at me, eyes as cold as a mackerel on ice. "This isn't over."

"You better believe it's not. Now give me my phone and gun."

He reached inside the car and retrieved my stuff, handing them over.

The door was still open. I leaned in, grabbed the cattle prod. The officer behind the wheel looked like he was going to protest but then thought better of it.

"What the hell do you think you're doing?" Lutz said.

I smashed the cattle prod on the asphalt, shattering it into a dozen pieces. What was left, I tossed on the hood of his car.

"See you around, Lutz." I headed to the Escalade.

CHAPTER TWENTY-ONE

Mia's personal office had a desk at one end and a sitting area at the other, a coffee table between two leather chairs and a sofa. The smell of lilies from the arrangement on the coffee table—Mia's weekly extravagance—filled the room along with the stench of sweat, which I realized was coming from me.

Mia was in one of the chairs, a yellow pad in her lap, when I walked in three minutes late.

The new client, a pudgy white guy in his sixties wearing a golf shirt and a gold Rolex, sat on the sofa.

Mia glanced at her watch and ever-so-casually said, "My, my, glad you could join us, Dylan."

I introduced myself to the man and sat in the second chair, scooting away from the table just a little so as not to be any more offensive than necessary.

The new client proceeded to tell an old story, one involving his second wife, a woman twenty-five years his junior, whom he suspected of having an affair with the tennis pro at the country club.

I tried not to react to the clichéd nature of his problem. Mia asked if I would start looking into the wife's movements while she discussed the couple's prenuptial agreement. I agreed and went to my office.

Sometimes my job was ridiculously easy, especially when the client wasn't adept at navigating the internet. Ninety seconds later, I found a picture on the Facebook page of one of the tennis pro's friends, the bikini-clad wife sitting on the tennis pro's lap, his hand resting on her thigh. I printed the picture and returned to Mia's office.

The man's face turned ashen as he stared at the image.

"You think you know somebody." He shook his head. "I thought she was different."

I wondered how much I didn't know about Rose, what reservoirs of secrets she'd kept hidden from me.

On her birthday almost four years ago, the last one we'd celebrated together, we'd eaten dinner at the French restaurant she liked. She'd seemed preoccupied, picking at her food. As we were waiting for the valet, she slid an arm around my neck, kissed me, and said thanks for a wonderful night. At home, she went to the bathroom and stayed there for a long while, silent except for an occasional sob.

"Do you want me to file?" Mia asked the new client. "The adultery's pretty obvious."

The man rubbed his eyes and nodded. He left without speaking as I wondered for the umpteenth time what my wife had been crying about.

*   *   *

Mia came into my office a few minutes later. "You want to tell me what's going on?"

"What do you mean?"

"You were late, and you look like you wrestled a bobcat while you sprinted here from Fort Worth."

My face felt hot and gritty. One elbow was scraped. My T-shirt was sweat-stained and wrinkled.

Without thinking, I touched the spot on my chest where Lutz had jammed the cattle prod. That was a bad idea because doing so hurt, which caused me to grimace. Which Mia noticed.

"What's wrong?" she asked.

"Nothing."

She focused on my torso for a few seconds and yanked up my shirt.

"What the hell are you doing?" I said.

"Are you going to tell me what happened?" She pointed to the two burn marks dimpling the skin on my chest.

"It's no big deal." I pulled the shirt back down. "Detective Lutz appears to be padding his salary, that's all."

"That's pretty much the definition of a big deal." She held up her phone. "Let me take a picture. We can file a complaint."

I pushed her hand away. "No, we cannot file a complaint. If we do, Lutz'll run straight to the judge and tell her that I'm investigating Rose's death."

Mia was silent for a moment. Then: "Do you need to see a doctor?"

I shook my head.

"This whole thing is a dumpster fire," she said. "I told you to walk away."

I didn't respond.

"Why are you doing this?" Her voice was heavy with emotion.

"Because someone killed Rose and I want them to pay." I tried not to sound angry. It didn't work.

"You 'want them to pay.' She was your *ex*-wife, emphasis on the ex part."

"Does that matter? She's still dead."

"You are so damn stubborn." Mia stalked to the doorway. "Do you even remember about tonight?"

"Of course I do."

Full disclosure: I only had a vague recollection about an event that evening.

"Traffic'll be a bitch," she said. "We need to leave in an hour."

*   *   *

It was late afternoon. I wanted to keep going, grinding through on the search for Boyd, learning all I could about Josh Gannon. I wanted to figure out what Gloria Doucette had meant when she said her second husband had tried to "take the money." Also, I needed to examine more closely the picture I'd snuck out of her room.

But then I remembered what tonight was about.

Mia's sister, her birthday. The good daughter, the one who married an Indian man, an engineer. The sister who had a baby the regular way, not in some bizarre fashion that caused certain members of the tradition-bound family to give each other the side-eye whenever Caleb was around.

Mia wanted me there, her plus-one, and I couldn't say no.

I kept a supply of clothes at the office, nicer duds than what I usually wore. I grabbed a pair of khakis and a lightweight denim shirt and took a shower in the bathroom connected to my office.

Thirty minutes later, I met Mia in the foyer. She'd changed out of the gray skirt and sleeveless blouse she'd been wearing, putting on a sari in a swirl of yellows and reds, colors that complemented her dark skin and hair. Caleb was in his car seat on the floor, next to the bag of baby stuff that traveled with him everywhere like the president's nuclear codes.

"Thanks for going with me tonight," Mia said.

"Thanks for bailing me out of jail yesterday. You look nice, by the way."

She smiled.

"Want me to drive? All day, people have been telling me how much they like my rental car."

She nodded, and we loaded Caleb and his accoutrements into the Escalade.

Fifty-five minutes later, we pulled up to the front of her parents' house, a one-story brick home in a subdivision on the north side of the DFW Airport.

I parked across the street. Mia wrangled the car seat while I grabbed the bag.

Inside, the party was in full swing, family members and friends of all ages everywhere.

The air was filled with the smell of cinnamon potpourri and wine, and the sounds of people talking in the singsong British accent of the subcontinent.

Arjun, Mia's father, approached us. He was short, maybe five foot five or six, and wore a white guayabera shirt, gray slacks, and leather sandals.

He hugged Mia and greeted me warmly, clasping my arm. "Do you want a beer, Dylan? I have Kingfisher, a very good Indian brand."

"Not right now. Thanks."

Mia's mother, Riya, appeared out of the crowd.

She said to her husband, "Dylan is driving. Why on earth would you offer him a beer?"

I wondered how she'd heard her husband ask if I wanted a drink. Then I wondered how she knew I'd been behind the wheel. Was she watching for us from the window or did she just make a reasonable guess?

Arjun shrugged. "What's one drink?"

"He is responsible for the safety of our grandson." She cast an appraising glance my way. "You are responsible, aren't you, Dylan?"

Mia rolled her eyes. "Mother, please."

A couple in their fifties entered the house. Arjun left to greet them. After a moment Mia waved at the couple and strolled over as well, leaving me standing with her mother in awkward silence.

"I'll have a soda," I said to Riya. "Can I get you anything?"

She stepped into the pathway between a sofa and a knot of people, blocking my access to the bar area.

"How is the detective business?" she asked, emphasizing the word "detective" with the same tone one might use for leper or male prostitute.

"I haven't had to shoot anybody today. So, I guess things are going well."

She frowned.

From across the room a woman called her name. She ignored the voice.

"You have a nice family," I said.

"Yes, I do." Her nose wrinkled like she smelled something bad. "I would like to keep it that way."

Before I could reply, Mia returned. She pulled me toward one of her cousins, a patrol officer for a nearby suburb who I'd met several times before.

"You had that deer-in-the-headlights look on your face," she said. "Everything okay?"

"Everything's fine. Your mother and I were just . . . visiting."

"She's pretty easygoing once you get to know her."

"I'll take your word for it," I said.

Her cousin shook my hand. He had a name that Western tongues had trouble pronouncing so everyone called him Tom.

Tom and I sat in a corner and talked about cop stuff for a while until Mia asked me to look for Caleb's teething ring, which must have dropped somewhere in the Escalade.

It was dark when I stepped outside.

The day had been long. I was tired, and my chest ached from Lutz's cattle prod, which I guess were the reasons I didn't notice the Chevy Tahoe sooner.

CHAPTER TWENTY-TWO

I was leaning into the SUV, groping around in the back seat for the teething ring, when I heard car doors shut. Then, feet on concrete, the sound getting louder.

I jerked upright. Looked in either direction.

A black Tahoe was two car lengths behind the Escalade.

The guy with the red hair and bandage on his nose was standing on the sidewalk a few feet from me. He wasn't wearing coveralls and a ball cap like earlier in the day when he'd conned his way into Mia's office. Instead, he was dressed for the neighborhood in a pair of chinos and an untucked knit shirt that accentuated his biceps.

Another man in similar clothes was next to him. The second guy was older, late forties, with short hair that was more salt than pepper. His face was pale, like he spent a lot of time indoors, but creased, wrinkles earned some other way than too much sun.

Like the red-haired guy, he reeked of ex-soldier—the fit body, his posture, the way he focused on me while taking in his surroundings.

I drew my gun from my waistband.

Two problems presented themselves. The first was the presence of these guys, an immediate threat. The second, to be dealt with later, was how they found me here in the first place.

Had they tailed us? (Unlikely.) Was there a tracker on the Escalade? (Also unlikely, but less so.) Or had they done such a deep dive on me they knew where Mia's parents lived? (The worst-case scenario—which meant it was most likely.)

The older one pointed to the pistol in my hand. "Think this through, Dylan. Shooting us would be a bad idea."

His point was valid. I aimed at his nose, nonetheless.

"This isn't the hood," he said. "People like their peace and quiet here in the suburbs. So do the local police."

"Who are you?" I continued to aim at him.

"You can call me Jax."

"Who are you working for, Jax?"

"Put the gun away and we'll talk."

I didn't move.

Jax looked at the guy with red hair. "You were right. He is a stubborn SOB."

"We're not going to hurt you," Red Hair said. "We just want a little chitchat."

I lowered the weapon slightly, keeping it at the ready.

"Thanks." Jax smiled. "Look, we got off on the wrong foot."

"Was that before or after you broke into my office?"

"Water under the bridge," Jax said. "You got your pound of flesh out of that."

Red Hair touched his nose and glared at me.

"We used the stick instead of the carrot," Jax said. "Let's have a do-over."

They wanted something and they wanted it bad. Showing up here, risking an altercation, none of that seemed like a sound strategy. Seemed more like something you'd do only if you were desperate.

"You've had a busy day," Red Hair said. "How about you tell us what you've found out about your ex-wife?"

"In exchange for what?"

"For us not telling the judge what you've been up to." Jax chuckled. "Let's start there."

"That's what you guys call a carrot?"

Jax sighed. "Don't be a smart-ass, Dylan. Tell us about Rose."

It always came back to Rose. Not about her death specifically, but about her. Something deep in her past.

"What about Josh Gannon?" I asked. "Don't you guys want to know about him?"

They glanced at each other; expressions blank.

"Or maybe we could talk about that one summer," I said.

Red Hair exhaled loudly.

"Look at you," Jax said. "Juggling chain saws."

"Who are you clowns working for?" I asked.

No answer.

"I'm not much of a carrot guy. Let's try the stick." I raised my gun.

Jax seemed to be the one in charge. He was about ten feet away, an easy shot.

I aimed at his leg. "I can't imagine shooting you in the knee would make my situation all that much worse right now."

He took a step back. "Let's not go nuclear. Especially outside your girlfriend's house."

"That Caleb, he's a cute kid," Red Hair said, a smile on his face that was anything but friendly. "You two are best buds. That's nice."

I took a sharp breath. The gun wavered, a torrent of rage coursing through my body.

The front door of Mia's parents' house opened. Light spilled out.

Jax glanced toward the house. "We're gonna bounce. But we'll be in touch."

They walked back to the Tahoe as Tom strolled across the street. He was a big man, a shade over six feet, unlike Mia's father. He watched them drive off and asked, "Everything all right?"

I didn't reply, too busy trying to control my heart rate.

"I got the license plate on the Chevy," he said. "You want me to run it?"

CHAPTER TWENTY-THREE

I used the flashlight on my phone to examine the undercarriage of the Escalade for a tracking device. The SUV was clean, so I resumed searching for Caleb's teething ring while Mia's cousin got a walkie-talkie from his car and called dispatch.

I found the ring on the floor of the back seat. A moment later, the walkie-talkie squawked, dispatch saying the vehicle belonged to a company called Reunion Investments.

A dead end without a lot more digging.

"Those guys in the Tahoe didn't look friendly," Tom said. "How about you tell me what's going on?"

I shook my head.

"You and Mia are a good team. Always have each other's backs." He looked down the street in the direction the Tahoe had gone. "Whatever you're involved in, keep my family out of it."

"Thanks for running the plates." I held up the teething ring. "I should get this to Caleb."

Inside, the party was still going full steam. Mia took the ring and said, "Where have you been? I thought you'd run off."

"I was outside, talking to your cousin."

"Everything okay?" She squinted at me.

"Of course."

Now was not the time to explain what had happened.

Mia nodded warily, like she knew I was holding something back. She led me into the living room where she introduced her grandmother Laxmi, a regal-looking woman in her late seventies who had only recently come to America.

Laxmi had coal-black hair streaked at the top of her forehead with gray. She wore a black and gold sari and ruby nail polish. She was by herself on the sofa, so I sat next to her as Mia drifted off to talk to someone else.

"Very nice to meet you, Dylan. I've heard much about you." She patted my hand.

"Really? Me?"

"Families love to gossip." She smiled, a vaguely mischievous look on her face.

I wasn't sure how to reply to that, so I smiled back and nodded.

Laxmi lowered her voice. "Do not tell anyone, but Mia is my favorite grandchild."

"Your secret is safe with me."

"She cares for you very much." Laxmi paused. "And I can see that you feel the same."

"We're very good friends."

"But nothing else?" She raised an eyebrow.

I'd be lying if I said there was no attraction between Mia and myself.

We were the same age and had similar outlooks on life. Our personalities meshed well. We laughed at the same things, trying to find a slice of humor in the casual cruelties our respective jobs caused us to witness on a daily basis. Our differences dovetailed nicely as well. She was cool and analytical when needed; I was more action oriented.

But I hadn't been in a real relationship since Rose had left me, and the idea of opening that door again anytime soon filled me with dread.

"When I was a young woman, there was a man who I loved dearly," Laxmi said. "But he was British and my parents did not approve."

"What happened?"

"I met Mia's grandfather and we married. He came from a very good family in our town."

"But everything turned out well for you, right?"

"Of course. We had a good life," she said, a wistful look on her face. "But not the one I imagined. What is the American expression . . . the road not taken?"

Mia stepped back in the room and told me it was time to get Caleb home. We said our goodbyes and left.

I waited until we were on the freeway headed back to Dallas before I told her about the two guys in the Chevy Tahoe and the company that owned the vehicle.

I expected anger. Instead, I got silence. She crossed her arms and looked in the back at Caleb, snoring softly in his car seat.

After several miles, she said, "He's my world."

"I know."

"I didn't really understand what love meant until he came along. It fills every crevice."

I didn't reply because there was nothing to say to that.

"So, what happens now?" she asked.

"You shouldn't stay at your place tonight."

Mia lived in the Kessler neighborhood south of downtown, in a two-bedroom cottage on a hill overlooking a park, the only part of the city that wasn't as flat as Kansas. The lot was large, the neighbors not close. The house wasn't very secure. A Cub Scout could kick in her front door.

"I have a hotel suite under a different name," I said. "We can stay there tonight."

"And tomorrow?"

"Tomorrow, I keep digging."

She stared outside at the darkness.

"I'd die before I let anybody hurt Caleb," I said. "You know that, right?"

After a moment, she nodded.

We drove in silence for a few minutes.

"You still keep in touch with your client at the school district?" I asked.

"Yeah," she said warily.

"I want to get a look at Rose's school records."

"People in hell want ice water too. Doesn't mean they get it." Her voice was shrill, the stress finally coming through.

"But records from that long ago still exist, right? They're in a file cabinet somewhere. Or online behind a firewall."

"I assume so." She rubbed her eyes. "The problem is it's a FERPA issue."

"A what?"

"That stands for the Family Educational Rights Privacy Act. It's like HIPAA but for schools." She turned to face me. "That means it's illegal to access those records."

The lights of downtown were visible now, soft and indistinct.

"We're way past worrying about what's legal," I said.

"Good point. But that doesn't mean I can just make a call and mosey through her records."

Caleb mewed. She leaned in the back and adjusted his blanket. He grew quiet.

"I'll see what I can do," she said. "No promises. That client's not someone I can lean on."

I thanked her. A few miles later, I exited the freeway and found a Target. Mia went inside and grabbed what she and the infant would need for the next few days. We drove the rest of the way without speaking.

Traffic was heavy because of some event across the street from our hotel, and it took a while to get there. Mia grew restless the longer we were in the Escalade, shifting in her seat.

Once we finally got to our hotel, Eagan my manager friend made a fuss over Caleb, promising to rustle up a crib.

The suite was composed of a sitting room with a sofa sleeper and the bedroom.

I told Mia that I would take the sofa, and she and Caleb could have the bedroom. She didn't argue. Eagan brought the crib himself and made sure we had everything we needed. After he left, Mia fed Caleb and put him to bed. Then she took a shower.

I stared outside at the lights of the city, the first time I'd been still all day. I was in the exact same spot as the night before, and I was no closer to understanding what had happened to Rose.

The grief visited me once more. I tried to turn away but to no avail. The why of it was hard to fathom. Rose wasn't perfect, but she was a decent human being.

I wiped my eyes, pulled out my phone, and found the picture of our wedding day again. I scrolled through more shots from that time. Our honeymoon in Cancun, Rose on the beach with an umbrella drink. Our first apartment.

I found a picture of Rose and me in New Orleans, a spur-of-the-moment getaway one weekend early in our marriage. We'd wandered the French Quarter, drinking beer from plastic cups, people watching. We looked happy. Because we were. Or so I thought.

Mia appeared next to me wearing a white robe, smelling of hotel soap, hair damp.

I closed out the pictures. There was nothing to be gained from wallowing in the old memories, for either of us.

"You okay?" she asked.

I nodded.

She leaned her head on my shoulder. "Thanks again for going with me tonight. Sorry about my mother."

"She wants what's best for you. That's the way mothers roll."

"We should get some sleep." She yawned. Her body felt warm and comforting next to mine.

"In a minute." I logged into my burner email account and pulled up the images from the picture Lutz had destroyed. "This is what I got from Rose's mother today."

"That's an old one," she said. "Look how young they were."

I opened the second shot, the one that showed the back of the photograph. Someone had written a line in pencil, the lettering hard to see. I enlarged the image, read what was there.

"Camp Eagle Bluff. 1993," I said. "You ever heard of that?"

She shook her head.

"I'll look it up. Maybe there's a webs—"

She pulled the phone from my fingers. "Go to bed. It's been a long day."

A deep fatigue settled over me. My limbs felt heavy. I plopped down on the sofa. Mia put the phone on the table. She leaned over and kissed me on the forehead.

"Good night, Dylan."

I wanted to respond somehow, to kiss her back at the very least. But an image of Rose's body in the parking lot flashed across my mind, mixing with the picture of our honeymoon, the beach in Cancun.

Mia patted me on the cheek, breaking off the kiss, and headed to the bedroom.

I watched her go, wondering how much danger she and Caleb were in because of my connection to Rose Doucette.

CHAPTER TWENTY-FOUR

The next morning, I ordered room service breakfast for both of us. Bacon and eggs, buttermilk pancakes. A vat of coffee.

While I ate, Caleb and I played peekaboo. Mia munched on a piece of dry toast and arranged her day via cellphone, in between telling me to go easy on the bacon and the butter. Cholesterol, processed meat, etc.

When she left the room, I gave Caleb a tiny piece of bacon to gnaw on. She came back suddenly and busted us, which caused much laughter for both me and Caleb.

Mia grumbled but had a piece herself. Then she opened the Texas secretary of state's website on her tablet computer and looked up Reunion Investments.

After several moments of tapping and scrolling she said, "It's a single member LLC."

"Great . . . I guess. So, who's the owner?"

"LLCs don't have owners. They have members."

"Dumb it down for the non-attorney."

"The member is the owner." She tapped the screen. "And the member of Reunion Investments is . . . another LLC. I bet there's more after that. Probably a string of them."

"What does that mean?"

"Means it's going to take a lot of digging to find a name. And then the actual owner might be a corporation. Which might be chartered in any one of fifty states."

"That's hours of work."

"Or days," she said. "This is a Russian doll. One layer on top of the other."

I asked to borrow her tablet. She handed it over and I googled Camp Eagle Bluff.

There wasn't much on the web, the camp apparently out of business. Some photos of campers and counselors, neither group containing anyone I recognized. A few blog posts. A half dozen mentions on forums devoted to the history of the area.

The facility had been located in southern Dallas County, in the bottomlands of the Trinity River, an area known as the Great Trinity Forest, thousands of acres of wilderness only a few miles from the skyscrapers of downtown. It was near a high point overlooking the river where early settlers had spotted a number of eagles soaring on the updrafts. Hence the name.

Camp Eagle Bluff began operation in the 1950s but was no longer in business, having shut down sometime around the turn of the new millennium. According to an archived website, the camp had been a nonprofit, its mission to "provide an outdoor experience for the less advantaged children of Dallas County." That explained how Boyd and Rose ended up there. I guessed Josh Gannon's family fell into that category too.

Caleb threw a piece of toast at his mother, the beginning of his morning meltdown. She sighed and picked him up. He cried and kicked, reaching out to me for help. I raised my hands in a what-are-you-gonna-do gesture as Mia carried him into the bedroom.

When the door shut, I stared at the tablet computer, remembering what Mia had said to me yesterday. *Anybody else you can ask about Rose?*

My ex-wife had a number of work friends, all connected to the police department and not likely to cooperate with me. Neither of us had much of a life outside of our jobs, so there wasn't a posse of girlfriends I could reach out to.

Except for Suzy, who I'd completely forgotten about. Out of sight, out of mind.

At the time of our divorce, Suzy had been living in Tuscany with her third husband, a retired hedge fund manager who'd bought a vineyard there.

Suzy and Rose were polar opposites. Rose was quiet and introspective; a couple of drinks was enough. Suzy was loud and boisterous, the life of a party that she kept going with a never-empty wineglass.

Despite having dissimilar personalities, Suzy and Rose had been close. They'd gone to elementary school, and then junior high together, before Suzy's family had moved to a more upscale area. But they'd kept in touch and remained good enough friends that Suzy had been the maid of honor at our wedding, Rose's only attendant.

Then they drifted apart. Rose and I were cops. Suzy dabbled at being an interior decorator, a career subsidized by her first two husbands, a doctor and a banker, respectively.

The times we'd been together, she and I had gotten along, mostly because her antics didn't faze me. I saw a lot of crazy on the street. Somebody drinking too many margaritas at Sunday brunch and getting loud was hardly a blip on my radar.

If I could locate her, she would talk to me.

I opened another search page, wondering how one went about finding an Italian phone number. After a few moments, I found something better.

Suzy Larson—she'd gone back to her maiden name—was in Dallas as of last night, according to the picture of her at a society function I found on a local gossip site.

In the photo she looked much as I remembered her. She was thin almost to the point of being unhealthy, except for surgically enhanced breasts. She wore a low-cut, sequined dress and a wide smile, teeth unnaturally white against scarlet red lipstick and overly tanned skin. The look was pure Dallas, and I imagined it hadn't played well in upper echelons of Italian society, no doubt a factor in her return.

I followed a link to the charitable event where her picture had been taken. After several more clicks, I learned that the event had been held at the hotel across the street from where we were staying, the reason for the traffic from the night before. I wondered if that meant she'd been a guest there last night as well.

I called the hotel, asked to speak to Suzy Larson. The operator said hotel policy was not to disclose information about guests. I hung up and called Eagan.

"I need a favor," I said.

He sighed. "Tell me something new. What?"

I asked him if he could find out if Suzy was staying at the place across the street. If so, what was her room number. He grumbled but said to give him a few minutes. Ninety seconds later, he called back with the information. I thanked him and hung up as Mia came back in the room.

"I'll be back in a while," I said. "I'm going across the street to talk to Rose's best friend."

CHAPTER TWENTY-FIVE

The hotel where I was staying had been built in the early 1900s by a robber baron. The facility had been remodeled often over the years, but the design remained traditional—wood paneled walls, thick carpeting, heavy furniture.

Suzy Larson's hotel across the street was modern and sleek, built only a few years ago. Marble floors, stark white walls, minimalistic furniture. According to people who followed such things, it was the flavor of the moment for society events and fundraisers.

I entered the lobby and headed straight to the elevators. I got out on the twentieth floor and headed left, turning left again. Suzy's room was at the end of the hall. I knocked and waited.

Movement behind the peephole. A moment later, the door opened halfway.

Suzy—wearing a robe, hair in a ponytail—stuck her head out. "Dylan? Is that you?"

"Hey. Long time."

"Like what, a decade?" She opened the door all the way and flung an arm around my neck, giving me a hug. She smelled like last night's perfume.

"What in the heck are you doing here?" She smiled, clearly happy to see me.

"I'm actually staying across the street."

"Small world, huh?" She motioned me inside. "C'mon in. You want some coffee?"

"I'm fine, thanks." I entered the room.

She was in a suite, the layout similar to mine, two separate rooms connected by a single door, one converted to a living area, the other for sleeping.

The dress she'd worn in the picture from last night was draped across the couch. A pot of coffee was on the table by the window.

"You look good, Dylan. How have you been?"

I shrugged.

"Rose shouldn't have let you get away." She poured herself a cup. "You always were a nice guy."

"I agree. At least on the first point."

She chuckled. "You two probably aren't talking much these days, but do you have any idea where she is?"

Suzy didn't know. I should have realized that and prepared myself to tell her. The grief emerged, an ache in my chest. I took several deep breaths.

"I sent her a couple of texts, left a voicemail too. I don't have a U.S. number so—" She looked up, saw my face. She frowned. "Hey. What's wrong?"

"Let's sit down."

She put her cup on the table. "Is Rose all right?"

"I'm sorry to just drop this on you, but Rose is dead."

Suzy tilted her head and frowned. She leaned forward slightly like she was having trouble hearing my words.

"Two days ago," I said. "She was killed."

Her face turned white. She covered her mouth with one hand, stance wobbly.

I grasped her elbow, guided her to the sofa.

She sat, legs pressed together, hand still over her mouth.

"That's why I'm here," I said. "I'm trying to find out who's responsible."

"Rose is d-dead?"

I nodded. "She was murdered."

"No-no-no." She gulped air. "That can't be."

"I'm afraid it's true."

Tears filled her eyes. She sniffed, rubbed her nose. "What happened?"

I didn't want to get into the details just yet. "Do you know about an incident during a summer? Something that involved Rose? Back when you were kids."

Silence.

"It might have been when she was in high school. Maybe before."

"Why are you bringing that up?" She crossed her arms. "They've been through enough, the hospital and everything."

"They who? What hospital?" I paused. "Talk to me, Suzy. This is important."

She didn't reply. Her mouth was open, eyes unblinking. Too much was coming at her too fast.

"I think whoever killed Rose is connected to that summer and to Josh Gannon," I said.

"First, that reporter. Now you?" She shook her head. "Rose didn't want you to know."

The reporter again, on the hunt just like I was, trying to put the pieces together. Pieces of what?

I waited, not speaking. Suzy was on the edge, and I didn't want to push too hard.

"You were her fresh start," she said. "A way to get past all that."

"Rose is dead." I spoke very slowly. "I don't want you to betray a confidence, but whoever killed her is still out there. Still a danger to others."

"Boyd and Josh." She didn't phrase it as a question.

"Not to Josh. He's dead too. Somebody staged it to look like a suicide."

She covered her mouth again, eyes wide.

"Do you have any idea where Boyd is?" I asked.

After a moment of silence, she shook her head.

Her cellphone lay on the coffee table. It buzzed, an incoming text. I looked at the screen.

ROSE DOUCETTE: HEY GIRL! GOT YOUR MESSAGES. I'M DOWNSTAIRS. CAN I COME UP?

Suzy peered at the phone. "What the hell is going on?"

Footsteps from the hallway, heavy sounding. One or more men.

"What did you say in the message you left?" I asked.

She looked at her phone, and then at me, brow furrowed.

"Did you mention the reporter contacting you? Or say anything about that summer?"

She nodded.

I pointed to the bedroom where there was a second exit. "We need to get out of here."

CHAPTER TWENTY-SIX

Suzy didn't move.

RAP-RAP. A knock on the door.

"Engineering." A man's voice. "There's a problem with the air-conditioning."

I grabbed her arm. Pulled her up from the couch.

They had Rose's phone, which was supposed to be part of her personal effects at the coroner's office. They knew that Suzy was privy to whatever had happened to Rose, Josh, and Boyd that summer.

RAP-RAP. "Is it okay if we come in?"

Suzy looked at the door, and then at me, her arms trembling.

The scratchy sound of a key card in a lock.

I dragged her toward the sleeping area of the suite as the door slowly opened.

Panic bubbled in the pit of my stomach. I tried not to think about Mia and Caleb alone in a room just across the street. One crisis at a time.

I shoved Suzy into the bedroom.

THPPT. A silenced weapon fired.

Splinters flew from the doorway by my head.

Suzy and I ran to the suite's second exit.

They were pros, which meant they'd have someone in the hall. Hopefully only one person.

I flung open the door as another bullet slammed into the wall. Suzy screamed.

I dashed into the corridor, pulling her with me.

The lookout guy was two feet from the door. He was wearing a suit but other than that he looked like the two guys from last night. Short hair and muscular.

He reached under his coat as I punched him in the nose with the heel of my hand. He fell backwards, his head hitting the far wall.

Suzy and I ran toward the elevators.

A maid stepped out of a room thirty feet in front of us.

"Go back inside," I yelled. "Call 911."

THPPT.

A red splotch appeared on her forehead, and she dropped.

Suzy screamed again, loud enough to crack a boulder.

I sprinted away from the shooter, dragging her with me.

The hall jogged one way, and then the next, getting us out of the line of fire for an instant.

A fire alarm switch was on the wall.

I yanked it.

The alarm blared. A couple of doors opened; heads peeked out.

A bullet shredded a picture on our left, showering us with glass. The doors shut.

Suzy was barefoot. She stepped on a shard, yelped.

Ahead of us, I heard the elevators ding over the sound of the alarm. Behind us, another round punctured the wall.

I grabbed Suzy by the waist and threw her over my shoulder in a fireman's hold, her legs dangling in front of me.

The alarm stopped. Voices from the direction of the elevator. A two-way radio chirped.

I ran as fast as I could, Suzy jiggling on top of me. I turned the corner, coming into view of the elevators.

Several police officers stood next to a guy in a suit with a name tag on the breast. The officers drew their weapons, aimed at me.

"Multiple shooters behind me," I said. "We need to take cover."

Two of the officers strode down the hall. The third continued to point his weapon at me.

"I'm gonna put her down, okay?" I asked.

He nodded.

I eased Suzy to the floor.

Blood pooled beneath her head. A bullet must have hit the back of her skull while I'd been carrying her. Her robe fell open, her breasts visible. I closed it.

The third officer called dispatch on his radio. He asked for backup and an ambulance.

The guy with the name tag said, "I'm the manager. What the hell happened?"

I stayed kneeling by Suzy, overcome with an emotion I couldn't name. Fear and grief and desperation, all rolled into one. I stared at her face. She looked like she was asleep.

"Hotel security saw these guys on their video feed," the manager said. "They came in right after you."

The officers who'd gone after the shooters came back and said the floor was clear but there was another victim.

The maid. I stood; the unnamed emotion replaced by a slow-bubbling rage.

One of the cops said to me, "Put your hands on top of your head and turn around."

CHAPTER TWENTY-SEVEN

I was getting tired of being in handcuffs.

Two of the officers took me to the lobby in a service elevator so as not to upset any more guests than necessary. The other two stayed behind with hotel security to wait for the crime scene techs and homicide team.

I told the officers in the elevator who I was, figuring I might as well get it out of the way.

Turned out one of them had been a rookie serving as one of my trainees from a decade earlier. We talked about our mutual connection on the ride down, and I learned the blue line wasn't completely broken between us since he agreed to take me across the street to the hotel where my attorney was waiting.

"Not like the homicide investigators couldn't find you there," he said with a laugh.

"No, it's not." I laughed back.

Eagan was wide-eyed when he saw me enter his lobby in handcuffs, escorted by two uniformed officers.

He rode with us up to my floor. "What the hell happened over there?"

"A small misunderstanding," I said.

Ninety seconds later, Mia opened the door to our suite, a crying Caleb on her hip.

"Hey," I said. "I'm back."

*   *   *

After Mia asked several times if I was under arrest, the officers removed the cuffs.

Eagan stood by the window, gesticulating wildly while talking on a cell. Every few seconds he glared at me; his lips pressed together. He'd done me a favor, finding out what room was Suzy's, and now that was biting him in the ass. I'd be mad at me too.

While Mia talked to the cops, I slipped into the bedroom and began throwing my stuff in a bag, figuring I'd worn out my welcome. I tried to ignore the voices in the other room as a sense of frustration smothered me like a wet blanket.

Two more innocent people dead. And all there was to show for it was one more bit of information.

The hospital.

One of the police officers came into the bedroom. Mia trailed after him carrying Caleb. The officer told me that Homicide was on their way to take my statement, and that I should stay put. He looked around, no doubt wondering what I was doing in a suite like this, and then left the room.

Mia put Caleb in the crib and asked what had happened. I glanced into the living room.

Everyone was out of earshot. I told her everything.

"The judge is not going to like this," she said.

"Not like what? I had coffee with the maid of honor at my wedding and a crew of unknown assailants gunned her down."

"She's not going to like that you've left a trail of dead bodies behind you."

I zipped up my bag. "Let's just hope the detective who catches this one isn't Lutz."

*   *   *

It wasn't Lutz. It was someone worse.

Rose's partner.

If there was an Olympic team for sanctimonious pricks, Detective Larry Weeks would be the captain. He was ridiculously honest, a deacon at the largest Baptist church in South Dallas. He made the average Boy Scout look like a Chicago alderman. When I was at Internal Affairs, we used to say there was regular law and Larry law, the latter much more stringent.

Despite a holier-than-you-heathens personality, the brass kow-towed to him because Larry's brother was a powerful state legislator.

Detective Larry Weeks sat down at the table in the living area of the suite, positioning his notepad so as to be at the optimum angle for writing. He laid out several sharpened No. 2 pencils, each equidistant from the other.

He was tall and thin, with a shaved head, his skin smooth and unlined, the color of eggplant. He looked like a penis wearing a Brooks Brothers suit.

I sat across from him, Mia standing behind me.

Finally, he said, "Self-indulgence is not my style, Dylan. But I am sorry not to have been there when they arrested you for killing Rose. That would have given me great pleasure."

I tried not to react. Contemplating what gave Larry Weeks pleasure made my skin crawl.

"My client looks forward to his day in court when he can be acquitted of this baseless charge," Mia said. "In the meantime, perhaps we could stick to the matter at hand?"

"Of course." Weeks selected a pencil. "Start at the beginning."

I did so, telling him everything except why I wanted to talk to Suzy Larson. I described the man in the hallway, the only one I'd seen.

He scribbled furiously for a moment. Then he put the pencil down and said, "According to the hotel's cameras, there were three of them, including the guy you hit. They escaped down the stairwell. A vehicle was waiting outside."

"A white van?" I asked.

He frowned. Reluctantly nodded.

"Can you ID any of the shooters from the video?" I asked.

"The techs are working on that right now," he said. "Unfortunately, we recovered this in the hallway near Ms. Larson's room."

He opened his briefcase and pulled out an evidence bag. The bag contained a piece of flesh-colored material about the size of a matchbook, irregularly shaped.

"Theatrical-grade prosthetic, a cheek pad," he said. "Designed to fool facial recognition software."

When I punched the guy, that must have come off. Mia whistled softly.

I said, "Try to forget how much you hate me, Larry, and give me your best guess. Who the hell are these guys?"

"I don't hate you." Weeks's lips puckered like he was tasting a lemon. "That would be a sin. I just want you to pay for what you did to Rose. For your sins."

The tone of his voice indicated a certain amount of bewilderment at the fact that I didn't embrace his divinely inspired notions of sin and retribution. Black and white, Old Testament style—that was the world of Larry Weeks.

I stared out the window. It was shaping up to be another cloudless, hot day.

"If I had to guess, I'd say they were ex-military," he said. "What else can you tell me about them?"

I looked up at Mia. She nodded.

"I've run into the same group before." I told him about the three guys at my office and the subsequent encounters at Mia's place of work and her parents' house.

Weeks tapped his pencil on the table. "What do they want from you?"

"Rose," I said. "They think I know about something in her past."

"Like what?"

Mia told him that Rose and Boyd and Josh Gannon had been involved in an incident during a summer long ago; an event that whoever hired these people wanted kept quiet.

"How did you come by this information?" Weeks asked.

She didn't answer.

"I've seen the Gannon file," he said. "That's a suicide."

I nodded. "Sure looks that way. But what if it's not?"

"I've also seen the file for Rose," he said. "The evidence against you is compelling."

They did have a lot—gunshot residue, my prints on the murder weapon, the fact that I was arrested at the scene.

"The *circumstantial* evidence might be compelling," I said. "But are you going to believe everything in a file put together by Lutz?"

Larry Weeks crossed his arms and stared out the window. He was not a big fan of Detective Lutz. There was the whole sin thing plus the fact that Lutz, while born in the modern age, had an outlook on life from a different era, a time when people of color sat in the back of the bus and were grateful they didn't have to walk.

"If I followed Rose across town and shot her twice," I said, "why would I try to save her life?"

"Remorse?" he said.

"C'mon, Weeks. I used to be a cop; you still are. Remorse is for others. Not us."

He closed the notepad, still staring out the window.

"I didn't kill Rose," I said, "and I think you know that."

He turned from the window. "Then who did?"

CHAPTER TWENTY-EIGHT

C aleb started to cry again. Mia went into the bedroom to get him. Detective Weeks packed his stuff, the pencils and the notepad, the evidence bag.

"Is that your child?" he asked.

I shook my head.

"The little ones are a blessing from above. Don't leave the county, Dylan. I'll have more questions."

"Of course. Anything I can do to help."

He furrowed his brow, obviously wondering if I was being sarcastic.

"Are you still active in the union?" I asked.

His expression became puzzled.

"I'm looking for somebody who worked northwest," I said. "Back in the nineties."

"Who?"

"Doesn't matter. Just somebody who will talk to me about an old investigation."

"Why on earth would I help you?" he said.

"Because you want to catch Rose's killer as much as I do."

*　*　*

We loaded up the Escalade, Caleb in his car seat in the back.

Eagan stood by the exit, watching us. When we were ready to go, I said to him, "I'm sorry about all this. If there's anything I can ever do—"

"Just leave." He went inside.

I climbed behind the wheel and drove to Mia's office, neither of us speaking.

Once there, everything appeared normal. Luna was in the nursery, waiting for Caleb, and Archie was behind his desk, fiddling with his phone.

When we were all settled, I called a retired Texas Ranger I knew and asked if he could spend the next few days with Mia and Caleb. Stodghill was in his sixties but ran five miles a day, his body as tough as an oak tree. He was also bored with retirement and said he'd be there in an hour.

Mia came into my office, and I told her what I'd arranged. Then I told her what I planned to do next. Track down Tito. It was time for us to compare notes.

"We could just leave instead," she said. "One of my clients has a place in Taos. Nobody would know where we were."

"That would violate my bail conditions."

Silence.

"And once we're there, then what?"

She didn't answer.

"Sometimes, the only way out is through," I said.

A moment passed.

"I'm scared, Dylan."

I was, too, but I didn't want to admit it. The events unfolding around us felt out of control, like everything was spiraling toward a terrible ending.

"Why don't you and Caleb go to New Mexico?" I asked.

"Do you have cop friends there too? Somebody to watch our back?"

The answer was no, and she knew it.

"Did Rose ever get scared?" Mia asked. "The way you talk about her, she didn't seem like the type."

They had never met, Rose and Mia.

"She was scared two days ago," I said, remembering the haunted look in Rose's eyes. I wished I had picked up on the depth of her fear sooner. Perhaps that might have made a difference.

"Maybe we could all go to Taos . . . just for a week or so," Mia said. "Just to let things cool down here."

"Don't you have court?"

She didn't reply.

"See if you can dig up Rose's school records." I left, trying to quell the guilt I felt over putting Mia and her child in harm's way.

* * *

From the parking area behind Mia's office, I called the main number for Tito Mullins PC.

I asked the woman who answered if I could speak to Mr. Mullins. She said he wasn't available. I told her that I had a gift for him, and I needed to deliver it in person as per the explicit instructions of the sender. She said I could leave the gift at the front desk, and she'd make sure he received it.

I sighed, doing my best to sound discouraged, and said that would work if there was no other option, especially since for some reason I couldn't reach the person who sent the gift.

Tito's wife.

A long period of silence ensued. The woman finally said in a hushed tone, "Rose sent him a present?"

Yes, I replied, confirming it was indeed Rose by describing her physically and noting that she was a police officer. I lowered my voice to a conspiratorial volume and told the woman it was a secret, but Rose had ordered the gift two weeks ago, a gun that Tito had long coveted, something to commemorate the anniversary of their first date. It was really pretty, I said, a nickel-plated Colt, engraved with their names surrounded by hearts.

From the other end of the line came the sound of sniffling. Then the woman told me where Tito was.

I thanked her and was on my way.

*   *   *

Tito saw himself as a cowboy, down to the sad country songs about crying in your beer and whatnot, so I wasn't too surprised at where I found him.

The Broken Promise had been around since before the First World War. The establishment was located in the Deep Ellum section of downtown, in what had been the old red-light district in the early part of the twentieth century.

The place was one long room lit only by neon beer signs. There was a bar on one side, booths on the other, a few tables here and there. A jukebox containing every country song ever recorded sat in the corner. The scent of pine disinfectant hit my nose first, followed by fried onions.

It was a little after noon on a workday, and the place was nearly full with people eating lunch. The menu was limited—burgers and cheeseburgers—thus proving the old adage: "Don't fix it if it ain't broke."

Tito Mullins was alone at a four-top by the pool table, sipping from a mug of beer and staring into space as a Hank Williams song played on the jukebox. He was wearing a gray felt cowboy hat and a white, western-style shirt with enough starch in it to stop a bullet.

I sat across from him uninvited.

"How in the hell did you find me here?" he asked, a look of amazement on his face.

"I'm in the finding business, Tito."

"Then find somebody else. Anybody else."

"Let's be pals. We're playing on the same team right now. You and I both want to track down Rose's killer."

He grumbled, took a swallow of beer.

"You have any leads on who broke into your house?" I asked.

He shot me a look of loathing—an odd reaction to a simple question. After a few seconds, he shook his head.

A waitress old enough to be Dolly Parton's grandmother shuffled over carrying a burger and a platter of fries. She set the meal down in front of Tito and looked at me.

"You want anything, sugar?"

I told her no and she left.

"What do you hear about Detective Lutz these days?" I asked Tito. "When I was on the job, he had the ethics of a crack whore, but he wasn't as honest."

Another Hank Williams song started, the one about a cold, cold heart.

"If I can get a lead on who he's tight with," I said, "then maybe I can start to unravel this thing."

Tito took a bite of the burger. He pushed the plate away, his expression one of anger and something else. Sadness perhaps, or distaste.

I pointed to the plate. "Burger no good?"

He called the waitress over, asked for another beer and a shot of Jack Daniel's. When she left, he stared at me for several moments, lips curled into a sneer. Something was bothering him above and beyond the obvious.

"What's wrong?" I asked. "Got a sick cow back at the Ponderosa?"

"I went through some of Rose's stuff this morning."

"Yeah?"

"Any idea why she'd save pictures of y'all's wedding?"

I didn't answer. One part of me was pleased. Another part wanted to get back to the matter at hand. The pleased part was larger, and I hoped I wasn't smiling.

"I think she still had a thing for you," he said.

"She had a funny way of showing it. What with the leaving and the divorce and all."

The waitress returned with his drinks.

"When was the last time you saw her?" he asked.

"Two days ago. Right before she died."

"Before that, I mean."

"When we signed the final divorce decree. The lawyer's office. Three years ago."

He crossed his arms, glared at me.

"You think Rose and I were fooling around behind your back?" I tried not to laugh.

A moment passed.

"Not sure what to think anymore." He downed the shot. "Why are you asking about Lutz?"

"Looks like he's working for the same people who hired the goon squad that broke into your place and mine."

"Lutz owes all over town." He took a sip of beer. "The guy thinks he's Jimmy the Greek, but he never met a sucker bet he didn't like."

"So he's for sale?"

"Past tense. He's been sold. Somebody bought up all his debt."

"You going to make me ask who?"

"A knuckle-dragger who works collections for a payday lender," he said. "One of those places in South Dallas. I forget the name . . . something Reunion."

CHAPTER TWENTY-NINE

I considered the potential for coincidences related to the word "Reunion."

It was a relatively common name in Dallas, a touchstone to the early history of the area. In the 1850s, a group of French settlers established a utopian society called *La Reunion* on the banks of the Trinity River, just west of what was now downtown. They only lasted a few years, utopia being no match for barren plains and the unpredictable Texas weather.

"How'd you come by this information?" I asked.

"Lutz is a witness in a case I've got coming up. I did a little digging."

The jukebox clicked to a new song. Willie Nelson's "Whiskey River."

He drained his beer. "The last couple weeks. She talked about you."

"Oh yeah? What'd she say?"

A waitress walked by. He ordered another round. I wondered if he was planning on driving.

"That you were one of the best investigators she'd ever known. She sounded—I guess the best way to put it is—wistful."

I chewed on this for a moment, wondering how that particular topic had come up.

"One of the reasons I'm good at what I do is because I can read people," Tito said. "Folks say things with their bodies and their faces that are different from their words."

"And what was Rose saying without her words?"

The waitress brought his next round.

"That something was wrong. Something big."

"Any idea what?" I paused. "Or where I fit in?"

He downed the second shot of whiskey. At least I hoped it was only the second.

His skin was flushed, eyes filmy, the veins in his neck throbbing. He stared off into the distance like he'd forgotten what we were talking about.

"Day drunk is not a good look on you, Tito. Why don't you have some coffee?"

He drained the second beer, all twelve ounces in one long gulp.

"That's impressive," I said. "If we were in college and this was spring break. But right now, you need to sober up. The Tahoe guys are dangerous."

"I'm not afraid of those punks." He reached into his pocket and pulled out a pistol about the size of a deck of cards. "I'm not afraid of anybody."

He wobbled in his seat—his voice was loud, the cadence off. Slurring appeared imminent.

"What are you going to do with that?" I pointed to the gun. "Go mouse hunting?"

"I've seen worse in my day than a couple of B&E losers."

"I'm sure you have, Perry Mason." I lowered my voice. "But I watched those *losers* kill two people this morning."

He stared at me, his eyes wide but struggling to focus.

"They're pros," I said. "They used silencers. Popped Suzy Larson and a maid in a hotel hallway three hours ago."

"R-Rose's Suzy?" He gulped.

"One and the same. Another person from her past who's dead."

He cradled the gun in his lap, his shoulders hunched.

"Let's get out of here," I said. "Being in public probably isn't a good idea right now."

He nodded slowly, like my words had great importance. He put the gun in his pocket, left money on the table, and stood, steadying himself by grabbing the back of the chair.

"Where's your ride?" I'd parked the Escalade in the front, a couple blocks down.

"Out b-back. In the alley."

The Broken Promise had a minuscule parking lot that was always full. Most people parked on the street or in a pay lot nearby. There were a few spaces in the alley, however.

"We'll take my car," I said. "More people out there."

Tito ignored me and staggered to the rear exit, moving quickly as only a drunk on a mission could. I chased after him, following him outside. The air was hot and humid, smelling of stale grease and cigarette butts. No one was around.

He pointed to the left. "Tha' way."

"Let's cut through to the front and get my ride. We can come back for yours later."

"Uh-uh. We're taking my car." He sounded belligerent, which was the last thing the situation needed, an angry drunk with a gun.

He marched off. I followed a few feet behind him, scanning our surroundings.

The alley was deserted. The buildings on either side were vacant, two or three stories tall, making it feel like we were in a brick canyon. Every few yards, there was a door inset or a passageway between structures, narrow and dark.

At the end of the block, just past a dumpster, I could see his pickup.

Tito tripped, almost fell. He leaned against a building to get his balance.

I reached out to help him but stopped.

Something didn't feel right. The hairs on the back of my neck tickled.

I pulled out my gun, remained very still and quiet.

We were about fifty yards past the back of the bar. The alley was empty, draped in shadows. His pickup was maybe another fifty yards ahead, gleaming red in the drabness of the alley.

"Wha' are you d-doing?" Tito asked.

I held a finger to my lips.

Footsteps from behind us.

I whirled around, pistol raised, hoping Tito wouldn't get caught in a crossfire.

CHAPTER THIRTY

A man wearing a filthy pair of sweatpants and a tattered Dallas Cowboys T-shirt emerged from the passageway we'd just walked by.

He stared at my gun. "Dude, don't shoot. I just want to bum a cig."

I let out a breath, holstered my weapon. "I don't smoke. How about some cash?"

"That'd be righteous."

I looked at Tito. "Give the guy some money, will you? We need to keep moving."

Tito blinked several times, trying to process the situation. After a few seconds, he tugged out his wallet and handed the guy a five-dollar bill.

"Bless you and yours." The man took the cash and disappeared back into the passageway.

When he was gone, I told Tito to give me his keys. He reached into his pocket, still holding the wallet. The simultaneous activities were too much for his inebriated brain, and he dropped the wallet. He frowned but made no move to retrieve it.

I swore under my breath and bent to pick it up. That's when one of the Tahoe guys slipped out of a passageway a few feet ahead of us.

I stood upright, wallet in hand. I hadn't seen this one yet. But he matched the others— early thirties with the same short haircut. He was built like a weight lifter, arms and legs thick with muscles, a massive chest that threatened to rip apart his T-shirt.

He rushed me, ignoring Tito.

I reached for my pistol, but he was moving too fast.

My fingers had just started to draw the gun when his head smashed into my chest. My weapon clattered to the asphalt. I fell. Disoriented, struggling for oxygen.

He kicked the gun away, aimed a silenced pistol at me. "Hands up."

I sat upright and raised my arms, gulping for air.

"W-what the hell do you think you're d-doing?" Tito asked.

"Shut up, drunkie. Get over there by your pal."

Tito wobbled a little but didn't move.

Muscle Man threw him to the ground beside me.

"You're making a big mistake," I said. "The police know where we are."

"The police don't give a damn about you," he said. "I'm gonna zip-tie your hands. Then we're all taking a ride."

Tito pulled out the tiny pistol and pointed it in the general direction of our attacker.

Muscle Man laughed. "What the hell are you planning to do with that?"

Tito aimed at his massive chest, hand wavering.

It would be an easy shot if he were sober. If he'd take it.

Muscle Man pointed his weapon at Tito's face. "Drop it."

Tito listed to one side like a ship taking on water. He lowered the pistol.

"That's what I thought," Muscle Man said. "You gun nuts are all the same. Big talk—"

POP.

Tito had raised his arm and fired. The tiny gun wasn't much louder than a champagne bottle opening.

The bullet hit Muscle Man's neck, right where one might cut a tracheotomy hole. Because of the angle, the slug traveled upward through the soft tissue of the larynx before penetrating the mass of nerves where the spine connected with the brain.

Muscle Man dropped, a puppet whose strings had been cut.

Tito shook his hand like he was trying to get rid of something sticky on his fingers, desperately trying to free himself of the gun. The weapon dropped to the ground.

I jumped to my feet, grabbed my pistol, and looked both ways. They wouldn't operate alone.

Tito leaned over and vomited on his gun, a forensics nightmare if there ever was one.

Other than the sound of retching, the alley was silent. No living thing around except the two of us.

I crept toward the side alley where Muscle Man had been hiding.

As I got close, I heard the faint sound of scuffling on the ground. A moment later a rat dashed out, scurrying across the alley.

I stopped three feet away from the opening of the passageway, pressed against the side of the building. In a loud voice, I said, "Quick. Hand me a flash-bang grenade."

Red Hair dashed into the open, silenced pistol in hand. He took in the scene.

Tito on the ground covered in puke, no grenade in sight. His dead partner. And me, just as I lunged at him and grabbed his pistol with my free hand.

THPFFT-PING. A silenced round fired, ricocheting off the ground.

He grunted as I twisted the pistol back against his wrist.

SNAP. The bone in his trigger finger cracked.

He screamed.

I ripped the pistol from his damaged hand.

He swung at me with his good arm, a clumsy blow, easily avoided.

I punched him in the stomach with the muzzle of my pistol. "That's for threatening Caleb."

He doubled over. I kneed his face, causing him to fall backwards.

My chest was heaving, and I struggled to regain my composure. We weren't out of the danger zone quite yet.

I aimed my weapon at his chest.

He didn't move.

I peered down the side alley from where he'd come.

The street was visible at the other end. Nobody else was hiding.

They must have tracked either me or Tito to the bar and planned to snatch us when we left. Red Hair had probably been assigned to stand watch at the front. Maybe he hadn't heard from Muscle Man and decided to investigate. I wondered how many more of them were lurking about.

Red Hair began to shake on the ground, limbs spasming. I took a closer look. When he fell, his head had hit a chunk of brick on the asphalt. A moment later, he exhaled loudly and then was still.

I knelt beside him, felt for a pulse. There was none.

Heads were tricky things. Just the right amount of impact at the right place, and it was lights out.

Tito appeared next to me, unsteady on his feet. He held his cell in one hand. "We have to call the police."

I yanked the phone from his fingers. "What we have to do is get the hell out of here."

CHAPTER THIRTY-ONE

We'd each killed a man. Our actions had been taken in self-defense, but neither Tito nor I were likely to get a fair shake from the police.

I was the main suspect in the murder of a decorated homicide investigator. Tito was a defense attorney whose job it was to thwart law enforcement whenever possible. He was also intoxicated and in possession of a weapon, a violation of numerous state laws.

I ran through all the scenarios. Each one ended with us in custody for a period of time, at the mercy of Lutz or another cop on the same payroll as the guys we'd just taken out.

Therefore, our only option was to run.

I plucked Tito's wallet from the puke, using an old plastic grocery bag as a glove. I did the same with the tiny pistol he'd used to kill Muscle Man.

"He-he-he's dead," Tito said.

"Yeah, I can see that." I patted down the bodies. "Find your empty cartridge. We need to clean this up as much as we can."

The Tahoe guys were each carrying burner phones, spare ammo mags, and tactical folding knives. What they weren't carrying were wallets or any IDs.

Tito didn't move. He started to take deep, sucking breaths, hands on his knees.

I grabbed him by the front of his pearl-snapped shirt and got in his face. "You don't get to have a breakdown right now."

He stood up and straightened his shoulders, took another slow, deep breath.

"Every second we're in this alley," I said, "puts us closer to being killed or in prison."

A tear leaked from one eye. He nodded.

I let him go and scanned the buildings on either side of us. No cameras visible, our only break. I dragged the bodies into the side passageway.

When I was done, I saw a glint of light on the other side of the alley. It was the empty cartridge from Tito's gun, a .25 caliber. I grabbed it and put it in the plastic bag.

I added the silenced pistols from the two dead guys. I didn't particularly want to have their weapons in my possession, but I didn't intend to leave two guns unsecured in an alley either. I smashed their phones and threw the remnants into a garbage can.

Then I tucked the bag under one arm, hoping it wouldn't fall apart, and pushed Tito toward his truck. He climbed in the passenger seat. I dropped the grocery bag full of hardware on the driver's-side floorboard and got behind the steering wheel, starting the engine.

"What's gonna happen?" Tito asked.

"These guys no doubt have a backup team. Hopefully, they'll find the bodies before a civilian does."

"I don't understand. They'll just call the police."

"They don't want the cops involved any more than we do." I put the truck in gear and pulled onto the cross street.

He leaned against the door, breathing shallow.

"If you're going to be sick again," I said, "put your head outside."

He groaned. "Where are we going?"

"I don't know." I turned on Elm Street. "We can't go anywhere we normally would."

"Go to Preston Center," he said, sounding remarkably sober. Maybe the adrenaline had killed some of the buzz.

"Why there?"

Preston Center was a high-end commercial district in the heart of North Dallas—an outcropping of luxury apartments and offices set amongst a greenbelt of expensive homes.

"I've got a place. Private elevator to the penthouse."

"Look at you with a love shack. Did Rose know?"

"It's not a love shack. Certain clients, they need a secure place to stay."

"Whose name is it under?"

"A company owned by my sister's husband. It's hidden, trust me."

The highway leading out of downtown was three blocks ahead. I stopped at a light. His idea wasn't bad. Better than what I had, which was nothing.

On the other side of the intersection was a black Chevrolet Tahoe.

Two men were in the front seat. Hard to tell much about them from my vantage point.

Were they checking on their buddies or looking for us? Were they even part of the same crew? Maybe they were just two guys who liked to drive around in a plain, nondescript SUV.

Tito's pickup, however, stood out like a stripper at a church social. If they were looking for us, we were easy to spot.

The light turned green.

I headed toward the highway, driving just below the speed limit. The Tahoe made a U-turn, tires screeching.

I jammed on the accelerator. The Tahoe sped up too.

A side street loomed ahead on the right.

I yanked the steering wheel. The truck rocked on two wheels as it turned.

"What the hell are you doing?" Tito asked, gripping the door handle.

I ignored him. The street was narrow. Bars on either side, closed until later in the day. I hit the brakes, threw the transmission into PARK.

"Get on the floor." I grabbed one of the silenced pistols and jumped out, not waiting to see if Tito did as requested.

No one was on the street. It was summer in Texas. Everybody was holed up inside.

The Tahoe squealed around the corner, locking up its brakes as it stopped about twenty feet from the back of Tito's pickup.

I pressed myself against the side of Tito's truck, trying to be as small of a target as possible. I flipped off the safety and fired twice into the Tahoe's radiator.

Steam hissed.

I aimed at the rearview mirror and fired three more times.

Bullet holes formed a triangle in the windshield about the size of a pie pan, the glass spiderwebbing.

The two guys ducked behind the dash.

I emptied the magazine into the vehicle—the hood, the front grille, the windshield. I lost count of how many shots. At least another ten. Probably more.

Pebbles of glass showered the inside. More steam erupted from the hood.

I jumped back in the truck and sped away. Tito looked out the back window for a few blocks, and then turned around.

He gulped once, his face pale, and vomited again.

*   *   *

I headed south, away from town. We'd get to Preston Center eventually. Right now, I needed to dispose of the two silenced pistols and Tito's gun.

Ten minutes later, I exited the highway and cut through a neighborhood south of downtown called the Cedars, a small slice of the city that was a fashionable residential area a century ago before people migrated to the suburbs. The neighborhood was rapidly transforming, the buildings being rehabbed for the young professionals who worked in the city center.

I stayed in the less gentrified areas until I got to a narrow street that dead-ended at the Trinity River.

No cams were visible. Very little traffic.

I parked under a cottonwood tree and broke down our attackers' pistols into their parts—frame and slide, magazine and barrel, suppressor. Then I exited the pickup and tossed the pieces in the river in as many different directions as possible.

Tito opened the passenger door and staggered out, shirt damp with the contents of his stomach.

"Try to clean up the truck," I said. "And yourself."

He nodded and rummaged around in a pile of junk under the tree.

"This is a long shot," I said, "but do you think you have a drill somewhere in this monstrosity?"

He glanced up from the junk pile. "Try the tool box."

There was a chrome-plated box attached to the bed of the truck by the cab.

I opened it and saw a cordless screwdriver with a single drill bit. The bit was too small, but I used it anyway on his gun to damage the rifling in the barrel, rendering a ballistics match impossible. Then I field-stripped the weapon and threw the parts into the river.

Tito found a hubcap and scooped some water from the river. He washed out the interior of the truck as best as he could, saving a little to clean off his shirt. It was better than nothing, but only just.

We got back in the truck and left, the windows open to flush out the stench of booze and vomit.

I stopped at a convenience store on the other side of downtown and smashed our cellphones, tossing the pieces into the garbage. I found a ball cap behind the seat of the truck. I put the cap on low over my eyes so I wouldn't be too identifiable, went inside, and bought two burners.

Twenty minutes after that, we emerged from a private elevator in a granite-faced building in Preston Center. The elevator opened onto a short hallway that led to the entrance of Tito's penthouse.

Tito fumbled for his keys and unlocked the door, displaying a marble-floored entryway that opened to a large living/dining room. The far wall was all windows, the downtown skyline hazy in the distance.

Two sofas bracketed a glass-topped coffee table. There was a fireplace on one wall, under a flat-screen TV. The decor was beige and light brown—bland, lacking any personal touch. I wondered what Rose had thought of the place. Then I wondered if she'd ever seen it.

Beyond the living room was an open area with a sink and about an acre of granite countertops, a section I took to be the kitchen.

A coffee maker sat by a wooden block filled with knives. I started a pot brewing and returned to the living area.

Tito was sitting on the sofa, staring at the unlit fireplace.

"You okay?" I asked.

"Rose and I were supposed to go to a party tonight for one of my old law partners," he said. "What the hell was she involved in?"

"I don't know. But I'm going to find out one way or the other."

CHAPTER THIRTY-TWO

A strange feeling, taking the life of another human being. What once was, is no more. All those tomorrows gone like water down a drain.

That impacts a person, whether they want to admit it or not. I could see it happening to Tito as he sat on the sofa in the penthouse apartment, sipping coffee. He continued to stare at the fireplace, his face blank, eyes unblinking.

"You all right?" I asked.

He didn't respond.

"I'm going to get a bottle of water from the kitchen. You want one?"

Silence.

"We're doing the right thing," I said. "Not calling the police. Those guys knew how their day might end when they got out of bed this morning."

He looked up at me. His skin was sallow, eyes bloodshot.

I knew what he was feeling. Remorse and anger and sadness, all blended into one indescribable emotion. A sense of desolate emptiness.

Ten years ago, I'd killed a man outside a bar on Samuell Boulevard in one of the city's most dangerous neighborhoods, the first and only time I'd ever taken the life of another person.

He was a low-level affiliate of a neo-Nazi biker gang, working as a drug dealer and a pimp, and he had just cut one of his girls for not hustling hard enough. The girl had given birth three weeks before, but that didn't mean she got a break from earning, maternity leave for prostitutes being pretty much nonexistent.

So, he took her into the parking lot, slapped her around a little, and then sliced her cheek, ear to chin. He was jacked on cocaine at the time, the autopsy later revealed.

It was about nine at night. My partner and I were on patrol when we drove by and saw them in the parking lot lights, right as the pimp pulled out his knife. Before my partner had come to a complete stop, I exited our squad car and ran across the street.

The pimp was wiping the knife blade with a bandana when I entered the parking lot with my gun drawn and told him to drop his weapon.

The cocaine and the need people like that have to be seen as tough meant that my request was a nonstarter.

He growled like an animal and ran toward me, the knife poised for an attack.

Thirty feet away, you'd think I would have had all the time in the world. In reality, I barely had a half second to decide he represented an imminent threat, get my finger on the trigger, and fire.

He was so close the muzzle flash left burn marks on his shirt, and the knife landed on my shoe as he fell.

My partner arrived seconds later. He called dispatch, asked for a supervisor and an ambulance. He told me to wait in the car, that he'd secure the scene.

I ignored him and approached the girl. She was still standing, holding a hand against the gash in her cheek, blood streaming between her fingers.

"Ambulance is on the way," I said. "You need to sit down. You're in shock."

"Why'd you shoot him?" She began to cry. "He wasn't hurting you."

I didn't point out that he was about to hurt me, figuring that wasn't going to help the situation.

The adrenaline shakes started. I felt light-headed. My arms trembled uncontrollably, legs quivering to such an extent that I didn't know if they'd support me much longer. I plopped down on the pavement.

On the street, two squad cars screeched to a stop, an ambulance behind them.

Red and blue lights swirled through the parking lot, giving the girl's skin an eerie, unhealthy glow.

"What was his name?" I asked.

No answer.

A paramedic and a cop ran over. They clustered around me. I told them I was fine, take care of the girl.

The cop helped me stand.

"I'm sorry," I said to the girl.

She didn't respond, and I didn't expect her to.

The cop walked me to his squad car. He gave me a bottle of water, told me to take deep breaths.

Rose had arrived ten minutes later. She'd sat with me, holding my hand as I'd tried to get my head around what I'd done.

I didn't have the same feeling now about the death of the red-haired man. Maybe because he had directly threatened someone I cared about. Maybe because I didn't mean to use deadly force on him. Or maybe he was just one more senseless death surrounding a situation I still didn't understand.

It was the middle of the afternoon, and Tito and I both needed food.

"I'm going to get us something to eat," I said. "You be all right for a few minutes?"

He nodded without looking up.

"Don't call the police, Tito."

No response.

"Tito?"

He sighed. "I won't call the police."

I took his key and left.

There was a deli across the street. I ordered two club sandwiches and two potato salads. Carbs were good in situations like these. While I waited for the sandwiches to be prepared, I called Mia's cell from my burner.

She answered hesitantly.

"It's me," I said. "I've got a new number."

"Do I want to know why?"

"How's Caleb?"

"Don't change the subject," she said. "Where are you?"

The deli clerk told me my order was ready.

"I've had a busy day. I'll tell you more when I see you."

In the background on her end came the sound of a man's voice, muffled. Mia replied to him, but I couldn't understand what she said.

I picked up the sack of food, headed outside.

Mia came back. "Sorry."

"Didn't mean to interrupt. Call me lat—"

"Don't hang up," she said. "How soon can you be here?"

That depended on how stable Tito Mullins was. The worst thing that could happen right now was he got an attack of guilt and decided to tell someone what had happened.

"The busy day I mentioned, it's still being busy."

"I found out something about Reunion Investments," she said.

I stopped in the middle of the street, the phone pressed to my ear. A car honked. I jumped out of the way.

"There's a man in my office right now," she said. "You need to talk to him."

CHAPTER THIRTY-THREE

On the evening of July 7, 2016, I'd been eating tacos at a place down the street from the county jail when my police radio lit up.

A sniper—a veteran of the war in Afghanistan, angry over the recent shootings of unarmed African Americans by white cops—had attacked a protest rally in downtown Dallas.

His target? The police.

Five officers died that night. Nine others were wounded along with two civilians, making the attack the deadliest single incident for law enforcement since 9/11.

The killings ripped the heart out of the city, but they also brought people together.

I worked the security detail for President Obama when he and the first lady came to Dallas five days later to attend a memorial for the slain officers. I remember standing offstage at the symphony hall where the service was held, looking out over the sea of faces in the audience. Black, white, brown. Everything in between. One thing in common—they were all grieving.

In the weeks that followed, an outpouring of support showered the Dallas Police. Fundraisers were organized, money was donated to the survivors, scholarships were established.

No one had given more than the McFaddens, though, a family descended from one of Stephen F. Austin's original settlers—the Texas equivalent of coming over on the *Mayflower*.

Blaine McFadden, the scion of the Dallas branch, was sitting on the sofa in Mia's private office when I got there thirty minutes later after dropping off the food and making Tito promise he wouldn't call the police.

Mia and Blaine were deep in conversation. I nodded hello and sat in one of the chairs facing the sofa, wondering how someone of his stature had ended up in this particular room.

McFadden and I had met before, but I doubted he would recall. He didn't seem like the type to remember a brief encounter involving someone of lesser social standing than himself.

He looked up. "You must be the investigator."

Blaine was in his late forties, thin like a runner, with hair the color of sand. His nose was long and pointed, matching an angular chin. He wore a charcoal-colored linen sport coat, a white button-down, and expensive-looking jeans.

"That's me. Dylan Fisher."

"Mr. McFadden is here to set up a guardianship," Mia said. "The beneficiary is his brother, who's missing."

The McFaddens began amassing a fortune early on, first with a ranching empire, then in oil, finally diversifying into whatever it was people with a boatload of money invested in. Real estate and banking, politics, buying and selling the occasional professional sports franchise.

"Call me Blaine," he said to Mia, not sounding very sincere. He turned to me. "My brother Rye is not well. He needs to be located as soon as possible. I understand you're good at that sort of thing."

"He was recently released from a, uh, institutional setting," Mia said.

"What kind of institution are we talking about?" I asked McFadden.

"Rye has an IQ of 170. He's also bipolar and on the autism spectrum. Both conditions have been worsened by heavy drug use." He paused. "That kind of institution."

Mia scribbled some notes on her yellow pad.

"He's a sadist, too, with a streak of cruelty that's hard to fathom." Blaine stared out the window. "I mean . . . we could never have pets growing up. Not sure what the clinical definition is for that."

"When did he get out?" I asked.

"A week ago. I have a sister who doesn't get how dangerous our brother can be. She took it upon herself to get him released."

"How long was he institutionalized?" I asked.

"Off and on for much of his adult life. I think the latest stretch was nearly three years."

"So, he probably doesn't have many friends on the outside," I said.

"He does have a sizable trust fund. That buys a lot of friends in a hurry."

"The guardianship," Mia said to me. "That's for the trust fund. Rye's assets."

Since my baseline emotional state these days was suspicious, bordering on paranoid, I decided to ask the obvious. "I'd like to know why you picked us."

He frowned.

"You've got access to the top law firms in the state," I said. "With that comes an ocean of private investigators."

"You came highly recommended." He named several prominent police officials. "Your investigative skills are second to none is how most of them put it."

I imagined that those recommendations had come before Rose's death.

"What about Mia, then?" I asked. "This seems like something one of your regular attorneys could've handled over lunch at the tennis club."

Mia's head slowly turned in my direction. Her expression conveyed the message that she was wondering the same thing, but this could be a big payday so please don't screw it up.

No one spoke for a few seconds. Blaine McFadden stared at me, his eyes half closed like a lizard's.

"If I go to our regular law firm, my sister will find out in an hour. That means a family squabble, which might become public." He steepled his fingers. "A public fight, well, that's not the McFadden way."

"We understand completely," Mia said in a soothing tone. "Let's go over the guardianship details and Dylan can get started on his end."

Blaine McFadden acted like he hadn't heard her, his entire attention focused on me.

"Why do I feel like there's another reason you're here?" I asked.

He stared at my face, his head cocked like I was an inanimate object he was studying.

McFadden's cell rang. He excused himself and took the call, strolling over to the window, his back to us.

Mia continued jotting on her pad. Without looking up, she asked in a lowered voice, "What the hell are you doing?"

"Trying to figure out why he's here."

"Other than his obvious need for a lawyer and an investigator?"

"You know what I mean. How did he even know who you are?"

"He got my name from my best friend from law school. She's a big-deal tax lawyer. This is going to be a nice chunk of business to finish out the quarter."

Blaine McFadden's voice grew louder, something about focus groups and the polling numbers. Whatever the situation was, it didn't make him happy. He glanced at us and turned back to the window.

Mia continued. "Before you got here, Blaine told me that a large portion of Rye McFadden's assets are held by Reunion Investments LLC."

"Really?" I said. "That's an interesting turn of events."

Mia nodded. "So, tell me about your busy day."

"Too long to go into right now." I wondered if the bodies had been discovered yet.

McFadden's call ended. He sat back down. "Where were we?"

"The other reason you chose us."

"Do you follow politics, Mr. Fisher?"

"Call me Dylan."

"Do you follow politics, Dylan?"

"As much as the next person, I suppose."

"I heard about your arrest. The situation with your ex-wife. I knew her, by the way. Years ago, we worked on a fundraiser for the Dallas Police Association. Seemed like a decent sort."

"What does Rose have to do with politics?" I said.

"As a person? Nothing. But her death, well, that's a different story."

The room turned silent. Mia put her pen down, stared at McFadden.

"Garofalo," I said. "The assistant district attorney handling the case against me. I'm guessing he's involved somehow."

"Very good." He nodded like I was a slow kid who'd just figured out how to tie his own shoes.

"I'm lost," Mia said. "Fill in the details for me."

"ADA Garofalo is planning to run for Congress," McFadden said. "His district is purple."

Texas had long been a Republican stronghold, but the demographics had shifted in recent years and a number of areas appeared up for grabs, red maybe shifting to blue.

"Prosecuting a capital murder case where the victim is a decorated police officer makes Garofalo seem tough on crime," McFadden said. "That appeals to the red."

I contemplated the corollary to his statement. It actually made some sense.

Before he could speak again, I finished his thought. "At the same time, nailing a recently retired cop will make the blue people happy. Garofalo has the potential to pick up voters from either side."

"Exactly." McFadden smiled for the first time.

I remembered the phone conversation from moments before. Polling numbers and focus groups.

"You've got your own person in mind, don't you?" I said.

"Let's stay in your lane for now, okay, Dylan?" He smoothed a wrinkle from his jeans. "How's the investigation going?"

"What investigation?"

"Your ex's murder. You are looking into that, right?"

Now we were getting somewhere, closer to the real reason Blaine McFadden was in this office instead of talking to a
fifteen-hundred-dollar-an-hour partner at a major law firm.

He wanted Garofalo to lose the election. Having someone
other than me go down for Rose's death was a small but significant factor in making sure that happened. McFadden was a
cover-all-your-bases kind of guy, clearly. No detail too small. Made
me wonder who his candidate was.

"I don't know what you're talking about," I said.

"You don't want to answer," he said. "The judge told you not to
get involved. I understand."

"Speaking of staying in your lane," I said.

He chuckled. "One question, for my own curiosity. Did you kill
your ex-wife?"

CHAPTER THIRTY-FOUR

I shook my head. "I did not kill my ex-wife."

One of my training officers at the academy used to say that muddy waters meant the catfish were feeding, so don't stick your hand in too deep or you might get bit. That folksy slice of wisdom was another way of saying that when things get complicated, proceed with caution.

Blaine McFadden had managed to stir up the mud nicely, all without getting me any closer to finding out who'd killed Rose.

Except for the new information about Reunion Investments. I planned to circle back to that momentarily.

"You don't seem like the type," he said. "But if the right buttons get pushed, people are capable of extraordinary actions."

"Rose and I were long past pushing each other's buttons."

A moment passed.

"We've met before," he said. "Do you remember?"

I had misjudged Blaine McFadden. Not much got by him. I wondered whose buttons he was mashing.

"Consuelo Navarro," I said. "Not an easy case to forget."

"The woman who got carjacked?" Mia asked. "My DA buddies told me about that one. What a mess."

"Her daughter was in the back." McFadden pointed to me. "Dylan saved the child's life."

Consuelo Navarro was a housekeeper for the McFadden family, part of the staff at their home just across from the country club.

She'd left work one winter evening and picked up her five-year-old daughter from day care. Due to road construction, she had to detour through a bad neighborhood to get home. Three men brandishing pistols—one of whom had been arrested the week before for child molestation only to be freed on a technicality— had come out of an alley when Consuelo stopped at a light.

The three men had been smoking meth for most of the past forty-eight hours. They yanked Consuelo from the car, pistol-whipped her a couple of times just for the hell of it, and then drove off, her daughter in a car seat in back.

I had met Blaine McFadden in the ER where they'd rushed the injured woman. When I entered the room, he'd been telling her not to worry about the cost of the doctors. He pulled me aside and said whatever help he could provide, he was more than willing to do so. Just find the child. I'd said thanks, and then tried to hustle him out of the way so I could talk to Consuelo before they wired her jaw shut.

He hovered nearby, making a series of calls, which I later learned were to the mayor and the chief of police. He was trying to be helpful in the way rich men often were—calling the boss, making things happen, dammit.

An hour later, after getting an earful from the chief, I was at the scene with two uniformed officers, men I trusted. From the outset, it had been clear that the perps were neighborhood punks. A contact in narcotics told me where to find the local dealer, a person who would surely know the location of the three.

The dealer hadn't wanted to talk, but with the help of the two uniforms, I persuaded him to divulge their location. Three hours after Consuelo Navarro had been pulled from her car, we found the perps and the kidnapped girl.

I wish I could say that we'd gotten there in time to stop the inevitable. Unfortunately, that wasn't the case.

One of the perps died at the scene. One was killed in a prison beef a few months after his conviction for aggravated sexual assault of a child. The third, also injured during his arrest, was still incarcerated, six years into his thirty-year sentence; hard time when you're in a wheelchair.

"You handled that situation very well," McFadden said. "You did what was necessary to bring about justice. Not everyone has what it takes to go the distance in those circumstances."

I did things that night that I still don't like to think about. The messy part of being a cop, the actions that don't wear well in the cold light of day.

"Consuelo and her daughter," I said. "How are they doing?"

"Fine, all things considered. The girl still has nightmares occasionally."

Mia made a sound somewhere between a groan and a sigh.

"They're in Laredo now," McFadden said. "We keep Consuelo on the payroll at one of our ranches down there. Mostly so she can get health insurance."

He was trying to do right by the woman and her daughter, but his comments came across as medieval, the lord caring for his vassals. Or perhaps I was reading too much into his kindness.

"That's very generous of your family," I said.

"To whom much is given, much is expected." Blaine McFadden crossed his legs and leaned back.

*   *   *

Mia left her office for a moment to ask her assistant to prepare the paperwork needed for a new client.

Blaine pulled out his phone and started scrolling and tapping, ignoring me.

I watched him work and tried to imagine what it was like to come from wealth that old and that immense. Nothing was free in this world, and I wondered what price he was paying.

A few minutes later, Mia returned with a sheaf of papers. She handed them to Blaine, and they discussed a few points before he signed where she indicated.

Mia slid the papers into a folder and glanced at me, one eyebrow arched. She said to Blaine, "I'll get the guardianship started today."

"In the meantime," I said, "can you tell us about Reunion Investments?"

"What about it? It's an asset vehicle, something my grandfather set up for Rye. My sister and I have similar entities."

"Can you tell us what kind of assets Reunion Investments owns?" Mia asked.

McFadden leaned forward, his posture relaxed and threatening at the same time. "Where are we going with this?"

"On an unrelated matter," she said, "we learned that a certain vehicle was owned by Reunion Investments, LLC. A Chevrolet Tahoe."

McFadden rubbed the bridge of his nose and sighed. "Rye and his soldier boys."

"Soldier boys?" I asked, trying to sound casual.

"Rye's always been fascinated with the military. A life of adventure he couldn't have due to his health. He bankrolled a group of former soldiers. A company named Warwick Services."

"What exactly does Warwick Services do?" I asked.

"They call themselves consultants. Threat assessment, private security. Executive protection."

"Bodyguards," I said.

"Or thugs in suits. These guys aren't exactly strangers to dishonorable discharges and the occasional court martial. My regular security people wanted nothing to do with them."

"Rye's just the money, right?" Mia asked. "Who actually runs Warwick Services?"

"I forget the guy's name. Jax something."

I tried not to react to the name of the guy who'd been with Red Hair last night.

"What's this all about?" McFadden asked.

Coincidences, of which I wasn't a big fan.

"Nothing," I said. "Just covering all the bases on a separate matter."

A group of ex-soldiers connected to rich, crazy, recently released from the nut-hut Rye McFadden, willing to kill to stop anyone from investigating the deaths of Rose Doucette and Josh Gannon.

At the same time, Rye's brother wanted me to investigate Rose's case based on some far-fetched scenario involving an upcoming congressional election.

McFadden stared at me for a moment before looking at his watch. "Are we done here?"

Mia nodded. "I'll get started right away."

He turned his attention to me. "What about you? Are you going to find Rye for me?"

I smiled. "That's going to be my number one priority."

CHAPTER THIRTY-FIVE

I went to my office and called Tito's burner.

No answer, which was worrisome to say the least.

In the hallway, Mia walked Blaine McFadden toward the front door. She was in full client mode, asking about the rest of his day, thanking him for the work, promising to do a good job.

I tried Tito again. Same result.

A few moments later, Mia came into my office.

"He's gone." I flicked on the computer screen.

"Do you think he's telling the truth?" she asked.

"About what?" I entered the phrase "Warwick Services" into Google.

"Any of it."

"I think he genuinely wants to know who killed Rose in order to defeat Garofalo. Beyond that, I have no idea."

The results popped up. The Warwick Services home page was the first line. I clicked the link.

Mia leaned over my shoulder and together we examined the internet presence for Rye McFadden's company of soldier boys.

Like many businesses, Warwick Services was good at talking a lot without saying much.

The first page was a word salad, containing phrases like "catering to our clients' needs" and "each situation is unique, so we develop a unique response for each situation." The page mentioned "strategic objectives" three times before I stopped reading.

I navigated to the SERVICES page. The company offered a number of options including personal protection, self-defense training, online and computer security, and something called "specialized services," which only said, "Please call for details."

I clicked the ABOUT page, and a picture appeared of the man who'd identified himself as Jax last night.

Carl J. Connell was his name. He'd founded the company in 2014 after a ten-year stint in the Army, including two tours in Afghanistan.

I opened a fresh page and typed in the address for the database I used most frequently. I entered Jax's full name and clicked on CRIMINAL/ARREST RECORDS.

"Damn." Mia stared at the results.

Jax was a thug, as Blaine McFadden had indicated. He'd been arrested for assault, assault and battery, and reckless endangerment, all since his discharge from the military.

"He probably started the company because no one would hire him," she said.

I switched over to the Warwick Services website and clicked the CONTACT tab, hoping they had something more than a fill-in-the-form method of reaching the company.

They did. A phone number and a generic email. And a physical address, a building in an industrial section of town near Love Field.

I called the number with my burner. It rang and rang and rang. I ended the call and pushed back from the desk.

"You're not going there, are you?" Mia said.

"You got any better ideas?"

"Better than jumping into the lion's den? Yeah, I can come up with a few."

"They tracked me to your parents' house. They threatened Caleb. They're also a direct link to whoever is connected to Rose's death."

"I'll go with you."

"Oh, that's a great idea. A single parent in the line of fire." Neither of us spoke for a moment.

She muttered something under her breath and left the room.

*   *   *

I needed to search for Rye McFadden, but the guys in the Tahoes, Jax Connell and his Warwick Services buddies, were the priority, a direct and immediate threat. The risk they posed had to be mitigated if at all possible. Also, there might be a bit of evidence at their office linking them to Rose's death or to Rye McFadden's location.

I grabbed a duffel bag from the closet. The duffel contained the tools needed to access a building without a key. Lockpicks and a selection of screwdrivers. A crowbar, bolt cutters. A hammer and a small, but powerful flashlight.

I slung the bag over one shoulder and went to the nursery to see Caleb.

Stodghill, my Texas Ranger friend was there, reading a gun magazine. We chatted for a moment while I played with the infant.

Then I left and headed toward the back where I'd parked Tito's pickup.

Mia was standing by the passenger door of the truck. She'd changed out of the skirt and blouse she'd been wearing and now had on jeans, a T-shirt, and a pair of Nikes.

"What happened to your Caddy?" she asked.

"Tito was overserved earlier today. What exactly do you think you're doing?"

"I'll stay in the car," she said. "But I'm going with you."

"What about Caleb?"

"My parents are coming to pick him up. They'll keep him for the night."

"Somehow that's going to make your mother like me even less."

"That's not really possible. Open the door. It's hot out here."

I chirped the locks. We got in, and I cranked the AC to as cold as it would go.

She sniffed the air. "Smells bad in here."

"Yes, it does." I pulled out of the driveway.

I wanted to pay a visit to Warwick Services as soon as possible, but before that I needed to make sure that Tito hadn't left the apartment or called the police.

"We have a stop to make first," I said.

*   *   *

Traffic was heavy, and it took a half hour to get back to Tito's high-rise apartment in Preston Center. I used the key he'd given me, and we entered through the front door.

Tito was passed out on the sofa, a half empty bottle of gin on the coffee table. Apparently, he'd given up on the coffee and decided to stick with booze.

While Mia wandered around the place, I left a note under his burner, right next to the bottle of gin. The note said to call as soon as he woke up and not to leave the apartment no matter what. I would have put something in there about not calling the police, but I didn't want Mia to see it.

She came back in the living room. "Why'd he get drunk?"

"Who knows? We need to roll."

She was crafty, that Mia. She squinted at me. "Are you avoiding my question?"

I hesitated for a nanosecond. "No."

"You still haven't told me about your busy day," she said.

Mia Kapoor was my lawyer, which meant anything I told her was bound by attorney-client privilege. That included the fact that I had accidentally killed a man in self-defense a few hours before.

But I wasn't worried about ethical obligations or legal niceties. I was concerned for her physical safety, and the less she knew, the better.

"It got a little rough today," I said. "Tito and I . . . we fled the scene of a crime."

Her eyes went wide. "What was the crime?"

"It's better if you don't know."

Tito shifted his head, started snoring.

"Maybe I should be the judge of that," she said. "You know, since I'm your attorney."

"But as your friend, not your client, I don't want to tell you."

She shook her head wearily. "It's *so* good to be your friend."

"What does that mean?"

She stared at me for a few seconds, lips pressed together tightly. "Is there any way to proceed other than what you're planning to do?"

I told her there was not. This was the best move right now. Afterwards, I could start the search for Rye McFadden.

"Then let's get to it," she said.

We headed to the door side by side. Our hands brushed together.

I slid mine into hers and our fingers intertwined, her skin warm and smooth.

Just for a moment I imagined that all the trouble was over and we were safe.

CHAPTER THIRTY-SIX

Warwick Services' headquarters occupied a small building at the end of a dead-end street, the back abutting a levee for the Trinity River.

This part of the city was nothing but warehouses, no shops or residences. It was early evening, and no traffic or people were anywhere to be seen. The nearest neighbors were a wild game processor and a tile wholesaler, one on either side of the street, Warwick at the end. All three businesses appeared to be closed for the day. No cars in the parking lots.

I stopped in front of the tile wholesaler and told Mia that we were going to change places. She would drive to Warwick's parking lot where I would get out. Then she would leave and wait at the end of the block by the cross street. I would text her when it was okay to come get me.

She grumbled but made the switch. A few seconds later, she pulled into the parking lot.

The front door was on the side of the building, not visible from the street.

The door was ajar.

I jumped out, slid the pistol from its holster inside my waistband, and strode toward the entrance, the duffel bag on my shoulder. Sweat dribbled down the small of my back. The air smelled like water and wet earth from the river on the other side of the levee.

When I reached the front steps, I glanced back.

Tito's pickup was still in the parking lot. Mia hadn't left like she was supposed to.

I debated whether to go back and make her follow the plan. Then I looked at the entrance again and realized it didn't matter. I'd gone through enough doors in my time to have a feel for what was on the other side of this one.

Nothing. Warwick Services was gone.

I pulled the flashlight from the duffel and held it in my weak hand, using that wrist as a brace for my pistol so the light and the muzzle tracked each other. I kicked the door open all the way, darted inside.

The first room was a reception area, and it was empty.

I found the light switch, turned it on.

A desk was in the middle of the room, all the drawers open. A few papers and empty file folders were scattered about. A network cable lay curled on the floor like it had been yanked from a computer.

On the far wall a door led to a hallway. There were four offices opening onto the hall, two on either side.

I crept down the hall, gun in hand. All four were in the same condition as the reception area. Computers gone; drawers emptied. A few pieces of paper and the odd pen or stapler were the only items left.

At the end of the hall was a break room with a refrigerator and a table and chairs.

I opened the refrigerator. It was empty except for a carton of milk, the expiration date four days in the future.

My phone buzzed, a text from Mia. *R U OK*?

Instead of responding, I called her. "The place is empty. They left in a hurry."

"I'm coming in." She hung up before I could tell her no.

I put the phone in my pocket and opened the door on the other side of the break room.

It led to the largest part of the building, the warehouse section, which was filled with fake plywood walls. The walls were movable, laid out to resemble the inside of a house or an office.

It was a training area, designed to teach someone how to breach a particular building and clear each room. I'd often been in similar facilities during my time as a police officer.

I wandered through the fake rooms. It took a moment, but by the time I got to the area with the crib I realized the facility was a mock-up of Mia's office.

My skin grew clammy, pulse racing. I took several pictures of the rooms, evidence should it ever be necessary, and then threaded my way back to the kitchen.

Mia was there, standing by the refrigerator. "What's wrong?"

"Nothing. Let's go."

She pointed to where I'd been. "What's in there?"

"We should leave. They might come back."

She headed toward the warehouse section.

I grabbed her arm. "Don't."

*   *   *

Outside, the sun was low in the sky, the clouds on the horizon streaked with purple and orange. A pair of cattle egrets glided over the levee toward the river.

THE LIFE AND DEATH OF ROSE DOUCETTE   183

I mopped sweat from my face and wondered if it was any cooler up that high.

We climbed into Tito's pickup, Mia in the passenger seat this time.

She flicked on the AC. "So they're gone. That's good, right?"

Good like a wounded tiger.

"Why do you think they left so suddenly?" she said.

Two dead bodies in an alley, that's why. Jax and what was left of his crew had gone underground, assuming their location was compromised. They were biding their time.

"I'm guessing it had something to do with what you and Tito got into this afternoon."

Sometimes Mia was too smart for her own good.

"Who knows?" I drove out of the parking lot.

"And what was in the back of the building that you didn't want me to see?" she asked.

"You are full of questions today, aren't you? Why don't you check on Caleb?"

She glared at me for a block or so before calling her mother. While they talked, I headed to Deep Ellum to pick up the Escalade, hoping it was still there and in one piece.

Twenty minutes later, Mia hung up as I stopped beside the SUV.

"Meet me back at Tito's." I got out before she could argue.

Twenty minutes after that, we parked next to each other in the underground garage.

It was dusk when we entered the penthouse.

The lights of downtown glowed on the horizon. The half-empty bottle of gin was still half empty. It was in the same spot as before, on the coffee table next to the note I'd left.

But the burner was missing, as was Tito.

Mia and I searched the apartment. No luck.

The apartment's patio stretched across half the building. I opened the sliding door, stepped outside. There was a built-in gas grill at one end and a sitting area at the other, an all-weather sofa, and several chairs.

Tito was sprawled on the sofa, staring at the sky.

I approached him, Mia a few steps behind me.

"Why didn't you call?" I asked. "Didn't you get my note?"

He turned, saw us both. "What the hell is she doing here?"

Mia said, "I'm helping Dylan find out who killed your wife, that's what."

He didn't reply, a glum look on his face.

"Let's go inside," I said. "We should talk about what to do next."

"I have to go home." He sighed heavily. "I need clothes."

"There's a dozen stores close by," I said. "Buy what you need in the morning."

"I want my black suit, the Brioni. That's the one Rose liked best." He paused. "The police chaplain planned everything. Tomorrow's the funeral."

CHAPTER THIRTY-SEVEN

The familiar ache returned; grief that had been shunted aside because of the day's activities. My limbs felt heavy, my throat swelling with sadness.

Rose was still dead, and I remained the number one suspect. At least it seemed like I was getting a little closer to discovering what had really happened to her. But only a little.

Tito stood. "Where are my keys?"

Mia handed them over.

He stuck them in his pocket, walked to the railing, and stared at downtown. His skin was pale, and he smelled of alcohol. Despite that, he appeared reasonably sober.

"What do you know about the McFadden family?" I asked.

He turned away from the view. "Other than they own half of Texas and they're richer than six feet up a bull's ass?"

"Yeah," Mia said. "Other than that."

He glared at her. She glared back.

"You got a husband somewhere?" he asked. "Does he know you're out running around with this guy?"

"I don't have a husband," she said, her tone icy. "But if I did, he wouldn't have any say over who I associated with."

I could tell from her clenched fists that it was all she could do to not throw him over the side of the railing. I felt the same way.

"Well, aren't you a feisty little lady," he said.

Tito's baseline mode of operation was attorney agitator. Factor that in with the physical and emotional upheavals all three of us had endured during the last forty-eight hours and it was a wonder we weren't all at each other's throat.

"Did I say something wrong?" Mia frowned. "I forgot that you like your women to know their place."

His face purpled with rage. "I like my women *alive*. Now, I gotta bury my wife tomorrow and here you two are—"

"Shut the hell up, Tito, and go pick up your damn suit," I said. "Watch your back though. You won't have me around to be your bodyguard."

His cheeks bellowed with each breath. He strode inside. I immediately felt bad about unloading on him.

"What a jerk," Mia said.

"Cut him some slack." I peered through the window to the interior of the apartment. "The anger bone's connected to the grief bone."

Tito stood by the sink in the kitchen, his head hung. After a few moments, he wiped his face with a paper towel and came back outside.

When he spoke again, his voice was ragged and low. "They asked me to speak at the service. I don't know what in the hell to say. Or how to say it."

I shrugged. "Just say no. You're the grieving husband."

He sniffled, rubbed his nose.

"We'll figure out a way to get your suit," I said. "Sit down so we can talk."

He plopped back in the same spot he'd been in when we got there.

"Let's get back to the McFaddens," I said. "Do you know Blaine?"

"We've run into each other a time or two. I went on a dove hunt at one of his places up near Wichita Falls."

"What about Rye?" I said.

"Don't know him. Why are y'all asking about that family anyway?"

"The guy who bought Lutz's debt," I said. "You told me he worked for a payday lender called Reunion something. Remember?"

Tito nodded.

"The people who broke into my office. They're with a company called Warwick Services. They're the same outfit that hit your house."

He lowered his voice to whisper. "That's the people from . . . today?"

I nodded. Mia's brow furrowed.

"Warwick Services is owned by Reunion Investments," I said. "And Reunion Investments is owned by Rye McFadden, Blaine's brother."

He leaned forward, elbows on his knees.

"Put all that together," I said, "and it makes me think Rye McFadden is interested in Rose for some reason."

"Makes me think that too." He stroked his chin.

"Did Rose ever mention Rye McFadden?" Mia asked.

He shook his head. "How did you two sleuths come by this information?"

Neither Mia nor I answered. She had an attorney-client relationship with Blaine McFadden that mandated confidentiality. By extension, I did as well.

"Warwick Services has pulled up stakes," I said. "Gone to ground."

"Where does that leave us?" he asked.

"They're not gone-gone," I said. "They'll be back."

He swore. Pointed at Mia. "And where is she on all this?"

"In the dark. Where she's gonna stay."

"You know what really chaps my ass?" Mia said. "When men talk about a woman like she's not even there."

"Would you mind going inside?" I asked. "Tito and I need to discuss some things privately."

I wanted to make sure he hadn't done anything stupid like call the police about the two bodies in the alley.

"You're not making it better, Dylan." She shook her head, expression angry.

"No, you stay here, darling." Tito grinned and slid his wallet from his pocket, pulling out a twenty. "I'd like to retain your services."

"Tito, don't do that," I said. "I'm warning you."

The look on his face made me think of a coyote about to eat a chicken.

"What's going on?" Mia asked.

Tito held up the twenty. "I find myself in need of counsel."

"She's got a kid," I said. "She needs to stay away from this, not get in deeper."

He knew dozens of qualified attorneys he could call if the police came after him for killing one of Warwick Service's operatives. He was hiring her just to be a jerk, because he knew I didn't want him to.

"I accept." Mia took the bill, glancing at me. "Now tell me what mess you guys got into today."

As night fell, Tito did just that.

CHAPTER THIRTY-EIGHT

When Tito had finished relating the events that had happened in the alley, he told us that he'd reached out to a cop friend and learned that there had been no bodies discovered or murders reported in the city that day, which most likely meant the Warwick Services guys had cleaned up their own mess.

That didn't mean we were in the clear, just that the police weren't looking for us. Yet.

Mia asked a number of questions, going back and forth with Tito over various aspects of criminal law. Finally, there was nothing left to say, and we all went inside.

I ordered pizza for delivery, two large all-the-ways from a restaurant called the Egyptian.

The place that had been around since Eisenhower was in the White House and had the best pie this side of Brooklyn. Comfort food for a distinctly uncomfortable situation.

Mia sat on the sofa in the living room and stared at the cold fireplace while Tito called his assistant and arranged for him to bring the suit to the apartment in the morning.

When the pizza arrived, we ate in silence.

Tito fell asleep on the couch, a plate with a half-eaten slice on his lap. I nudged him awake and told him to go to bed.

He trudged into one of the apartment's two bedrooms.

I put the plates and leftover pizza away and found Mia in the second bedroom staring outside at the lights of the city.

"I'm your attorney," she said without turning around. "You could have told me about what happened today."

I didn't say anything.

"I'm also your friend," she said. "You can confide in me."

"Sometimes it's better to know too little rather than too much."

"Did you think you were protecting me?"

"This is more than you signed up for," I said. "I don't expect you to take a bullet so I can find out who killed Rose."

She shook her head, lips pressed tightly together.

"Maybe I was thinking about Caleb too," I said. "Why are you mad at me?"

"Caleb." She nodded. "Sure, let's go with that."

"I'll take the couch again."

"Was that only last night? You can have the bed."

The room was bland but tasteful, like a suite at a resort hotel, a beige area rug, light green drapes, a nondescript painting of the ocean over the king-sized bed.

"Before she died, did you think about Rose a lot?" Mia asked.

"That's out of the blue. What do you mean?"

"Just what I said."

Divorce was a horrible thing, almost like a death. Two people sworn to be as one, torn apart, a hole where the other once was. The pain might lessen but the memory remained, like a phantom limb.

I thought about Rose every day. But we'd been together for a long time so that was only natural.

"Guess so," I said. "Every now and then."

"When we get to the other side of this mess, I think I should find a new investigator."

Breath caught in my throat. The room felt frigid all of a sudden.

"Whatever our . . . situation is," she said. "It's not working for me."

I found my voice. "Uh, if that's what you want."

"What. I. Want." She laughed without humor. "That's a good one."

"What are you saying, Mia?"

"You're a great guy, Dylan. But you are dense." She headed toward the living room. "The bed is yours."

"Wait." I touched her arm.

She stopped, took my hand in hers. Her skin was soft and smooth.

"I don't understand what's going on," I said.

"You're still hung up on Rose. Could be a pride thing since she dumped you. Or she's the damsel in distress." A moment passed. "Or maybe you're still in love with her."

I tried not to sound angry. "You don't know what you're talking about."

"Maybe not. But I know what I see. Whatever's going on, it's clouded your vision and—" She stared at me.

"And what?"

"It's changed you. You're a different person from a week ago."

"That's ridiculous." I let go of her hand. "I'm trying to clear my name."

"Yeah, but there's more to it than that."

I didn't reply. Was she right?

"G'night, Dylan." She left the room.

CHAPTER THIRTY-NINE

Rose's father reentered her life for a very brief period not long after we were married. She hadn't seen him since grade school, nearly twenty years earlier.

I'd been working narcotics at the time, a tiny cog in the War on Drugs, the misguided initiative that any street cop could tell you was an abject failure.

Due to the nature of my assignment, I kept odd hours. So, it was normal for me to come home in the middle of the afternoon to grab a bite to eat.

What wasn't normal was finding my wife outside on the back deck with a man in his fifties, the latter puffing on a joint, a cloud of marijuana smoke wafting across the yard.

Rose introduced me to Charlie, her father, whom I'd never met.

Charlie said hello and offered me a hit.

I politely declined and glanced at Rose questioningly.

She looked away.

I turned back to this stranger who was my father-in-law and took a closer look at the man. Based on his appearance, it seemed obvious that he was going to die soon.

His skin was blotchy and hung on his face like it was a hand-me-down that didn't fit quite right. He wore a pair of jeans and a threadbare, button-down shirt, both of which had obviously been acquired when he'd been a larger man. He wasn't bald, but his hair was thinning in an unnatural way, clumps gone here and there. What remained was coarse, gray at the roots, a deep chestnut brown everywhere else.

I said, "What brings you to town, Charlie?"

"Came to see my girl." He smiled at Rose. "And I wanted to meet you."

"What about your son, Boyd?" I asked. "You gonna see him while you're here too?"

Charlie shifted in his seat but didn't reply, an expression on his face that could have been discomfort over my question or something pertaining to his medical condition. Or anger.

Rose filled the silence. "Do you want some iced tea, Daddy?"

"Sure, honey, that'd be great."

She stood. "Dylan?"

"I'm good."

Her demeanor was different from what it had been that morning. She seemed shy, almost subservient. She scurried inside as her father took another hit.

When the door closed, I said, "Put that thing out, Charlie. We're cops."

"I have a prescription."

"Can I see it?"

He exhaled loudly and stared at me for a moment before he snuffed out the joint and dropped it in his pocket.

I was new to this particular dance, and I didn't know the steps that were comfortable to everyone. Screw it, I thought, I'll ask the obvious.

"Are you here for money?"

"You don't mince words, do you?" He chuckled. "I just wanted to see Rose."

We stared at each other for a few moments, each sizing up the other.

"She was the light in my life," he said. "I don't expect you to understand why I wasn't around."

"That's good. Saves me the trouble of trying."

He touched his chest like it ached. A moment later he asked, "How's Rose's mother?"

"Gloria?" I looked at my watch. "She's about to have her first Chablis of the day."

"She always had a thing for the fruit of the vine. What's your vice?"

"Running deep background checks on people who appear out of nowhere and upset my wife."

He laughed. "You are a spicy enchilada. Things played out different, you and me woulda been friends."

"But things didn't play out that way, now, did they?"

"Don't blame you for not liking me," he said. "I wasn't around when my kid needed me."

"Kids. You keep forgetting your son."

He sighed. "How is Boyd?"

"Scared of his own dryer lint. Was he that way as a child?"

Charlie rolled his eyes, a sneer on his lips. "He always was weak."

"Maybe if you slapped him around more as a kid, he'd be stronger."

"What happened to them, that's on Gloria. She's the one who—" He coughed, something rattling deep in his lungs.

"You okay?"

He nodded.

"What do you mean 'what happened to them'?" I asked.

"Nothing." He waved a hand dismissively. "Boyd always was a little slow. He never understood that you take things like a man, or they take you."

Rose returned with a tray of ice-filled glasses and a pitcher of tea. The glasses and the pitcher and the tray were wedding gifts that we'd never used before. She poured a glass for herself and Charlie, and we all made small talk, discussing the weather and the Dallas Cowboys' chances for the playoffs and what movies we'd seen.

After about fifteen minutes, Charlie put his glass down and coughed again. This time he didn't stop, the rattle in his chest sounding like marbles in a paint can. His face turned red as he struggled to get enough air.

Rose—one of the most levelheaded people I'd ever seen during a crisis—froze, hand covering her mouth, eyes unblinking.

I helped Charlie stand, told him to lean over, put his hands on his knees.

After a few moments, the coughing fit subsided and he sat back down, his eyes watery.

Rose's brow furrowed. "What's wrong, Daddy? Are you sick?"

"Nothing you need to worry about." He pulled a phone from his pocket. "I should go."

"Where are you staying?" Rose asked. "We've got a guest room."

He ignored her question and sent a text. Then he looked at me. "Take care of my baby girl, Dylan."

"It's usually the other way around," I said. "She takes care of me."

He pushed himself to his feet and lumbered inside, Rose trailing after him. I followed them both through the house to the front door.

Outside, an early 1980s Cadillac Eldorado was parked by our mailbox, the top down. The car was turquoise, with white leather upholstery.

A man in his thirties got out from behind the wheel. He wore a pair of faded Levi's and a white sleeveless undershirt. His hair was dyed an inky black and greased back against his skull.

Charlie introduced him; Axel was his name.

Axel took Charlie by the arm and helped him to the passenger seat before he walked to the other side and slid behind the steering wheel.

Charlie grasped his daughter's hand. "See you soon, little girl."

Rose had tears in her eyes. She kissed his forehead, and we watched them drive away. After they were gone, she leaned against my shoulder but didn't speak.

Three days later, Axel called me at the station and said that Charlie had passed away that morning at a Holiday Inn on the interstate south of town. He wanted me to tell Rose.

I asked if any arrangements had been made for a service.

He didn't answer, his confusion evident. After a moment, he said that Charlie was still at the Holiday Inn. He thought that since I was a cop, I could take care of all that. Before I could ask any more questions, he hung up.

The funeral was small. Me, Rose, and Boyd. Maybe a half-dozen friends from the force and a preacher who didn't seem to know much about the deceased.

Rose sat between me and her brother and displayed no emotion throughout the service. At the end, she clasped Boyd's hand as a single tear rolled down her cheek. Then the two siblings stood and abruptly left.

*   *   *

I was dreaming about Charlie's plain wooden coffin when I woke up.

The room came into view. Tito's apartment. A thin stream of daylight coming through the window. It was early, just after dawn.

Mia was sitting on the edge of the bed, nudging my shoulder.

"Dylan. Wake up."

I yawned, rubbed my eyes. Our argument from last night drifted back into my consciousness.

"You asked me about Rose's school records," she said.

I stopped yawning.

"My contact at the school district." Mia stood. "She's got something for us."

CHAPTER FORTY

Two years ago, before we started working together, Mia Kapoor made a fair amount of money and a lot of headlines when she sued the Dallas Independent School District on behalf of a district employee named Nancy Lindahl.

The cause of action was sexual harassment, specifically a pattern of unwanted touching and lewd comments from Nancy's supervisor. The troubling behavior culminated with the supervisor masturbating in front of Nancy while telling her what a dirty girl she was.

One would think this would be an open-and-shut case, a slam dunk for the plaintiff.

One would be correct. Except for a tiny wrinkle.

Nancy had recently broken up with the supervisor's brother, a man with whom she had enjoyed an adventurous sex life, one involving multiple partners they located online. Everyone was a consenting adult, and obviously Nancy's private life mattered not one iota when it came to workplace harassment, at least in a legal sense.

The court of public opinion was a different matter, however, and that's where the attorneys for the school district chose to wage their war.

With the help of a PR consultant, opposing counsel placed a steady stream of damaging stories in the media, resulting in the plaintiff acquiring the nickname "Nympho Nancy."

Coming forward to accuse someone with power over you was a hard choice, guaranteed to be an unpleasant experience. Having your name dragged through the muck turned "unpleasant" into a special kind of hell, one that caused Nancy Lindahl to almost drop the lawsuit. But Mia Kapoor encouraged her client to stand her ground, arguing that the supervisor shouldn't be allowed to impact the lives of any other women in the way he did Nancy's. So, Nancy Lindahl steeled herself against the dirt and refused to back down.

Mia was able to mitigate the impact of the smears by getting seven women on the jury, and she won a big settlement for her client, who elected to stay in her position at the school district, despite everything that had happened. Or maybe because.

As we drove to the district headquarters, I said, "Thanks for doing this. I know it wasn't easy to ask."

No answer.

"I'm sorry about last night."

Mia stared out the window. "I don't want to talk about that."

It was a little before eight and traffic was heavy. The clouds in the west were high and dark, the temperature in the eighties despite the early hour.

After several stoplights, she said, "You don't have anything to be sorry about."

No one spoke for the rest of the drive.

The headquarters for the Dallas school district was an office tower on North Central Expressway, a building covered in mirrored glass that reflected the sun's heat onto the city like a blast furnace.

I parked the Escalade in the visitor section, and we entered the atrium. A security guard photocopied our IDs and gave us visitor badges before directing us to the fifth floor. There, a receptionist took our names and buzzed Nancy Lindahl while we waited in an area decorated with artwork from a fifth-grade class.

A few minutes later, Nancy appeared. She was in her mid-thirties, dressed like a CPA or an insurance executive with a gray blazer and matching skirt, a beige blouse. Brown hair in a bun, a sport watch her only jewelry.

She worked in the human capital management department, what used to be called human resources. Her clothes and demeanor appeared designed to be unremarkable. I wondered if that was how she'd always been or if it was a recent, post-lawsuit thing. Maybe that was just how all people in human capital management looked.

She ignored Mia's outstretched hand and pointed to me. "Who's he?"

"A friend," Mia said. "He and I work together."

Nancy Lindahl didn't like that answer. She frowned, crossed her arms.

"You can trust him," Mia said. "I wouldn't have brought him otherwise."

A moment passed.

"Okay," Nancy said. "Let's go to my office."

We followed her into a drab, windowless room about twelve feet by twelve, the only bit of color coming from a framed reproduction of van Gogh's sunflower painting. Nothing else was in the room except a desk, several chairs, and a filing cabinet.

Nancy sat behind the desk and motioned for us to take the chairs on the other side. She shifted in her seat, shuffling papers, her brow wrinkled.

"Everything all right?" Mia asked.

"One of the new board trustees," Nancy said. "His wife's cousin is my former supervisor."

"What are you saying?" Mia frowned.

"I shouldn't have stayed here. You told me not to."

"I *suggested* you not stay. I think you're very brave for continuing to work in this place."

No one spoke for a few moments. Nancy rearranged some pens, a faraway look on her face.

"Do you like working here?" I asked.

"I'm good at what I do." She looked up, focusing on me instead of the pens.

"That's great," I said. "But do you like it here?"

Nancy leaned back in her chair, staring at the van Gogh print.

"If you're in an uncomfortable situation," Mia said, "something that could be construed as a hostile work environment, there are legal remedies."

Nancy snorted. "Like I want to take that road again."

I had strong feelings when people weren't being treated right. Part of my DNA, I supposed. Nancy Lindahl may have won a big settlement, but she was still paying the price for speaking up.

"What's the trustee's name?" I asked.

Nancy glanced at Mia but didn't speak.

I said, "Maybe he could put the word out that you're to be treated in a decent manner."

"Why would he do that?" Nancy said.

"Sometimes I'm able to persuade people to do the right thing."

Nancy shook her head. "I don't need a man to take care of me."

"I'm not taking care of you," I said. "Just offering to return a favor."

She stared at me for a few seconds before turning to Mia. "You asked if there was any way to access the records for a student named Rose Doucette. Class of 1999."

"I understand you're going out on a limb," Mia said. "Those records are confidential."

"They're more than that," Nancy said. "They're gone."

Mia and I looked at each other.

Nancy pulled a manila folder from her desk drawer. "But maybe I have something better."

CHAPTER FORTY-ONE

Nancy Lindahl put the folder on the desktop. "Transcripts are usually destroyed after seven years. That's the protocol. The diploma becomes the record."

I felt a tiny sense of relief. The information had been wiped as a matter of procedure, not because the Warwick Services guys had hacked into a server and erased one more chapter from the life of Rose Doucette.

"I have a friend who's the principal at Rose's old school," she said. "I asked him if there were any files from back then. He found a box of stuff in a storeroom. This was in it."

Nancy slid the folder across the desk. Handwritten on the outside was, "*Young Life 1994–95–Mrs. Callahan, sponsor.*"

"What's *Young Life*?" Mia asked.

"An extracurricular group that met at the school," Nancy said. "Religious. What we call faith-based these days. Like the chess club, but they read the Bible."

I opened the folder, slid out a stack of papers printed on a dot matrix machine, the pages yellowed and curling.

"Callahan was the principal in the 1990s," Nancy said. "The box has more stuff in it, which you're welcome to look through. This seemed the most relevant."

The top page was a list of members for that particular chapter, a total of twelve including Rose and Boyd Doucette. The next few pages were about the organization, the goals, and the structure of a typical meeting.

At the bottom of the stack were four pages stapled together. The heading said *PRAYER REQUESTS*.

I scanned the first page. The entries were dated from September 1994 onward, a snapshot of troubled lives.

Please pray that Tanya's father will find a new job.

Carlos's mother has cancer again. Please pray for a speedy recovery.

Jimmy hasn't been to class in a week. Please pray that his family is OK.

I flipped to the second page and found what I was looking for. It was at the top, dated October 15, 1994.

Please pray for Boyd and Rose. Pray for healing for whatever has happened to them. They were such good kids last year! Pray that Boyd and his friend J. will stop taking drugs! Pray that Rose will open up. She's so different now!

Below that paragraph was a handwritten note that read, *Rose & Boyd didn't come back after Thxgiving break. Find out what's wrong!!*

Mia had been reading over my shoulder. "Does that mean Rose dropped out of school?"

"Sounds like it." I flipped to the fourth page.

Another handwritten note was at the bottom: *April '95. No sign of Rose or Boyd. Pray for them, health & well being.*

Rose was a straight A student, or so I thought. But she'd dropped out for at least a semester, maybe more; another slice of her personal history I didn't know about.

Mia looked across the desk at Nancy. "Is there any way to tell what happened?"

Nancy shook her head. "Everything's been destroyed. Plus, there wouldn't be a record of why someone didn't come to school."

"What about Josh Gannon?" I asked. "Can you tell if he dropped out too?"

Nancy tapped on her keyboard, squinted at the screen. "Josh never graduated. So, yeah, he dropped for sure."

The timeline made sense. They returned to school after the summer break and that's when the trouble started. Something happened that caused the Doucette siblings to undergo a change so radical their principal noticed and beseeched a higher power to fix it.

Mia asked, "Could we see the box?"

"Sure." Nancy pulled a cardboard container out from under her desk.

Mia and I rummaged through the contents. It was filled with office tchotchkes, items that might be left behind when someone changed jobs.

"What about Callahan, the principal?" I asked. "Do you know how to reach her?"

Nancy shook her head. "She died several years ago."

I returned everything to the box.

"Rose Doucette," Nancy said. "That's the cop who was killed a few days ago, right?"

I nodded. "A homicide investigator."

Nancy put the box back under her desk. "She sounded like a strong woman."

"That she was." I stared at the van Gogh print, pondering what to do next.

"Women like that, they make powerful men fearful," Nancy said. "A threat to the status quo."

I thought about Rye McFadden as I stood up. "Thanks for your help."

*   *   *

Outside, the sky was cloudy, the heat and humidity oppressive like the tropics. Once we were back in the Escalade, I asked, "Do you have your tablet computer?"

Mia nodded.

"Let's go somewhere quiet. I need to look for Rye McFadden." She suggested a nearby shopping venue, which wasn't a bad idea.

Northpark Mall was more or less between Tito's apartment and the district's headquarters. It had a number of coffee shops and secluded areas, a large food court. It was midmorning, so the place wouldn't be packed. Yet it would be busy enough for us to remain anonymous.

"You need to do some shopping too," Mia said.

"Seriously? Now?" I pulled out of the parking area.

"Just go to the mall."

Ten minutes later, we stepped through one of the main entrances, a Chinese restaurant on the left, an Italian one on the right. Department stores and specialty shops loomed ahead.

"The food court's on the second floor," I said.

"We're going somewhere else first." Mia pointed me in the opposite direction.

Skylights lit the public areas. The air smelled like lemon furniture polish and damp potting soil, the latter from the containers of plants along the walkways.

"Where are we going?" I asked. "I need to get online."

"This won't take too long." She pointed to a menswear store. "You need a suit. Rose's funeral is this afternoon."

I stopped. "Are you nuts? I'm not going to Rose's funeral."

"Oh, yes, you are. You need closure."

"In case you've forgotten, I'm the main suspect in her murder, and 99 percent of the people who are gonna be there want to see me on death row."

"But you didn't kill her. Her husband knows that, and maybe her partner does too."

"I am *not* going to that funeral."

Mia's eyes narrowed into slits. "Yes, you are, Dylan. This one's not open for discussion."

I wanted to argue more but I couldn't think of anything to say.

Thirty minutes later, I emerged from the store in a ready-to-wear black suit, white dress shirt, and a maroon tie, the clothes I'd had on in a shopping bag. The pants fit perfectly, but the jacket was a little loose. That was okay. My gun wouldn't show as much.

I stared at myself in the reflection of the store's window.

Mia stood behind me. "You look good," she said.

"Thanks. Now it's your turn."

She raised her eyebrows.

"I'm not going to this thing alone," I said.

"You don't need a date for a funeral."

"That's not what I meant."

"Really?" she said.

I didn't reply.

"We're not a couple, Dylan. We went over that last night."

"But you're still my friend, right?"

*   *   *

We ate an early lunch at the food court, both of us wearing our new duds. Mia had found a black, sleeveless dress that fit perfectly and a pair of dove-gray pumps.

As we ate, I searched for Rye McFadden on Mia's tablet.

He was a ghost, much like Boyd Doucette. Entries were sporadic, except for links to various corporate entities connected to his family's wealth, among them Reunion Investments. Beyond that, all I could find were a driver's license from twenty years ago, a dormant checking account, and an expired passport.

His last known address was from a decade before, a home belonging to his aunt. Despite the staleness of that info, I wrote down the address anyway, and then stared into the distance, trying to figure out another angle.

According to Suzy Larson, Rose, Boyd, and Josh had been hospitalized for a period during the summer before everything fell apart for them at school.

On Google maps, I located Camp Eagle Bluff in the southeastern part of the county, a remote, undeveloped area.

I searched for hospitals nearby. Most were in the central part of the county near downtown, a long distance away. A couple were closer in South Dallas. I made a list of those. No idea how I'd find out if Rose had been a patient at any of them in the mid-1990s, but it was a start at least.

Mia asked what I was doing. I told her. She reminded me to look for places that had closed too. I entered that as a search and found a number of healthcare facilities in the area that were no longer in operation.

Only one was close to Camp Eagle Bluff though.

McFadden Memorial Hospital.

CHAPTER FORTY-TWO

M ia and I took turns reading the Wikipedia page for the hospital, closed for the past eighteen years. The facility had been nonprofit, 145 beds, funded by the McFadden Foundation in honor of one of their ancestors who'd been a physician during the Civil War. On the losing side.

The hospital, established in 1982, sold to a healthcare conglomerate in 2001. The conglomerate had closed the facility several years later in a cost savings measure. The building was still there, empty and boarded up.

"The name could be a coincidence," Mia said. "Don't jump to conclusions."

"Where should I jump?"

"What I'm saying is you don't know if that's the hospital where Rose was."

"Let's look at what we do know," I said. "Something happened during the summer of 1994, the summer they attended Camp Eagle Bluff."

Mia pushed her empty plate away.

I continued. "They ended up in a hospital. And the one closest to the camp was McFadden Memorial."

"Maybe there's a connection," she said. "Maybe not. The problem is how do you find out if a person was a patient at a facility that's been closed for nearly twenty years?"

"How about I ask Blaine McFadden if he has access to any hospital records?"

She sighed. "Those things you're grasping at. Those would be straws."

I crossed my arms but didn't speak.

"Just because he has the same name doesn't mean he has the old files in his attic," she said. "And that's before you consider HIPAA."

She was right. I was reaching for things that weren't there, desperate to break whatever logjam was holding back the information.

"Then I'll concentrate on Rye McFadden," I said. "Track him down. He's the key."

She stood. "We need to get going. The service starts soon."

I didn't move.

She placed a hand on my shoulder. "It'll be all right, Dylan."

*   *   *

Rose Doucette's funeral was graveside at a cemetery in northwest Dallas not far from where she'd grown up.

Crown Hill Memorial Park, the final resting place of another, more notorious daughter of Dallas, Bonnie Parker.

By the time we got there, the sky had darkened. The clouds were gunmetal gray, the air heavy with the promise of a summer thunderstorm.

A tent had been set up by the grave. Seating for about fifty people faced a closed casket.

A large photograph of Rose in her dress blues rested on an easel nearby.

Most of the seats were occupied when Mia and I walked up, about half the mourners in uniform. We took a spot in the back row. Tito and his family were in the front.

I scanned the crowd but didn't see Boyd. If he was missing his sister's funeral, I wondered if he was even alive.

Lutz was two rows ahead. He turned and stared at me for a long moment before facing the front again.

The police chaplain, a frail man with straw-colored hair, leaned on the podium and read several passages from the Bible, concluding with a verse from Matthew. "Blessed are those who mourn."

I didn't feel very blessed. Maybe that would come later.

The police choir stood to one side of the grave. They sang "Amazing Grace" a cappella, their voices melding into one melodious outpouring, uplifting and sad at the same time.

As they sang, I felt myself sink into the chair, the grief becoming a physical presence, a weight pressing down on my shoulders as a dull thread of pain wormed its way up the back of my skull.

Mia slid her hand into mine, squeezing my fingers.

I wiped my eyes and fixated on the casket, imagining Rose's body beneath the lid, dark and cold. The song ended. The chaplain returned to the podium and talked about the blue line and what it meant to be a police officer.

Thunder cracked in the distance.

The chaplain stepped aside for the chief of police, who gave the eulogy. She was a political hire, brought in from a midsize West Coast city four years before. Rose had loathed her. The woman had little knowledge of Dallas and didn't seem inclined to learn much about her adopted city, beyond who the power brokers were.

It was obvious from the chief's comments that she didn't know Rose either. Her words sounded like little more than an expanded LinkedIn page, except when she talked about Rose's commitment to the job and to helping others. When she was finished, the choir sang again, and the chaplain gave a short sermon followed by a prayer.

Then it was over.

Mia and I stood.

A few people I knew from the force drifted our way and said hello. We'd been in tight situations together, a bond that superseded anything else. Nonetheless, our topics of conversation were shallow; no one asked what I'd been up to. A number of people, some of whom I thought of as friends, saw me and pointedly turned away.

After twenty minutes of visiting, we headed toward the Escalade.

The sky had grown darker still, gusts of wind whipping through the trees. The air smelled like rain and tilled earth.

As we threaded our way through the tombstones, Detective Lutz and the officer who'd been driving his unmarked unit appeared from behind a mausoleum, blocking our path.

I stopped, Mia beside me.

Lutz put his hands on his hips, gun visible. "You got a lot a nerve coming here."

"Just paying my respects," I said. "You can get out of our way now."

"Or what?" he asked. "You gonna kick my ass?"

The other officer flexed his fingers and took a step closer. We were fifty yards from the tent and the remaining mourners. No one appeared to be paying us any attention.

"We're all here for the same reason," Mia said. "Let's keep that in mind."

Lutz snorted. "Y'all bumping uglies? That's very woke of you, Dylan, as the kids say, her being colored and all."

The other officer snickered.

I resisted the urge to punch Lutz. He was trying to provoke me, and he almost succeeded.

Mia's lips pressed together. She pointed an index finger at him like she was about to rip him a new one.

I waved her off. "I know about your gambling debts, Lutz. Do you report to Warwick Services or to Rye McFadden directly?"

His eyes narrowed. The other officer exhaled loudly.

"Move." I snapped my fingers. "We're leaving now."

"You won't get three blocks before you're pulled over," he said. "I'm gonna shut you down once and for all. Whatever you think you know—"

The other officer whistled, pointed toward the tent. Lutz cut his eyes in that direction.

BOOM. A flash of lightning, the crack of thunder a millisecond later.

Detective Larry Weeks appeared out of the gloom, his tie flapping in the wind. "Am I interrupting anything?"

Mia said, "I was getting ready to explain to Detective Lutz how one goes about filing official oppression charges against a police officer."

"A fascinating topic," Weeks said. "Maybe you could revisit that later. I need to have a chat with Dylan right now though."

Lutz glared at me.

Weeks said, "Is that going to be a problem, Detective?"

Lutz muttered under his breath and stalked off, his buddy trailing after him.

The first raindrop fell.

"Let's get out of this weather," Weeks said. "There's someone who wants to talk to you."

CHAPTER FORTY-THREE

The closest cover was where Rose's service had been held.

We jogged toward the tent, Mia sliding off her pumps to run barefoot as the scattered rain became more pronounced. The air smelled musky, parched earth suddenly moist.

Only a few mourners remained. A handful of officers. Tito and several of his family members. The police chaplain, the chief, and her security detail.

Tito glanced at us as we entered at the rear but didn't react.

Standing on the other side of the casket were three men wearing khaki work clothes and heavy boots. The gravediggers who would put Rose in the ground.

I positioned myself to be looking in a different direction.

Weeks mopped raindrops from his gleaming pate with a handkerchief, his skin glistening like polished onyx. "Sorry about that cracker Lutz. He can be overzealous on occasion."

"That's one way to put it." Mia slid her shoes back on.

Weeks asked me, "You know who Maney Bossert is?"

"I've heard the stories. He still alive?"

Maney Bossert had been a rookie in 1963, barely twenty-one years old. That was the year President Kennedy had been assassinated.

"By the grace of God, he is indeed," Weeks said. "Not in good shape though."

By luck or happenstance, Maney had ended up helping escort Lee Harvey Oswald through the jail parking garage when Jack Ruby killed Oswald and gave birth to a thousand and one conspiracy theories. He'd been one of the officers partially visible in the famous picture of Oswald reacting to the bullet plowing into his stomach.

"What does that mean?" I asked. "Define 'not in good shape.'"

Maney had enjoyed a certain amount of celebrity after Oswald's death. He gave interviews, exaggerating his proximity to Ruby when the gun went off, pontificating on who might have really been responsible for the death of JFK. He'd even been a guest on *The Merv Griffin Show* a couple times.

With fame came a proclivity toward excessive drinking, which worsened when his wife and two children were killed in a single-car automobile accident in the 1970s.

"He's sober," Weeks said. "Lives with his niece up in Frisco. He'll be eighty in a month. If he makes it."

At various times the brass had talked about firing Maney. They never did, however. In addition to feeling sorry for him, there was a golden aura surrounding the officers involved in the Kennedy and Oswald cases. They had touched history.

The rain started in earnest, a hard downpour that peppered the tarp over our heads. We moved closer in order to hear each other.

"He and I keep in touch," Weeks said. "This morning I told him I was going to Rose Doucette's funeral. He wants to talk to you."

"Any idea why?"

Weeks shook his head.

THE LIFE AND DEATH OF ROSE DOUCETTE   217

"Did you find somebody who used to work northwest back in the nineties?" I asked. "That's who I really need to talk to."

"Do you understand that you're not on the job anymore?" he asked. "And that most cops think you killed your ex-wife?"

Mia's phone rang. She stepped away and answered.

"What's your point?" I asked.

"You're radioactive. Nobody's gonna want to talk to you."

"Except for Maney Bossert."

"Maney doesn't count. He's an old drunk who happens to have my cell number."

He didn't have to explain further. No harm would come to Weeks's reputation if word got out that he had hooked me up with Maney Bossert. The same couldn't be said for anybody else, active or retired.

Mia ended her call and walked back over. "We need to leave as soon as possible. I'll tell you more in the car."

"I'll text you Maney's info," Weeks said. "I'd talk to him sooner, rather than later."

*   *   *

Before we could leave, Tito Mullins made his way over to where we were standing.

The rain had slowed. Sunlight peeked through the clouds. Weeks greeted Tito and offered his condolences. They exchanged pleasantries for a few moments before Weeks left.

Tito's skin was pale and drawn.

"Where did you two go this morning?" he asked.

"We had an appointment," Mia said. "And we've got one now too."

"Thanks for coming," Tito said to me. "She would have wanted you here."

"It was a nice service," I said.

"All those cops and one little old defense attorney. I felt like a hen at a fox convention."

"Do you mind if I ask you a question about Rose?" I said.

I didn't much care for Tito, but they were about to bury his wife, and I thought maybe I should be a little sensitive to what he was going through. Next to me, I could feel Mia's displeasure at having to wait any longer to leave.

He nodded.

"Did you know that she dropped out of school for a period of time?" I asked.

He frowned. "Say what?"

"Rose, Boyd, and Josh Gannon all dropped out after the summer they attended a place called Camp Eagle Bluff."

"I've got her diploma. Saw it a couple days ago."

"She graduated," I said. "Couldn't have been on the force otherwise. But she and the rest of them missed a chunk of school."

Mia shifted her weight from foot to foot, glancing at her phone.

"And you still think this has something to do with one of the McFaddens?" he asked.

"Rye McFadden," I said. "The one nobody knows anything about. I've got an old address for him. We'll start there."

Mia tugged on my sleeve. "Let's go."

"What's got your knickers all twisted?" Tito asked.

"Rye McFadden." She held up her phone. "He's surfaced."

CHAPTER FORTY-FOUR

Tito walked with us to the parking area. After the rain, the trees in the cemetery glistened with moisture, the air so humid it clung to my flesh like a second skin.

As we hiked across the wet grass, I said to Mia, "Tell me what's going on."

She took a gander at Tito but didn't speak.

When we got close to the Escalade, she turned to him. "This is where you exit the train."

"If whatever you're doing involves Rye McFadden," he said, "then I'm going with you."

"Dylan and I are meeting with a client. Afraid not."

Attorney-client confidentiality was sacrosanct, right up there with don't bill more than twenty-four hours in a single day.

"I rode here with my sister," he said. "My pickup's still at the apartment."

Mia didn't reply, an *I-don't-care* expression on her face.

"There might be a police officer or two around who could give you a ride," I said.

He crossed his arms, not budging.

"Aren't you supposed to be at a reception or something?" I asked.

"There's a department thing at a bar," he said. "Thought I'd skip that. A defense lawyer and a bunch of drunk cops. That's a dumpster fire looking for a place to happen."

I would have passed on that one, too, if I'd been in his shoes. With a start, I realized there was no family reception because there was no real family left.

"Where was Boyd today?" I asked.

He shrugged. "Beats me. I don't even know how to get a hold of him."

"C'mon, Dylan." Mia pointed to the Escalade. "We need to hurry."

"I just buried my wife and you two are leaving me in the cemetery parking lot." Tito wagged a finger at me. "Rose would be disappointed in you, Dylan."

I ignored the dig. It was easy see what was happening. He was sublimating his grief into a desire to keep busy, to concentrate on a task. Focus on that hard enough, and you could postpone thinking about how your wife was never coming home again.

I arched an eyebrow and glanced at Mia.

She closed her eyes for a moment and took a deep breath. "All right, you can go. You'll be an associate of my firm. That gets us around the confidentiality."

"I accept," he said. "Thank you."

"Now will you tell me what's going on?" I asked her.

"Our newest client called. Rye was at his house just a little while ago."

*   *   *

Blaine McFadden and his family lived in a Mediterranean-style home as large as a Borgia palace, with a blue tile roof, white stucco walls, and a fountain big enough to swim laps in.

A number of vans were parked on the street in front of the house. Caterers and event rentals. Apparently, the McFaddens were getting ready for a party.

I pulled the Escalade into the circular driveway and stopped between the entrance and the fountain. The front door was wrought-iron and glass, a story-and-half tall.

As soon as I slid the transmission into PARK, Blaine McFadden emerged from the house. He was wearing khaki shorts and an old University of Texas T-shirt.

The three of us got out of the Escalade.

Blaine pointed to Tito. "Who's that?"

"Rose Doucette's husband," Mia said, "who, coincidentally, is a new associate of mine."

Blaine considered each of us in turn, obviously noticing our clothes. "The funeral was today, wasn't it?"

I nodded.

Blaine spoke to Tito. "Sorry for your loss. Please, come in. All of you."

We followed him inside. The entryway was cavernous, with a domed ceiling and double staircase on the far side.

Service people scurried about, carrying trays of glassware and bottles of wine.

"Having a party?" I asked.

"Yes, tonight." He pointed toward a hallway. "Let's talk in the study."

He led us to a room that was wood paneled, floor-to-ceiling shelves filled with books and photographs. Two leather sofas bracketed a coffee table in the middle of the room. A tablet computer sat on the coffee table.

"My brother, Rye, showed up here a couple of hours ago," Blaine said to me. "I'm guessing you haven't had much luck finding him."

"He hasn't left a very prominent trail," I said.

"What have you learned so far?"

I told him about the last known address from ten years ago, the aunt's house not too far from where we were at the moment.

"I'm sure he's not there," Blaine said.

"A 100 percent sure?" Mia asked.

He nodded. "She's scared of Rye, as most of us are. I could call her if you want verification."

"I'd rather just drop by," I said. "Tell me what happened here."

Blaine crossed his arms. "This is a difficult situation. I have two children. I don't want them exposed to any of this."

He picked up the tablet. Scrolled to a paused video, held up the screen for all of us to see.

The image was grainy in the way that security cams often were, especially those that were outdoors. It showed a portion of a backyard, the lush landscaping matching the front of the McFadden home.

A boy stood on the lawn, wearing a swimsuit. He was small and slight, maybe eleven or twelve years old.

"That's my son," Blaine said. "Fortunately, my daughter was upstairs with my wife."

A few yards away, a man sat on a bench holding a Frisbee. He and the boy looked like they were in the middle of a conversation.

The man was thin like Blaine and had the same bearing, head tilted slightly back like he was not quite engaged in whatever was before him. His hair was light-colored, shoulder length, tied in a

THE LIFE AND DEATH OF ROSE DOUCETTE   223

ponytail. He wore jeans and a polo shirt like one would expect in this neighborhood.

"Run it from the beginning," I said.

Blaine tapped a control and the two people disappeared, replaced by an empty lawn. The time stamp read 1:48 p.m., about when the chief of police was giving Rose a generic eulogy.

At 1:49 the Frisbee landed on the grass. Blaine's son ran into the frame and picked it up. A few seconds later, Rye McFadden came into view. He ruffled the boy's hair and sat on the bench. They talked for a short period.

The son sat next to Rye, who placed an arm around him. A few seconds later, the boy stood, Frisbee in hand.

He moved to a spot a few feet away, obviously wanting to play catch. He tossed the Frisbee to Rye, who caught it but didn't throw it back.

A few more seconds went by. Rye stood. He hugged the boy and wandered out of the frame.

"What about the other cameras?" I asked. "You've gotta have more video than that."

"He came in from the alley. That's all there is for that part of the yard. The cam is hidden pretty well. I'm guessing he didn't notice it."

"If Rye's been in and out of an institution all these years," Mia said, "how does your son even know who he is?"

"We have a call with my brother every Christmas, a video chat. My sister sets it up." Blaine shook his head, a rueful expression on his face. "Everyone gets to visit with Uncle Rye."

"What did Rye and your son talk about?" I asked.

"Sports. Whoever the kids are watching on YouTube these days. That sort of thing."

"Innocuous stuff," I said.

"There's nothing innocuous about Rye." Blaine's voice was angry. "My brother should not be . . . around children."

I thought about the video in a new light. Rye's behavior not that of an uncle with his nephew. More of a predator and a victim.

Tito had been in the corner, quietly looking at books. He pulled a card from the shelf and said, "Congratulations."

"On what?" Blaine asked.

"The party tonight," Tito said. "The kickoff for your congressional run."

CHAPTER FORTY-FIVE

Tito handed me the invitation.

It was made from linen card stock, expensive, thick like a charge card.

Eagles flanked an American flag. Below that, gold and blue lettering read, "You are cordially invited to join the Blaine McFadden for Congress Exploratory Committee." The date and time were tonight. The location was the house where we all were at the moment.

A list of supporters was at the bottom, people who'd signed up for the committee already. There were thirty or so names, many of them recognizable. Philanthropists and business leaders, a couple of billionaires, several people with Super Bowl rings.

"Looks like you have a busy evening," Mia said.

Blaine shrugged.

"Why didn't you tell us you were the one running for Congress?" I asked.

"What does that have to do with anything?" He plucked the invitation from my hand.

"Your brother, who you hired me to find, may be involved in the murder of a police officer," I said. "That means everything has to do with everything."

He put the card back on the shelf on top of a stack of others.

"What's the buy-in for tonight?" Tito asked. "That's a stout list you got so far."

Blaine rearranged several photographs on the shelf. He spoke without turning around. "Twenty-five thousand."

I whistled. "And they say lawyers are thieves."

Mia shot me a withering glance. Tito chuckled softly.

"The official sponsor for tonight is a super PAC," Blaine said. "Everything's legal."

"No wonder you don't want Rye hanging out in the backyard," I said. "Crazy's not a good look with that kind of money inside eating hors d'oeuvres and sipping champagne."

He continued to fuss with the photographs.

"What else aren't you telling us?" I asked. "You've moved that one picture like five times now."

He dropped his hands to his side.

I strolled over to the bookshelf. The picture Blaine had been moving from one place to another was old, the colors faded. The image showed a man who had to be a McFadden standing next to Lyndon Johnson in the Oval Office.

That shelf was obviously the political one. There were pictures of Blaine and other McFaddens with governors and senators, the odd president, both before and after Johnson.

I pointed to the photo. "Who's this with LBJ?"

"That would be my grandfather." He spoke the words softly, with reverence bordering on fear, and I wondered how much baggage was in that particular closet.

Celebrity pictures dominated the next shelf. Blaine with various actors and musicians, household names. Apparently, Bono had played an impromptu acoustic concert in this very room at some point.

"What do some old pictures have to do with finding my brother?" Blaine asked.

I turned away from the photos. "I need to talk to your son."

"My wife and children just left for the airport. They're on their way to Aspen. We go every year at this time."

"Your wife is missing your party tonight?" Mia asked.

Silence.

"It'll be nice for the kids to get out of the heat," I said. "You joining them?"

"Later in the week maybe. The campaign is keeping me busy."

"The campaign that you didn't tell us about," I said.

"I do a lot of things I don't tell you about. Perhaps we could focus on finding my brother. Maybe you could give me your action plan."

"How about a list of family members who live within five miles?" I said. "That'll be a good start after I visit your aunt."

"Other than her, no one lives nearby."

"What about the sister who got Rye out of the institution?" I asked.

"He's not at her place." Blaine rubbed his eyes. "My brother-in-law, let's just say he wasn't a fan of Rye being released."

"Still, I'm going to need her contact information," I said.

He sighed and grabbed a pencil and notepad from the coffee table.

"Will she be here tonight for your congressional kickoff?" Tito asked.

Blaine shook his head as he wrote.

"What about other family members?" I said. "Anybody coming in from out of town?"

From what I remembered of their history, the McFaddens were scattered across the state.

Houston and San Antonio. Austin. Midland. The centers of power.

McFadden handed me the slip of paper. "No family members will be joining me tonight."

Something about the way he spoke the words made me take notice. There was a hint of disappointment in his voice.

"How come?" I asked.

"I need to attend to some matters related to the party. Can you show yourselves out?"

No one moved.

Blaine looked at each of us, his expression indicating confusion at the fact that we didn't immediately do as he had requested.

Tito turned and examined another shelf, perusing book titles.

"My family has a certain way of doing things," Blaine said, "that's been ingrained in us since we were born."

"No public squabbles?" I remembered his comments in Mia's office.

He didn't speak. After a few seconds, he nodded.

"They don't want you to run for office, do they?" I said.

No reply, which was answer enough. The man was nearing fifty and still at the beck and call of others, unable to follow his own path. He was rich beyond most people's imagination, but there was a price to pay for that wealth.

"My cousin in San Antonio," he said. "The one married to a Latina. He's being groomed for a Senate run."

"But not you," I said. "You have to stay in your lane."

"I'm available tomorrow," Blaine said. "But I do need to get back to the party details now."

"We appreciate your time." Mia headed to the door.

Across the room, Tito stood up from a kneeling position, holding another photograph.

"Interesting picture," he said. "Camp Eagle Bluff. I think I've heard of that place."

CHAPTER FORTY-SIX

I took the picture from Tito. It was another old one, this time from the 1950s or before, black and white. Blaine's grandfather with two other men in front of a sign that read, "Camp Eagle Bluff Grand Opening."

The men were wearing casual clothing of the era, high-waisted khaki pants and plaid shirts, short-brimmed Stetsons. In front of them stood several children. Everyone was smiling.

I held up the picture. "Before we go, we're going to need to discuss this."

He looked at his watch. "Fine. But we have to be quick."

I put the photo on the coffee table, sat on one of the sofas, waited.

After a few seconds, Blaine said, "Well? What do you want to know?"

"Start at the beginning," I said.

Mia sat next to me. Tito plopped on the second sofa, loosened his tie.

"What do you mean, 'the beginning?'" Blaine asked.

"Neanderthals were hunting wooly mammoths with pointy sticks," I said. "Start there."

He stared at each of us, no doubt wondering how he had lost control of the situation.

After a moment, he said, "My family made a strategic decision after the Second World War to add to their land holdings. Eagle Bluff, that was part of what they acquired."

"You're doing great," I said. "Keep going."

He continued, telling us a story about generational wealth, a peek behind the curtain of old money, how the rich got richer.

The most lucrative play was north of Dallas, he told us, the direction of growth. Huge tracts of farmland were acquired with the idea that one day the real estate developers would come calling and the family could cash out at fifty or a hundred times their purchase price. Land bought by the acre would sell by the square foot. The family followed the same strategy in the major metropolitan areas of the state, and it paid off handsomely, a nice addition to the wealth created by their oil and ranching empires.

The price for land in southeastern Dallas County where the camp had been located was so cheap, bordering on free, the family also acquired vast swaths along the Trinity River, figuring why not?

Blaine's grandmother had the idea for the camp. She'd been active in a number of charities and saw a need for children from low-income families stuck in the city during the summer. We have all this land, she'd told everyone, beautiful acreage that was not ever going to be suitable for construction. Why not put some of it to use?

So, the family created Camp Eagle Bluff, seeding the nonprofit organization with money and a donation of two hundred acres, a small portion of which was out of the floodplain, a suitable location for camp buildings.

Another plus, the grandmother had argued, was the opportunity for the McFadden offspring to be around those less fortunate.

"What do you mean by that?" I asked.

"My grandmother wanted the younger generation to work at the camp," he said. "You know, as counselors."

Mia took a sharp breath.

"In the sixties and seventies," Blaine said, "just about every McFadden of a certain age worked at the camp. They came from all over the state. It was like a rite of passage."

"What about you?" Tito asked. "Did you work there?"

He shook his head. "The tradition started dying out in the 1980s. The camp had begun to fall apart. My grandmother was old. You know how it is."

"Tell me about Rye," I said. "Did he work there?"

A caterer stuck his head in the study. "Sir, when you have a second, I need to talk to you."

"I'll be there in a minute," Blaine said.

The caterer left.

"What do you care where Rye worked?" Blaine asked. "I don't understand how this helps locate him."

"Just answer the damn question," I said.

A flash of anger appeared in his eyes. He took a deep breath. "Rye was already showing signs of, well, not being quite right. The family thought it would be a good experience, a way to get him back on track."

"To be around children," Mia said. "The family thought that was a good idea?"

Blaine crossed his arms, avoiding our gaze.

"Has Rye ever assaulted anyone?" I asked. "Sexually abused a child?"

"I don't know how to answer that," Blaine said, his voice soft, hard to hear.

Tito leaned forward. "How about yes or no?"

"To the best of my knowledge, no." Blaine paused. "But I couldn't swear to that."

"When did Rye work at the camp?" I asked.

"I don't remember. Late high school, I think. That would have been the mid-1990s."

Mia, Tito, and I all looked at each other.

"We need you to remember exactly," I said. "And then we want to know about McFadden Memorial Hospital."

"What about the hospital?" Blaine asked. "That's another branch of the family foundation. I don't see—"

BZZZ. A cell rang. Blaine pulled a phone from his pocket, looked at the screen.

"This is the governor," he said. "I need to take the call."

He left the room.

CHAPTER FORTY-SEVEN

With my phone I took a picture of Blaine's grandfather in front of the camp. Then I hurried to the corner of the room where Tito had found the image. A number of photographs were there, family snapshots mostly. Blaine and his wife and children, holidays and vacations, that sort of thing.

There was a shot of Blaine and Rye in their teens with the grandfather on the front steps of what appeared to be a large home, all three unsmiling.

I was struck by the similarities between this image and that of Rose and Boyd and their mother in front of the modest house on Lively Lane. Someone trying to preserve a slice of time, no matter if the participants wanted them to or not.

"What now?" Mia asked. "We're not going to get much more out of him today."

"We go see the aunt," I said. "We have to find Rye."

The three of us left as a caterer carrying a tray of glasses entered the study.

There was plenty of activity in the house—people running around carrying party stuff, a bar being assembled in the entryway—but no sign of Blaine McFadden.

Outside, several valets were setting up shop by the front door.

Tito hopped in the back of the Escalade, Mia in the front passenger seat. I walked around to the driver's side, opened the door, but didn't get in.

A card had been left under the windshield wiper.

I grabbed it and slid behind the wheel.

"What's that?" Mia asked.

It was a business card identical to the one given to me by the manager at the halfway house in East Dallas, Josh Gannon's last address.

"It's for a reporter." I flipped the card over and read out loud the handwritten note on the back. "Give me a call. Trying to find Boyd Doucette."

A caterer's van pulled up behind me, obviously wanting my spot to unload. I put the Escalade in gear and left.

*   *   *

Blaine's house was on Beverly Drive, a wide, tree-lined thoroughfare. The street was named for Beverly Hills because the man who designed this part of Dallas more than a century before also fashioned the Southern California enclave.

The homes were all similar to Blaine's—large and well-appointed, no expense spared in design or construction. Blaine's aunt lived not far away on a more secluded, but no less luxurious, street.

I was headed there when Mia's phone rang.

She answered. Her body tensed up. She put a hand on the dash as if that would stabilize her movements.

I pulled to the curb. She held the phone pressed to her ear, saying things like, "Is he all right?" and "I'm on my way."

She hung up. "Caleb is sick." Her voice was shaky.

"What do you mean, sick?" I said. "Where is he?"

"That was my mother. He was throwing up. They couldn't get him to stop."

I put a hand on her arm. Her skin was cold. "Mia. Tell me where he is."

"At the ER." Her teeth chattered. "With my parents."

Tito poked my shoulder. "Don't just sit there like a bump on a log. Let's get to the hospital, speedy-pronto."

Mia told me the location. I made a U-turn and hoped traffic wasn't too bad at this time of day.

Fifty minutes later, we met her parents in an ER waiting room on the north side of town. Mia and her mother hugged each other. Riya's face was haggard, her sari rumpled. She nodded hello to me. A moment later she and Mia disappeared into the treatment area.

Her father, Arjun, said to me, "Caleb most probably has a stomach bug."

"Is that good or bad?" I asked.

"It is scary because he is so young, but the doctors do not believe the situation to be dire." Arjun introduced himself to Tito. "Why are you both dressed up?"

"We've all been at a funeral," I said.

"Ah, yes." Arjun nodded. "Rose Doucette. Your former wife."

I pointed to Tito. "And his current wife."

Arjun looked at me for several seconds. Then he turned his attention to Tito, who held up his hand to display a wedding ring.

One eyebrow raised, Arjun said, "How nice for you to be close at this time."

"That's us," I said. "Nice people."

We found three chairs together and sat down.

"Caleb is a good boy. So sorry he is ill." Arjun paused and turned his attention to me. "Are you romantically involved with my daughter?"

A sucker-punch. Who knew the old man had it in him?

Tito cocked his head, a smirk on his face.

"Mia and I are very close," I said. "We also work together."

"That is not an answer." He shook his head. "Perhaps you should be an attorney too."

Tito chuckled.

"Do not let my wife bother you," the father said. "You are not a desi, so you will never be good enough for Mia."

I frowned, not understanding the term.

"Desi means you are not from India or Pakistan," he said.

"Riya wants what's best for her daughter," I said. "In her mind, I guess that means a, uh . . . desi. I respect that."

"As do I." He stood. "Do you wish for something from the vending machine?"

I shook my head and he left.

Tito picked up a magazine. "You got a complicated life."

Twenty minutes later, Mia came back to the waiting room. Caleb was doing well and would be discharged in a little while. She planned to take him back to her parents' house for the night. Tom, her cousin who was a police officer, was coming over for dinner. She'd be fine, don't worry.

"I'm not leaving you and Caleb," I said.

"Yeah, you are." Tito pointed to the door. "We got some hay that needs baling."

"He's right," Mia said. "You need to finish what you started. We'll be okay."

I stared at her for a moment.

She gave me a hug and returned to the treatment area.

I headed to the parking lot with Tito, wondering how big of a mistake I was making by continuing the investigation and not staying with her.

Turned out, pretty damn big.

CHAPTER FORTY-EIGHT

I called the reporter as we drove back. Madge Boatwright was her name. When Madge's voicemail picked up, I left a message—my name and number, nothing else.

We were on the Dallas Tollway, the highway that split the northern half of the city in two. It was rush hour, heavy traffic, the office buildings on either side of the road disgorging workers.

From the passenger seat Tito stared outside without speaking.

"Where do you want me to drop you?" I asked.

He shrugged.

"How about your sister's?"

Silence.

"Your wife's funeral was a few hours ago," I said. "You ought to be with your people."

"Rose was my people."

"You know what I mean."

"We were headed to the aunt's house," he said. "Before the detour."

"You sure you're up for that?"

"I gotta keep busy. Best way I know to do that is to find the SOB who killed my wife."

*　　*　　*

It was seven in the evening when I parked in front of the aunt's place, a white columned home that looked like Tara without the cotton growing out back.

"Let me do the talking." Tito opened his door. "I know how to handle rich old ladies."

"Did you put yourself through college as a gigolo?"

He ignored my comment and exited the SUV, marching up the sidewalk. I followed.

Several rocking chairs were on the porch. They were dusty, covered in cobwebs. The mailbox was overflowing.

I knocked on the door, rang the bell. No response.

Tito peered through a window, but the blinds were down.

I knocked and rang again. Nothing.

"She's not home," a woman's voice said.

Tito and I looked around.

"Over here."

I walked the length of the front porch toward the sound of the voice, the shrubs bordering the aunt's house with the place next door.

There was a break in the vegetation, and a woman stood there holding a cat.

"Are you looking for Carol?" the woman asked. "She's out of town. I'm her neighbor."

The woman was in her seventies with hair that had been dyed henna red. She wore a housecoat and slippers. Another cat threaded its way between her ankles.

Her home next door was hard to see because of the trees and bushes, a mass of greenery that looked like it hadn't been pruned in decades.

"Do you know when she'll be back?" I asked.

"She summers in Maine," the woman said. "Bar Harbor."

"How nice," I said. "So, she's gone for a while?"

"Can I help you with anything?" the woman asked. "I pick up her mail."

I glanced back at the mailbox.

"We're looking for Carol's nephew," Tito said. "Rye McFadden. Have you seen him?"

"Goodness. Is Rye in trouble?"

"No, ma'am." Tito smiled. "We just want to talk to him."

She stroked the cat in her arms but didn't speak.

"Do you know Rye?" I asked.

"Of course I do. Rye's mother and I were debutantes the same year."

Tito asked if she knew any of the current debs and what parties she planned to attend during the upcoming season. She smiled at their point of connection, and they talked for a few moments about that particular demographic, people who knew how to curtsy.

I listened to them chatter, wondering what the upside was to being a debutante, other than learning skills necessary should you ever time travel back to the sixteenth century and need to be presented to the court of Marie Antoinette.

"What about Blaine?" Tito asked. "I bet you know him too."

"They were sweet little boys, both of them."

"And when they grew up?" he said.

She clutched the cat to her chest.

"Would you do us a favor?" I handed her one of my cards. "If you see Rye, call me."

The number was my old one, but I'd forwarded it to my burner.

She took the card. "Well, if you must know, Rye was here several days ago."

Tito arched an eyebrow. I held my breath and waited. Interviewing people was an art. Rarely could the most direct path be taken. They liked to mosey around a topic, taking their time, sniffing the air.

"I saw him in the backyard." She slid the card in the pocket of her dress.

"Would you show us?" Tito asked.

"Why, of course." She stepped through the bushes and led us to the other side of the house and down the driveway.

The rear of the aunt's home was dominated by a flagstone patio, an outdoor kitchen, and a small pool. Beyond the pool was a narrow strip of lawn. Beyond that was a three-car garage with an apartment on the second floor.

I peered through the back door into the kitchen of the house. No lights or sign of activity.

Tito said, "Where exactly did you see Rye, ma'am?"

"There." She pointed to an outdoor table and chairs in a shady area by the pool.

Tito stroked his chin. "And what was he doing?"

The question seemed to perplex her. She frowned. After a moment, she said, "Why, nothing. What do you think he would be doing?"

"Was he alone?" I asked.

She guessed so, but she'd only seen him for a moment because she was watering her day lilies. She was going to come over and say hi but by the time she finished, he was gone.

I asked her what Rye looked like these days and her description matched what we'd seen on Blaine McFadden's video—a skinny guy in his forties with a blond ponytail.

The question of when she saw him proved to be problematic. Three days ago. Or was it four? Come to think of it, maybe it was two days ago.

After much discussion, Tito narrowed the range down to between two and three days ago, which meant absolutely nothing beyond the fact that we now had concrete evidence placing Rye at his aunt's house.

I climbed the stairs to the garage apartment. The door was locked. Through a window, I could see a bed and a sitting area. The bed was made, and no luggage was visible.

I returned to the back patio where Tito and the neighbor were still talking.

"How long has it been since you've seen Rye?" I asked. "Other than recently."

No answer.

"We heard he's been away for a long time," I said. "Only just got back to town."

A moment passed as she stared at me, her eyes narrowed into slits. She squeezed the cat to her chest until it meowed.

"I have to go now." She headed to the front, looking over her shoulder as she went.

*   *   *

We trudged back to the Escalade, got inside.

I cranked the ignition, flipped the AC to max. "You did a good job with her," I said to Tito. "Much as that pains me to admit."

"Flies and honey. I've picked up a thing or two over the years going after witnesses on cross." Tito adjusted a vent. "Where're we going next, Mister Big Shot Private Investigator?"

Good question. The reporter Madge Boatwright hadn't returned my call yet. Maney Bossert, the retired cop who Detective

Weeks said wanted to talk to me, lived in a suburb north of town. It would be pushing nine o'clock by the time we got there, too late to talk to someone his age who had health problems.

I slid the transmission into DRIVE and stared down the street. "I don't know."

CHAPTER FORTY-NINE

Tito told me I was looking a might peaked and suggested we get something to eat. He said anywhere was all right with him so long as it was Mexican food.

In Texas, that doesn't narrow it down much. People have their favorites, places their parents took them to as children, much like lobster joints in Maine or strip clubs in Florida. Passions ran high in the Lone Star State when it came to enchiladas.

We finally settled on Ojeda's on Maple Avenue, a family-owned restaurant that had been around since *Laugh-In* was on the air. The chips were hot and greasy, the best kind, and they served a chili con carne sauce that was close to ambrosia.

The place was decorated with pink and yellow holiday lights hanging from the ceilings and posters of Mexican movies from the 1950s on the walls.

We left our coats and ties in the Escalade. Inside, we sat in a booth and ordered—cheese enchilada dinner for the both of us, iced tea for me, a frozen margarita for Tito.

I texted Mia and asked how everything was going. Fine, she replied. Caleb was okay but sleepy. Her father was fixing dinner while she and her mother fussed over the infant.

I put the phone away.

Tito drank a third of his margarita in one gulp. He was wired, jumping from topic to topic, talking about how the Mavericks were looking for next season, asking what I thought about the new Ford pickups, if I'd ever been spring skiing in Vail. He gesticulated with his hands a lot, his voice booming.

After another slug of his drink, he said, "I ever tell you about the stripper and Judge Schmidt?"

"We've only been hanging out a couple days. So, no, you haven't told me that story." His skin was flushed from the alcohol, a watery sheen over his eyes.

"Believe it or not her real name was Candy," he said. "She was in Schmidt's court for ag assault."

I'd testified in front of Judge Schmidt on several occasions. He had the personality and sense of humor one usually associated with driftwood. Only without the warmth.

"Candy was giving this guy a table dance and he got all handsy with her," Tito said. "So, naturally she reacts by coldcocking him with a beer bottle."

"Naturally." I took a drink of iced tea. "Sounds like the guy had it coming."

"Without a doubt. She wouldn't have been in trouble either except the guy's brother was a city councilman, and, well, you can see there wasn't a happy ending in store for Candy."

The waiter brought our food.

"Is there a point to this story?" I asked. "Other than the undue influence politicians have on our judicial system?"

He ignored my question, leaning forward to continue the story.

"So, Candy's all nervous about being in court. And—unbeknownst to her attorney, yours truly—she's popped a couple Valiums and washed 'em down with a freaking pint of vodka."

He paused to take a bite of his food.

"Let me guess," I said. "Candy flashed the judge."

"Dammit." He dropped his fork on the plate. "Why'd you have to spoil the punch line?"

"Sorry," I said, not sorry in the least.

He grumbled and drained his drink, ordering another one. When the second margarita arrived, he licked some salt off the rim but didn't drink any. He seemed to sink in on himself, the animated behavior from seconds before evaporating like a drop of rain on hot asphalt. Grief was a strange phenomenon, the path it took hard to predict, especially when fueled by booze.

"What's our next step?" he asked.

I told him about Maney Bossert, the retired cop.

He didn't reply, a glum look on his face. Discussing the investigation brought everything back into focus. We finished our meals in silence. He tossed his napkin on his plate, shifting in his seat like he was uncomfortable.

"You okay?" I asked.

"Something I want to tell you." His voice was soft.

"Yeah? What?"

"Me and Rose. We didn't get together until she left you."

"The timing of everything might give one pause. You can understand that, I'm sure."

"She wasn't a cheater."

I wanted to believe him. Rose was fundamentally a good person, honest and forthright at her core. Except for what she had kept hidden from both of her husbands.

I yawned. It was after nine. My eyes felt gritty, my limbs heavy.

"Let's go back to the apartment," he said. "I got to get some sleep."

*　　*　　*

Frisco, Texas, where Maney Bossert lived with his niece, was once a small farming community thirty miles north of Dallas.

Now the pastures had been devoured by shopping malls and subdivisions, twenty-story office towers and gleaming corporate headquarters, the family farms gobbled up as if a land-eating virus were chomping its way toward the Oklahoma state line.

I'd talked to the niece earlier and arranged a meeting time of nine thirty that morning.

Her house was in a subdivision only a few blocks from the head-quarters of the Dallas Cowboys, an enormous facility called The Star, a conglomeration of buildings beyond what was needed for the football franchise, offices and hotels and apartments overlooking the team's practice fields.

Tito and I grabbed breakfast and headed north. Technically, I would be violating the terms of my bail since Frisco was in another county, but at this point I didn't really care.

Of bigger concern was convincing Tito that the day's activities didn't include overthrowing a Central American junta, so he didn't need to bring multiple firearms. After much back-and-forth, I managed to persuade him to only carry on his person one small pistol.

Guns were like power tools. If you weren't trained in their proper use, you could get hurt really easily, and most firearm aficionados were not well trained, to put it mildly.

The niece's house was two-story, new within the last ten years like the rest of the homes in the subdivision. The front was brick, the sides wooden, the builder's effort at keeping construction costs low.

It was Saturday morning and children were playing up and down the block, interspersed with people puttering in their yards.

I parked in front of the niece's house. "This time, let me do the talking."

The niece answered the door. She was in her thirties, with eyes that were a little too far apart, giving her a perpetually vacant expression. She directed us to the family room at the rear of the home, a large area, the den and kitchen combined, overlooking a pool that took up the entire backyard.

Maney Bossert sat in the middle of a U-shaped sectional sofa that faced a fireplace and a TV.

I introduced myself and Tito.

Maney wore sweatpants and a T-shirt, both too large. His skin was mottled like a moldy tomato, his hair thin and gray. An oxygen tank sat next to him, a plastic tube snaking to the cannula in his nose.

I sat across from him; Tito by my side. "Larry Weeks said you wanted to talk to me."

He looked at Tito. "I've heard a you before. You're a lawyer, aren't you?"

His voice was raspy, like the air in his lungs was at a premium.

Tito nodded.

"A *defense* lawyer," Maney said.

Unless you were married to one, most cops loathed defense attorneys.

"That's right," I said. "Tito is also Rose Doucette's widower."

Maney squinted at me. "You were married to her too."

"Yep."

He coughed, phlegm rattling in his throat. "That's a puzzler. You two hanging out together."

Tito sighed, stared at the backyard.

"What did you want to talk to me about?" I asked.

He adjusted the oxygen tube. "Right before I retired, I worked patrol, southeast division."

Southeast was the equivalent of Siberia. A career killer.

"They didn't know what else to do with me, I guess." He shifted in his seat.

The effort to speak seemed to be taking a toll on the man. Or maybe it was what he was remembering.

"You ever heard of a place called Camp Eagle Bluff?" he asked.

CHAPTER FIFTY

There it was again. A location I'd never heard of forty-eight hours ago.

"That name rings a bell," I said, hoping to sound casual. "You ever been there?"

Maney stared at the blank TV, a faraway look in his eyes. "Long time ago. Summer of 1994."

The Venn diagram for cops, poker players, and shrinks overlapped at a single point—don't let your reactions impact the game.

I tried to keep my face blank. "Tell me about that summer."

"July in Texas. Hot as hell's attic." He seemed to be speaking to no one in particular. Almost talking to himself. Unburdening his mind. "I was at the VFW the night before, late. Me and booze, we were a bad combo back then."

He told us how hungover he was when the missing persons call came in midmorning from a place called Camp Eagle Bluff.

At the time, he'd never heard of the camp either.

He knew the general area, though, as did I. There wasn't much in that part of Dallas, only a few neighborhoods filled with shotgun shacks, low-lying areas prone to flooding, the residents overwhelmingly poor and Black.

The Great Trinity Forest, the location of the camp, was wilderness, untouched by human hands. Thousands upon thousands of acres of cypress and post oaks and dogwoods, century-old trees draped with honeysuckle and milkweed, an impenetrable mass once you got off the few roads leading in and out of the area.

Maney told us it took him several tries before he found the right road to the camp, a caliche path more like a tunnel due to the canopy of limbs overhead.

The camp itself was built on high ground that had been cleared of vegetation.

There was an administration building and a dining hall / activity center at the front, cabins arrayed out on either side. An archery range was beyond that.

It was obvious the buildings needed maintenance, he told us. The paint was peeling, or in some instances gone altogether, roofs were missing shingles, windows cracked. The place had obviously been nice at one point, but that day in 1994 it seemed as if the powers that be had stopped caring.

"The camp administrator," Maney said. "Kevin was his name. He met me at the front of the main building before I even got out of the car."

"And what did Kevin say?" I asked.

"Three campers had disappeared."

Tito and I glanced at each other.

"I asked when he noticed they were gone," Maney said. "I figured he was going to say earlier that morning or something like that."

The first question a good cop would ask. If children were missing, every hour that passed meant the likelihood of finding them unharmed got smaller.

"He stares at the ground like he doesn't want to tell me." Maney paused. "Then he says, 'Three days ago.'"

Tito let out a breath and crossed his arms.

"I ask him if he's notified the parents," Maney said. "He says, 'No, *they* told me not to.'"

"*They?*" I said.

Maney rearranged some pill bottles on the coffee table. "Soon as he realized the three campers were missing, Kevin had called his boss, who said everything was fine. Just sit tight, we'll get back to you."

"Who was the boss?" I asked.

"He never said. What happened later, it didn't really matter."

Tito leaned forward, elbows on his knees.

"Kevin gets that I'm pissed, obviously. But he's scared. Says this is just a summer job, and he doesn't want any trouble." Maney looked at me. "What would you a done?"

"Call my supervisor," I said.

"Exactly." Maney explained how he was reaching for his radio when he heard the sirens and saw a swirl of dust in the distance. A moment later, a small convoy of squad cars barreled down the driveway, shuddering to a stop behind his unit.

The passenger door of the lead car opened, and a plainclothes officer in his fifties got out.

Deputy Chief Wally Watson, long dead by the time I joined the force, but a man whose reputation lingered in the shadows years after his passing.

Watson had the political instincts and morality usually associated with a medieval pope. He always wore the same outfit, a buttermilk-colored suit, a bolo tie, and black cowboy boots, a pearl-handled Smith & Wesson on his hip in a hand-tooled leather holster. He was old school, too, violent and mean, a slap here, a nightstick there.

"Then a bunch of officers get out of the other cars," Maney said. "People I'd never seen, not from the southeast."

Watson ambled and addressed Maney by name, despite the fact that they had never met, and suggested they take a walk. Once they were out of earshot, the deputy chief told Maney that they were in for rough weather on this one. A real shitstorm.

"Watson told me I had two options," Maney said. "I could stay outside and get the stink on me. Or go to a place where it was dry and safe."

CHAPTER FIFTY-ONE

The people who ran Eagle Bluff, people who worked for the McFaddens, wanted to handle the situation internally.

They'd convinced Kevin not to contact the police, but after three days he'd gotten worried. He was the guy on site, the one whose neck would be on the chopping block if anything happened to those kids. So, he decided to call 911, and that changed everything. The call meant there was a record, something that couldn't be swept away. Secrets would have to be dealt with now.

The call had alerted people in the department beholden to outside forces. They had made some calls themselves and before Maney Bossert could even start filling out the forms, a high-ranking police official and a number of other officers arrived.

Deputy Chief Watson took charge of the investigation right then and there. He directed Kevin and Maney inside the administration building, somewhere with air-conditioning.

"We sat at this conference table," Maney said. "Me and Deputy Chief Watson across from Kevin."

"Anybody else there?" I asked.

"Two cops I didn't know. Big guys. They stood behind Kevin."

25625

A standard intimidation tactic. Split the subject's attention. While he's talking to someone in front of him, he's worrying about whoever's lurking behind him.

Maney continued. "Watson leans back in his chair like he owns the place and tells Kevin to go over all of it again."

"Anything new this time?" I asked.

"Yeah. Turns out the campers didn't just leave; they were taken off property."

"By who?"

"A counselor, Kevin says. Totally against the rules, but the guy had a car and nobody stopped him."

Tito swore softly.

Maney told us that Kevin started to say the counselor's name, but Deputy Chief Watson barked at him to be quiet. Then Watson asked for details on the campers, something that should have been done at the very outset.

"Two boys and a girl," Maney said. "The girl was thirteen. One of the boys was her brother, just turned twelve. The other was a neighbor, the same age as the brother."

No one spoke for a moment. Maney stared at the floor, avoiding my gaze.

"What are you leaving out?" I asked.

"Watson . . . he was a bad guy."

"No argument from me."

"He asked Kevin about the girl." Maney licked his lips like he was trying to find the right words.

I leaned forward. "What did he want to know about her?"

A short period of silence passed before Maney said, "He asked if she was fucking either of the boys."

Tito got to his feet and stalked across the room to the TV, the tendons in his jaw visible beneath the skin. Several seconds later, he walked back and sat down.

"Kevin bows up, says of course not. They're barely in their teens and one of the boys is her brother."

I was sorry Deputy Chief Wally Watson was dead. I'd like to find the man and give him a nice throat punch.

Maney told us that Watson asked for names and contact info for the parents of the three. No request for physical descriptions of the missing children or anything that would help track them down. The two burly officers escorted Kevin out of the room to get the information.

"Then it was just me and the deputy chief in that conference room," Maney said.

I wondered if Watson had offered the carrot or the stick. Or both.

"I was the first on the scene." Maney seemed to get smaller, the cushions on the sofa swallowing him up. "Watson wanted me to write up the report in a certain way."

"Without mentioning the counselor," I said.

Maney nodded. "He handed me an envelope full of cash . . . and I took it."

CHAPTER FIFTY-TWO

The niece came into the family room of the house in Frisco. She asked if we needed anything.

Maney shook his head. She checked his oxygen tank and went outside to the backyard.

When the door closed, I asked Maney, "Who was the missing girl?"

It felt faintly ridiculous to ask, but I needed confirmation.

"Your ex. Rose Doucette."

"And the counselor?" I was pretty sure I knew the answer already.

"McFadden boy. Rye, like the whiskey." He pursed his lips. "You think I was wrong to take the money?"

I didn't answer. That was not for me to say. Everyone has to live with their decisions. Nobody gets to slip off this mortal coil without some blemish on their soul.

"Every night when I go to sleep, I see my dead children," he said. "Who gets to decide what's right and wrong in this world anyway?"

"Why'd you reach out to me?" I asked. "It's been almost thirty years."

"That case was my white whale." He adjusted the valve on his tank. "You know how it is. Some of them just get a hold of you and won't let go."

I understood completely. Every cop lugged a case like that with them to the grave. Sometimes they went to the grave early because of those cases.

"I heard when Rose joined the force," Maney said. "She was a go-getter from day one, from what they tell me. Then she married a cop. You."

"Then she got murdered," I said.

"Yep." Maney scratched his chin. "Right after one of the other campers supposedly killed himself."

"How'd you know about that?"

"Larry Weeks told me. He was my union rep back when."

Tito spoke for the first time. "So, Rye McFadden takes the kids and three days later the police are brought in. Then what?"

Maney cranked the valve on his oxygen tank again and the hiss of airflow grew louder. His skin was pale, and his lips had a bluish tint.

"You doing all right?" I asked.

He pointed to the array of medications on the coffee table. "The one on the left."

I handed him the bottle and he popped a pill under his tongue. A few moments later, his breathing eased and his coloring improved.

"Congestive heart failure and emphysema." He took several deep breaths. "I'd kill for a Marlboro right now though."

"Were you there when they found Rose?" I asked.

Maney Bossert closed his eyes and continued the story.

*   *   *

Kevin came back with the names of the parents and their contact info, Maney told us. By that time a half dozen other officers were in the room, cronies of the deputy chief's.

"Watson was on his cell, one of them brick phones," Maney said. "He hung up and took the list. Told his men he'd just heard where the three campers were. Said the girl and her brother conned a counselor into getting them some booze."

Tito crossed and uncrossed his legs several times, lips pressed together tightly.

"One of Watson's men asks if that meant they were out partying somewhere," Maney said. "Watson nods and everyone laughs."

I did the math in my head. Rye McFadden was eighteen or nineteen at the time, maybe twenty, an adult with three preadolescents. A wave of rage emanated from my core, the skin on my arms and legs feeling hot.

"What else did Watson say about Rose?" Tito asked, his voice husky.

A moment passed before Maney replied. "Watson told everyone that he heard the girl was a real tramp, so there was no telling what was going on."

A story as old as dirt. When in doubt, blame the victim, in this instance a thirteen-year-old girl at summer camp.

"Watson orders a couple of his men to round up the parents," Maney said. "Says to tell 'em their kids are in trouble, but the police are gonna do what they can to see that they don't get charged with anything."

A smart move if you were on Team McFadden. Put the victims on the defensive.

Maney told us he and Watson left the building, followed by the other officers. There were more squad cars outside than before along with a handful of civilian vehicles—a couple of Cadillacs and a Suburban.

Several men in expensive-looking suits milled about. They were lawyers, Maney learned, there to represent the interests of the McFadden family.

In addition to the lawyers and the cops, there was an old man standing by the Suburban, an unlit cigar in his teeth. He wore a pair of khakis and a short-brimmed Stetson.

The grandfather. I remembered the picture in Blaine's study.

Deputy Chief Watson approached the man with deference, Maney said, telling him they were handling everything, and as far as they could tell, the press didn't know about any of this.

"The old man talked about what a handful Rye was," Maney said. "And Watson went into the boys-will-be-boys routine, all that bullshit."

I envisioned the scene, the grandfather and the deputy chief sharing their worries about Rye McFadden while showing no concern for the three children being held against their will.

Maney continued. "Then the old man said he hoped Rye turned out better than Rye's father, since the best part of him dribbled down his mama's leg."

I tried to imagine what it had been like growing up in a McFadden house, the dysfunction magnified by all that money.

"How did it play out?" I asked, swallowing my anger.

"Watson wanted to take my car," Maney said. "So he and the grandfather rode with me and everyone else followed."

"Where did you go?"

"The old man gave directions. Wasn't very far away, maybe a mile or so, but it took damn near twenty minutes to get there."

They drove deeper into the forest, down a one-lane dirt road, the trees on either side like the walls of a canyon. Finally, the squad car bounced over a cattle guard and followed a narrow track to a patch of high ground. There, a stone house sat in a clearing beside a rusted windmill. A late-model BMW was parked in front.

"Place didn't look like much," Maney said. "The house had to be a hundred years old if it was a day. Part of some ranch he'd bought a long time ago, the old man said."

"Who went in first?" I asked.

"The grandfather and Watson."

"That's not the way it should have gone down," I said. "A hostage situation like that, a SWAT team should have handled the entry. Not a civilian and a deputy chief."

"Watson wasn't happy about it either, but the old man insisted."

It was one thing to bring a civilian along on something like that. It was another to let him direct the activity. But power trumps procedure, especially with a crooked cop like Watson, one who'd already sold his services to the McFadden family.

Watson and the old man went into the house, Maney told us, while the others waited outside in the sun.

"Maybe a minute later," Maney said, "I heard shouts from inside. Then Watson ran out, scared-looking, his face all pale."

Tito perched on the edge of the sofa, listening as intently as I was.

"Watson yells at me to call an ambulance. I ask what am I supposed to tell 'em?"

Neither Tito nor I spoke.

"Watson's shaking now, he's so scared," Maney said. "He grabs my arm and says to tell the ambulance to fucking hurry."

CHAPTER FIFTY-THREE

For several moments the family room of the home in Frisco was silent except for the hiss of the oxygen tank.

Maney told us Deputy Chief Watson instructed him to cordon off the area and that nobody was to go in the house except for Watson's people or the paramedics. That included Maney.

"I stayed by the front door. Directed traffic." He popped another pill under his tongue. "It got crazy real fast. The lawyers running around. More cops showed up. Then the paramedics."

"Did you see inside?" I asked.

He ignored my question. "I kept everybody out except for who Watson told me was okay."

"But you had to see something," Tito said.

"I stayed outside." Maney crossed his arms. "That's what my orders were."

Tito and I looked at each other but didn't say anything.

"What was I supposed to do?" Maney's voice was plaintive, heavy with emotion. "Watson was a damn deputy chief."

"It's okay," I said. "This is all ancient history. We just want to know what happened to Rose."

"The guy that took them, he shouldn't a been around kids." Maney wiped his eyes. "He shouldn't a been around anybody."

I tried to speak to Maney in a soothing voice. "Let's stop now. We didn't mean to upset you."

"Like hell we're stopping. I started this and I'm a gonna finish it."

And he did, telling us what he'd pieced together while standing by the front door.

The three teenagers were conscious but non-responsive, the paramedics talking about dehydration and various physical traumas, Watson saying how he didn't want this to get blown out of proportion so if any of the paramedics talked to the media, he and every cop in Dallas would make that person's existence extremely unpleasant.

What Maney didn't hear was anything about the counselor Rye McFadden or the grandfather.

"Then they brought the three campers out," he said. "On stretchers."

A knot of pain formed deep in my chest. The ordeal that Rose had endured seared itself in my mind.

"The way they looked." Maney shook his head. "So young, so scared. Hooked up to IVs. I couldn't help myself. I asked Watson where the counselor was. If I could be in on the arrest. Get a little pound of flesh."

"What did he say?" Tito asked.

"He told me to forget the counselor or he'd make my pension disappear."

"What happened next?" I asked.

"They rushed all three to the hospital."

"McFadden Memorial." I sighed. "Where the family could control the situation."

Maney nodded. "Convenient, huh? After that, I guess the law-yers went to work because it was like nothing ever happened. No charges filed. The DA was never even brought in."

It was easy to imagine how it unfolded. The McFaddens paid off two low-income families in exchange for not pressing charges. Cashier's checks traded for non-disclosure agreements. If the money hadn't worked, there would have no doubt been hints of unpleasant consequences for not accepting the McFadden family's generous offer.

If both money and threats failed, Deputy Chief Watson had already laid the groundwork for blaming the victims. In the end, the 911 call had been the only record of what happened and with Maney filling out the reports, that had been taken care of too.

I remembered Gloria Doucette at the nursing home, talking about her second husband wanting some of the money. She'd traded justice for a pile of cash. I wondered if she'd ever regretted that decision.

"Did you go to the hospital?" Tito asked.

Maney shook his head.

"What about Rye?" I said. "What happened to him?"

Maney told us about the three men who showed up with one of the lawyers. The first man had a black bag, the kind a doctor might have carried. The other two were dressed in some sort of uniform, like they worked at a hospital. Those two were big men, tough-looking and fit.

The grandfather emerged from the house and told Maney to let the three inside.

Maney did as requested and a few minutes later, one of Watson's officers came out and told Maney he could leave.

Tito closed his eyes for a moment, massaging his temples.

"Thanks for telling us all this," I said to Maney. "Sorry to put you through it again."

"They say enough time goes by, that takes care of everything." He ran his fingers over the oxygen tube like it was a rosary. "That's bullshit."

*   *   *

Back in the Escalade, Tito and I stared outside without speaking.

My mind was blank except for images of the three campers that July day.

"Just so you know," Tito said. "When we find Rye McFadden, I'm gonna kill him and there's nothing you can do to stop me."

I offered no argument.

A deep sense of regret settled over me, sorrow that I hadn't known about what had happened to Rose. The emotional pain she carried must have been enormous.

If I'd known, I might have been able help somehow. Or not.

Tito rubbed his eyes. "I can't believe neither of us knew."

"Would knowing have made a difference?"

"In what?" He cranked his head in my direction.

"Any of it."

A moment passed.

"Good question." He shrugged.

My phone rang.

I looked at the screen. "It's the reporter."

*   *   *

I was a private investigator and before that a cop. Most of my working life had been spent on the streets of Dallas. Good neighborhoods and bad ones and every kind in between.

I knew every bar and saloon in the city.

Or thought I did, until Madge Boatwright suggested an early lunch at a place called the Tipsy Turtle.

I entered the address in the Escalade's GPS.

The Tipsy Turtle was by White Rock Lake, south of where Rose had been killed.

Before we left Frisco, I checked in with Mia by text. She replied that everything was fine.

I pulled away from the curb and headed toward the freeway, hoping that Madge Boatwright might give us some clue as to where to find Rye McFadden.

She gave us more than that.

CHAPTER FIFTY-FOUR

The Tipsy Turtle occupied the middle slot in a strip center on the east side of the lake, a narrow storefront with blacked-out windows. It sat between a laundromat and a place that loaned money on car titles.

The strip center parking lot was nearly full, people either doing their laundry or borrowing money at usurious interest rates. Or getting their midday drink on.

Tito and I stepped into the bar, a dimly lit room with a TV on one wall, currently showing a golf tournament with the sound muted.

As one might surmise, the theme of the place was turtles.

They were everywhere. Pictures of turtles. Stuffed turtles. Inflatable turtles. Turtles wearing sports jerseys. An eight by ten black velvet painting of the Teenage Mutant Ninja Turtles playing poker hung on the wall by the jukebox.

As my eyes adjusted to the low light, I saw that the place was empty except for the bartender by the beer taps, and a woman sitting at a table in the rear next to a pinball machine.

Tito and I headed to the back.

The woman was eating takeout, a Styrofoam container in front of her next to a glass of iced tea.

"Look what we have here," she said. "Rose Doucette's two husbands."

Madge Boatwright was in her late thirties with prematurely gray, shoulder-length hair.

She was dressed like a Grateful Dead groupie, wearing a tied-dyed peasant blouse, jeans, and a pair of Birkenstocks.

"Sorry, I forgot to tell you," she said. "If you want to eat lunch here, you need to bring your own."

"We didn't come for the food." I sat across from her. "How'd you know we were both married to Rose Doucette?"

Tito slid into the chair next to mine.

"I'm in the knowing business." She paused, a somber expression on her face. "Sorry for your loss, both of you."

Tito nodded in acknowledgement. I didn't reply, not caring much for Madge Boatwright even though we'd only been acquainted for a few seconds.

"What's it like, you two hanging out together?" she asked. "Given the circumstances and all."

"We didn't come to talk about that either," I said.

She was working her way through what looked like a Reuben sandwich. She ate one more bite and closed the lid on the container.

"You reached out to me," I said. "What's on your mind?"

"Don't be coy." She pushed the container away. "You're dying to pick my brain."

I didn't say anything. She was right, of course.

She eyed Tito. "Any idea where your brother-in-law is?"

"Haven't heard from him in two years. Not sure he's even alive."

"He's alive," she said. "At least he was a few days ago."

I tried not to react to that new bit of information.

"We want to talk to him too," I said. "Why don't you tell us what you know, and we can compare notes?"

Madge Boatwright laughed. "Have you ever actually dealt with a reporter before?"

Tito crossed his legs and settled back in his chair, a picture of relaxed confidence. "Let's do a trade," he said. "One piece of information in exchange for how you know Boyd is alive. See where that takes us, huh?"

I wondered where this was going, but I didn't want to interrupt. He seemed to have a game plan, which was more than I did at the moment.

Madge peered at him for a few seconds. "Okay. You first."

"We know about the families' non-disclosure agreements," he said.

Not exactly true. We thought there were NDAs but we didn't know for sure. Still, it was a worthy bluff.

Madge Boatwright would have made a good poker player. But not a great one. Her eyelids lowered for a split second as her nostrils flared.

"Your turn," Tito said.

She didn't speak, clearly trying to figure out how much we really knew.

"We had a deal, Madge." He pulled out his cell. "One of my fraternity brothers is an editor at the *New York Times*. I can call him right now and hand over the whole enchilada."

Everyone has a button and Tito had just mashed hers by threatening to give the story to someone else.

"Fair enough." She turned to me. "Who do you think Rose was meeting the day she was murdered?"

I shrugged. Then it hit me. "Boyd?"

She nodded.

I ran through everything from that day. Meeting with Rose at the hotel. The altercation with the manager. Walking a half block behind her and noticing the Toyota Camry. Following them both to the park where I stopped on the side of the road by the—

"The stables," I said. "Boyd works at the place across from where Rose was killed. He always was an animal lover."

Madge Boatwright smiled. "Look at you, being smart and all. Guess that's why you're an *ex*-cop."

"Is he still employed there?" Tito asked.

"Unfortunately, no. Boyd Doucette left work the day his sister was killed, and no one's seen or heard from him since."

"The people at the stables must have records," I said. "Home address. Contact info."

"He was paid in cash to clean up horseshit." She took a drink of tea. "Not a real big file in the HR department for that class of employee."

I drummed my fingers on the table. "And I'm guessing Boyd didn't have many friends at work. Kept to himself."

She nodded.

"He's gone completely off the grid," I said. "Even more than before. He's the only one of the three left alive."

"Scared shitless," Madge said. "That's how I'd describe Boyd Doucette right now. Unfortunately for me, I need him to corroborate a story since my sources keep dying."

"Rose was a source?" I paused. "No, scratch that. Josh Gannon was your source."

Once more her poker face didn't quite work, and I realized I was on to something.

Josh Gannon had threatened to expose Rye McFadden, wanting more money or he would tell his story to Madge Boatwright, the non-disclosure agreement be damned. A dangerous move to make against someone who wasn't mentally stable.

"What's your story about?" I asked. "Rich family covers for their crazy offspring, who then goes on a killing spree to keep his secrets from being revealed?"

She glanced at Tito.

He smiled sheepishly. "I don't really know anybody at the *New York Times.*"

She pushed back from the table. "We've traded enough info. You guys are shooting in the dark."

I didn't want her to go. She had more to share, that was clear.

"What about the hospital?" I asked. "McFadden Memorial. Do you know about that?"

"I know all about the hospital. It's obvious you don't."

"Give us something else," I said. "We want to find Boyd too, before Rye gets to him."

"Sorry, fellas." She stood, headed to the door.

Tito and I got up from the table.

She was halfway across the bar when she stopped and turned around. "My life coach says I need to work on being a better person. Practice random acts of kindness, shit like that."

"How's that going for you?" I asked.

"Not so good. Turns out I'm not a kind person. But I will give you guys one more tidbit."

I waited.

"Rose was pregnant," she said.

CHAPTER FIFTY-FIVE

Madge Boatwright left the Tipsy Turtle.

"What the hell did she mean?" Tito said. "Pregnant when?"

"I don't know."

"We have to go after her." He pointed to the exit. "Make her tell us what she knows."

"What are you gonna do, Tito? Beat it out of her? She's tougher than you are. You're liable to come out on the losing end."

Fists clenched; he eyeballed the door.

"Do you mind if I ask you something personal?" I said.

He frowned.

"Why didn't you and Rose have a baby?"

His head jutted forward like he was having trouble understanding the question.

"We tried for a while, but we gave up," I said. "I'd have kept going but Rose didn't want to."

"We never tried. She told me she couldn't have kids. Endometriosis."

That was news to me. But so was the fact that Rose had been pregnant, which I was assuming had to be the result of the incident at Camp Eagle Bluff.

More secrets. Untruths. Layer upon layer.

"Besides, she wasn't the mom type," Tito said. "The job, that was everything to her."

Making things right. Seeking order. That was what mattered to Rose Doucette. I pondered how much of that drive stemmed from the summer of 1994.

"You guys want a cocktail?" the bartender asked. "Looks like you could use one."

I told him no, and Tito and I left.

Outside, the heat and the humidity felt like a steam bath.

"We have to find that reporter," Tito said. "Make her talk somehow."

"No. We have to find Blaine McFadden."

*   *   *

I pulled into the driveway of the house on Beverly Drive and parked by the fountain, the same spot as the day before. There were no catering vans around this time, no valet stands by the entrance.

I rang the bell and waited, Tito beside me. Through the glass of the door, the home appeared empty.

After nearly a minute, Blaine appeared from the back of the house. He peered at us, a curious expression on his face. He strode across the entryway and opened the door partially, sticking his head out to greet us.

"Gentlemen," he said. "To what do I owe the pleasure?"
"We have a couple follow-up questions." I pushed the door open all the way, forcing him to step back.

Tito and I entered the home.

"Now's not good for me." Blaine glanced at his watch. "I have a tee time in thirty minutes."

He was wearing plaid golf slacks and a knit polo shirt, an insignia for the country club across the street on the breast of the shirt.

"You don't have very far to go," I said, "and this won't take long. Hopefully."

He sighed. "What do you want?"

"To talk about how Rose Doucette attended Camp Eagle Bluff the year your brother was a counselor there."

He looked at the floor without speaking.

"But you knew that already," I said. "A fact you neglected to mention when you hired me, and again yesterday when we saw the picture of your grandfather in front of the camp."

He crossed his arms.

"Why don't you cancel your golf game?" Tito said.

McFadden pulled a cell from his pocket and sent a text.

"We're going to deconstruct that summer," I said. "Day by day. Everything you know."

"You think that's going to bring her back?" His voice was weary. "You have no clue what's going on."

"We know you're not being truthful," I said. "We'll start with that."

"The problem is not me. The problem is my brother. Always, it comes back to Rye."

No one spoke for a moment. Blaine's face was a stew of emotions simmering just beneath the surface. Anger and sadness. Frustration.

"Rye was the chosen one," he said. "The best and the brightest. I got good grades too. But it was never enough."

"My heart goes out to you," I said. "Growing up with a mean, crazy brother. All there was to comfort you was your family's extreme wealth and social status."

"Your sarcasm is wearing thin," he said.

I grabbed the front of his shirt, shoved him against the wall. "Your brother kidnapped three children and your grandfather covered it up."

His face filled with rage. "And they put Rye away because of what he did. At least some justice was served. From where I sit, I'd call that a win."

"Except now he's out, and two of the three campers are dead, back-to-back," I said. "From where I sit, that's not a win."

"Two? What are you talking about?"

I told him about Josh Gannon, just out of prison, and his alleged suicide. "Boyd Doucette's the only one left alive, and he's in the wind."

Blaine's face drained of color. "You have to find him. He's not safe."

"No kidding," Tito said. "Why do you think we're here?"

"How on earth would I know where Boyd Doucette is?" Blaine asked. "But we have to locate him. Rye could be using his Warwick people to—"

"Warwick closed up shop." I let go of his shirt and explained what Mia and I had learned yesterday.

"Why would they do that?" Blaine frowned.

"No idea," I lied, not wanting to mention the two dead bodies we'd left in the alley. "Tell us about that summer."

After a moment he did, most of which we already knew.

The grandfather, wanting to control the situation, paid certain people at the Dallas police to handle the investigation. The lawyers stepped in with the money and the NDAs.

He told us the Gannon family balked after seeing the condition of their son in the hospital, almost derailing the whole payoff scheme. One of the police officers—Deputy Chief Watson, if I was to guess—had a private conversation with the mother and father, and soon after that they accepted the McFadden's offer. Gloria Doucette, on the other hand, signed off immediately. No need to apply pressure. Just gimme the check.

"Tell us what happened to Rose," I said.

"They got excellent treatment, all three of them. My grandfather made sure of that. Didn't cost them a dime."

"How magnanimous," I said. "But you're not answering my question."

"My brother is an animal. What do you want me to say?"

Tito pushed me aside, jammed a finger in Blaine's chest. "What did he do to Rose?"

Blaine slapped his hand away. "He raped her. Is that what you want to know?"

A wedge of coldness formed in my chest as my throat tightened. Tito balled his hands into fists, lips curled into a snarl.

"And she ended up pregnant." Blaine took a deep breath, lowered his voice. "And that's where it got sticky."

No one spoke for a moment.

"She carried the baby to term," Blaine said. "Put it up for a private adoption or something. No paperwork anywhere."

I digested that information and understood the implication. "Rye doesn't give a damn about Boyd. The child is the problem."

"What do you mean?" Tito asked.

"The abuse is one person's word against another's," I said. "Something from nearly thirty years ago. The child is proof though. DNA doesn't lie."

"That's a big part of it," Blaine said. "But my brother also wants revenge against the three children he kidnapped because in his mind they're responsible for what happened to him."

"And Rose's child?" I asked.

"It was a girl." Blaine paused. "He wants her, too, but not to harm her. Physically anyway."

"What then?" I said.

"He wants her to be his family. Even crazy people crave a degree of normalcy."

I wanted to ask why he hadn't told me this at the beginning, that day in Mia's office. Then I realized he probably would have had trouble articulating the reasons.

Blaine McFadden was part of a family that thrived on secrecy, and he was running for public office against the wishes of that family, in a race where in his mind the hint of scandal might derail his aspirations. Add that to the residual fear of his dead grandfather, and it was a wonder he could articulate as much as he had.

"How do you know all this psycho mumbo jumbo about your brother?" Tito asked. "What he really wants and all that?"

Blaine rubbed his eyes. "After the first hundred hours or so of group therapy with Rye—a family requirement by the way—I managed to piece things together."

"Do you have any leads on where Rose's daughter might be?" I asked.

He shook his head. "I've had people look, but they haven't found anything."

"You could have asked me to look for her," I said.

A moment of silence.

"I'm asking now. She has to be told that she's in danger."

Tito swore, paced back and forth.

"Rose has a daughter," I said more to myself than anyone else. With a start, I realized that for a period of time I'd had a stepdaughter.

Everything about our life together became a little less murky, a flashlight piercing the darkness.

"You two know Rose Doucette better than anyone," Blaine said. "Do you have any clues as to where the girl could be? Something that wouldn't show up during a regular investigation."

Tito slumped his shoulders like he was tired. "Not me. I'm still trying to get my head around all this."

I walked to the door, stared outside at the fountain, the water glistening in the sun. I tried to fathom the burden Rose must have carried around most of her life.

Blaine came over and stood beside me. "What about you?"

Everything that had happened so far ran through my mind, a catalogue of all the data, every bit of seemingly extraneous information.

"Yeah," I said. "I've got an idea where she might be."

CHAPTER FIFTY-SIX

I told Tito that we needed to leave.

"Where do you think she is?" Blaine asked.

"I don't know for sure. It's just a hunch."

"Can you at least keep me informed?"

"Sure," Tito said. "That's not a problem."

He and Blaine sent each other a text to exchange numbers.

"Thank you both," Blaine said. "It's a huge relief to be able to share this with someone."

I opened the front door.

"When this is over, I want you both to be my guests at the ranch, the least I can do. I owe you more than money."

"First, let's see if we can actually find Rose's daughter and Boyd." I had no intention of ever being his guest anywhere.

"And Rye," he said. "You have to find him too."

Tito and I left.

Outside, I tossed him the keys. "You drive. I need to make a call."

We climbed into the Escalade.

"Where are we going?" Tito cranked the ignition.

"Swing by the aunt's house one more time." I dialed a number. "Then I'll tell you, depending on what this phone call comes up with."

Six years ago, I had helped take down a prostitution ring, arresting an Albanian couple wanted by the FBI for human trafficking.

There was only one prostitute on the premises at the time, a girl from East Texas who'd made a series of bad decisions over the course of her young life, culminating with falling in love with the Albanian man. I cuffed her even though I figured she wouldn't be charged, the DA's policy at the time being to look at sex workers more as victims than as criminals.

I asked her if there was anyone I could call on her behalf. She gave me the name and number of her older sister's husband, a special agent at the local office of the US Secret Service. The special agent was most grateful for the call and even more so when I offered to cut her loose, telling me if I ever needed a favor, he'd be happy to oblige.

As Tito drove, I reached him on the first try and said he could repay the favor now. I recited Rose's phone number and asked him to check the incoming and outgoing calls and texts on the day she died.

It was a big ask, one I'd thought about making earlier in the investigation. But there was the whole ex-husband-accused-of-killing-his-former-wife situation that I was worried would stop people from helping me.

Turned out the special agent had no such compunction, and because the feds had great tools at their disposal, he was able to accommodate my request while I stayed on the line, telling me that Rose had communicated with two numbers that day. Mine and one more, an anonymous, pay-as-you-go cellphone.

He then offered to get a rough location for the anonymous phone.

While I listened to a keyboard clicking on the other end of the line, Tito pulled up to the aunt's house and stopped.

A Lexus SUV was parked in the driveway.

Tito slid the transmission into park as the special agent came back on the line. "Whoever owns that phone spends a lot of time in northeast Dallas," he said. "Somewhere near Audelia Road."

"Thanks." I ended the call and said to Tito, "I think I know where Boyd is. Probably Rose's daughter too."

"Where?"

"A house that Rose's uncle used to own. Just off of Audelia Road."

"Let's roll." He put his hand on the gearshift.

I pointed to the Lexus. "Let's see what's going on here first."

*   *   *

We didn't ring the bell. Instead, we walked down the driveway to the rear of the property.

They were in the backyard by the pool, sitting at the table eating lunch, what looked like chicken salad with sides of freshly cut fruit.

A waif of a woman in her early forties and a man a few years older with his hair in a ponytail. The woman was facing us, the man across from her, with only the back of his head visible.

The woman had blonde hair and the McFadden nose and chin, and it was obvious she was the sister. Mary was her name.

She looked up from her food, fork in hand. "Uh, can I help you?"

Tito's cell rang. He stepped away, turning his back to us, and answered.

With my elbow, I felt the comforting presence of the pistol under my shirt. "I'm here to see your brother."

Rye McFadden, the man with the ponytail, turned, and I realized something was wrong.

I'd made a mistake somewhere along the way.

While Rye might have had a stratospheric IQ at one point, those days were long gone. The face in front of me was that of a child trapped in the body of a middle-aged man. The eyes were without emotion of any sort, the jaw slack, the mouth neither smiling nor frowning. The overwhelming feeling that radiated from Rye McFadden was that of a long vacant building.

Mary stood. "What's this about? You realize you're trespassing?"

I pointed to her brother. "What's wrong with him?"

"Who the hell are you?" She pulled a phone from her purse. "I'm calling the police."

"We're not here to cause any problems. I just want to ask your brother about a woman named Rose Doucette."

Rye plucked a strawberry from his plate and ate it.

"Who?" Mary said.

"Rose Doucette. She attended Camp Eagle Bluff in the summer of 1994."

Mary swore. "You need to leave. That's all behind us now."

Rye McFadden stared at me, chewing on the strawberry, one eyelid drooping.

"We're not talking to reporters," she said. "About that or anything."

"I'm not a reporter. Rose Doucette was my ex-wife."

Silence. Mary rubbed the bridge of her nose between her thumb and forefinger, her lips pressed together.

Rye pointed to his food and smiled at me. "Do you want some lunch?"

I shook my head.

"Why don't you finish eating inside?" Mary said to her brother. "It's hot out here."

Rye picked up his plate and shuffled into the house.

When he was gone, she said, "He's been overmedicated for years, both prescription drugs and the other kind. He's not on anything at the moment, however. This is just who he is now."

"Is he staying here?"

"What's it to you where he stays?" she asked. "He did some very bad things early on in his life. He's paid for them. Trust me."

A similar sentiment to what Blaine McFadden had articulated fifteen minutes ago. The subtext: We're rich. We cleaned up our mess. You can show yourselves out now.

"I heard about your former wife," she said. "My condolences."

"I'd like to talk to your brother about where he's been the last few days," I said.

"You think Rye had something to do with her death? You can't be serious."

I didn't speak.

"He's been with me most of the time since . . ."

"Since he was released from the latest institution?"

"You seem to know a whole lot about our situation, but I still don't understand why you're here."

Tito's call ended and he returned to stand next to me.

"I'm a private investigator," I said. "Blaine hired me to find Rye."

Her face contorted with rage. "Get the hell out of here, now."

"What is going on?" Tito said. "Was that Rye?"

She held up her phone. "I am calling the police right this second."

"We're leaving." I raised my hands. "We mean you no harm. Sorry for the disturbance."

She lowered the phone. "If you really mean no harm, you won't mention us to Blaine."

"How come?" Tito asked.

She crossed her arms, stepping back from the table. She was no longer angry. She was fearful.

"Are you scared of him?" I asked.

"Of course, I am," she said. "He's the most dangerous person I've ever encountered in my life."

I looked at the backdoor where Rye had gone, not knowing who to trust.

"You don't believe me, do you?" she said. "Blaine told you Rye was dangerous and needed to be locked up. Right?"

I didn't reply.

"Did Rye look dangerous to you?" she asked.

I hesitated, shook my head.

"He can manipulate anyone," she said. "That's his superpower. Take Rye, for example. Blaine keeps getting him committed to mental institutions."

"Why?" I asked. "I don't understand."

"You've already mentioned it," she said, sounding exasperated. "The summer of 1994. He doesn't want Rye to talk about that."

Despite the heat, my skin grew cold.

"Those poor campers who were kidnapped," she said. "Blaine was the instigator. He talked Rye into taking them."

"You mean he was there?" I said, trying to comprehend what she was telling me. "He was at the farmhouse with Rose and the others?"

Mary rubbed her eyes, the expression on her face that of a teacher whose student couldn't quite grasp the idea that two plus two does in fact equal four. She nodded slowly.

The pieces began to fall into place. I'd been played.

If Blaine was part of what had happened in 1994, and if the surviving victim started talking, he had much more to lose than his brother. The implications for Rose's daughter chilled me to the core.

"Shit," Tito said. "That phone call. I think I screwed up."

CHAPTER FIFTY-SEVEN

Tito Mullins told me who had called.

Blaine McFadden, asking if we could check in every hour or so. He was worried, just wanted to stay in the loop.

Mary gasped, covered her mouth with one hand.

Worse was to come. Tito had told him about my hunch regarding Boyd and the uncle's house. About the possible location of the house.

"Did you tell him about Rye?" I asked.

He shook his head. "He called before I knew who was sitting at the table."

"Did you tell him where we were?"

Tito gulped, nodded.

"I thought we'd be safe here," Mary said, "Blaine wouldn't dream we'd be so close."

Something didn't add up.

"Doesn't Rye know that Blaine is dangerous?" I asked her.

"After what he's been through? Of course, he does."

"Then why would he drop in on Blaine?" I told her about the video of Rye with Blaine's son. How that had led us to discover the picture of Camp Eagle Bluff, to realize the connection to the McFadden family.

"That wasn't Rye," she said. "Trust me. Wouldn't be the first time Blaine has impersonated him to get what he wants."

Rye and Blaine did look alike. Same facial features, same build. All it took was a wig with long hair and the graininess of a video camera to throw me off.

"You didn't discover anything either," Mary said. "There's no way he would have left that picture out unless he wanted you to make the connection."

It dawned on me she was right. Everything we knew about Rye had been fed to us by his brother. Little by little, Blaine McFadden had been throwing us off the scent, making us think Rye was the bad guy. His wealth and stature had blinded me.

He was smart, manipulating us into tracking down the surviving victim, Boyd Doucette, the only person left alive who could implicate him in the crimes of 1994.

Other than Rose's daughter.

"Did you tell him we found anybody here?" I asked Tito. He shook his head.

I turned to Mary. "Just to be safe, get Rye and go to the neighbor's house, the woman with the cats. Lock up everything, close all the shades. Whatever you do, don't answer the door."

"I'll pull my car behind her house too," she said.

"Good idea." I looked at Tito. "Send Blaine a text, say the aunt's house was a bust, and we'll check in later."

Tito thumbed out a message on his phone.

"Be careful," Mary said. "Enough people have been hurt by my brother already."

*   *   *

THE LIFE AND DEATH OF ROSE DOUCETTE   289

Midday on a Saturday, the streets weren't too crowded.

I obeyed the traffic laws as much as possible, speeding where there weren't many cars but not blowing through red lights or stop signs. It wouldn't do at this point to get pulled over or involved in a wreck.

"Tell me again what you found at Rose's uncle's old house," Tito said.

"A woman working in the yard. She was in her mid to late twenties."

"That's the right age."

I accelerated through a yellow light. "She was maybe five-foot-four or so. Dark hair but a fair complexion."

Rose had dark hair and was about the same height, but her skin was olive. The McFaddens were all blond with fair skin.

I sped past the grocery store parking lot where Lutz had stopped me. Three blocks later, I turned onto the street where the uncle's former home was located.

I circled the block. Then the next block. Then I drove down the alley. Nothing appeared out of the ordinary. No black Tahoes lurking anywhere, no guys who looked like ex-soldiers loitering about.

I finally parked two houses down, on the other side of the street.

Under normal circumstances, I would have staked out the home for a few hours just to be sure there were no hostiles present. But these weren't normal circumstances. Time was trickling away. If this wasn't the location of Rose's daughter and Boyd, I needed to know that as soon as possible.

No one was in the front yard of the house this time. To be fair, no one was in the front yard of any of the other houses. It was in the mid-nineties and getting hotter. Only a few cars were parked on the street, none of them near where we were headed.

"How do we do this?" Tito asked.

"You knock. I'll stand to one side of the door."

"How come I'm in the line of fire?"

"We can do it the other way around. You okay with pulling the trigger on another person?"

He muttered something under his breath.

"This is a long shot anyway," I said. "We're just covering all the bases."

"Fine. We'll do it your way."

We exited the Escalade and marched across the street.

The curtains on the front windows of the house were shut. No vehicles were in the driveway and the garage was closed.

Tito stood on the doormat while I pressed myself against the wall by the mailbox.

He knocked.

A moment later, the door opened.

Tito's mouth fell open. "Boyd? Is that you?"

I sensed movement behind me. I whirled around, bringing my pistol up.

Jax, the founder and head of Warwick Services, emerged from the shrubbery by the house, a Taser in his hand.

I raised my weapon, but he fired first.

*   *   *

When I came to, I was in the living room of a home that had a passing resemblance to the one Rose and I had shared when we were married. Area rugs on polished hardwood floors, a leather sofa, a coffee table covered with takeout boxes.

I was on the floor, my back against the wall, legs splayed. I tried to move but my hands were behind me, tied with what felt like plastic restraints. Duct tape covered my mouth.

Tito was on the floor next to me, gagged, hands bound in the same position as mine.

My pistol was gone, but the folding knife I always carried was still in my waistband at the small of my back. Whoever had tied me up had been in a hurry.

On the other side of the room Boyd Doucette sat in a chair, hands behind his back, duct tape over his mouth. The twenty-something woman I'd seen working in the yard was next to him on the floor, bound and gagged too. They were terrified, their eyes wide, breathing rapid.

I heard the soft thud of footsteps from somewhere else in the house.

A moment later, Blaine McFadden, still wearing his golf clothes, appeared, followed by Jax Connell.

Jax approached me, a malicious grin on his face. "Look who's awake."

I struggled against the restraints.

"You killed two of my people," Jax said. "When this is over, you'll have to answer for that."

"Where are their weapons?" Blaine asked.

Jax pointed to a bookcase.

Blaine reached to the top shelf and retrieved two pistols, mine and Tito's. "Which one is Dylan's?"

"The one in your right hand. The Glock."

KABOOM.

Blaine shot Jax with my gun. A single round to the forehead.

The noise was deafening in the enclosed area. Jax fell, dead before he hit the floor.

The smell of spent gunpowder filled the air, followed a moment later by the copper tang of blood. Tito squealed beneath his gag as the girl started crying. Boyd bounced in his chair but couldn't free himself.

Blaine knelt beside me. He wiped off the Glock before pressing the weapon in my hand, getting my prints everywhere. Then he ripped off the duct tape covering my mouth.

"How many people have you killed this week?" he asked. "You must have a lot of unresolved anger."

His eyes sparkled, lit by a new intensity, a faint smile creasing his lips. We were in the dark territory where he thrived, a land populated by the pain of others, the wafer-thin boundary between life and death.

"There's a SWAT team in route," I said. "They'll be here in less than five minutes."

"No there's not. Lutz would have told me." He returned both pistols to the shelf, a location where it would be impossible for somebody with bound hands to access. He then pulled a small semiautomatic from his back pocket.

"Reunion Investments, that's controlled by you, isn't it?" I said.

"Of course it is. I filed guardianship papers on Rye years ago. You and your dot-head lawyer were too stupid to figure that out."

He sauntered across the room, stroked Boyd's head. "How are you doing today?" Boyd leaned back to get away from Blaine's touch, his eyes full of fear.

"Leave him alone," I said.

"Or what? You're not exactly in a position to issue demands right now."

I tried to work the knife free from my waistband without letting him notice.

"Where's my brother?" Blaine pointed his gun at me.

"I have no idea."

I'd managed to press a finger on the handle of the knife through my jeans. If I could ease the weapon upward without moving my arms too much and attracting Blaine's attention, I could theoretically grasp it, open the blade, and cut myself free.

That was a lot of theoreticals, however.

"You know more than you're telling me," he said. "I can see that in your eyes."

"I don't know where your brother is."

He stomped across the room and yanked me to my feet, just as I pushed the knife free from my waistband. It fell to the floor, hitting the rug silently near Tito.

Blaine's eyes were inches from mine. "Last chance. Tell me where he is."

"I don't know."

He dragged me toward the rear of the house and shoved me down a hallway to a closed door. He opened the door and threw me into a bedroom where after forty-three years on this planet, I finally understood what true fear really meant.

CHAPTER FIFTY-EIGHT

The first thing I saw was Mia Kapoor bound and gagged, sitting on a chair.

The second was Caleb in his car seat on the bed, sleeping like he'd been drugged, his mouth hanging open in an unnatural way.

"Jax picked them up this morning at her office." Blaine slid the pistol back into his pocket. "They were in my pool house when you and that moron Tito Mullins stopped by. So close but yet so far."

Mia's eyes welled with tears.

Blaine sighed. "Everything was going so well until Josh Gannon got out of prison and started talking to that reporter."

"If you harm either of them, I will hunt you down to the ends of the earth."

"Again with the empty threats." He chuckled.

The plastic handcuffs bit into my wrists. I took several deep breaths, willing away the rage and the fear. I needed a calm head. The anger could come later.

"How did you arrange Gannon's death?" I asked. "Everybody but Rose thought it was a suicide."

I had to keep him talking so Tito would have enough time to cut himself free.

"Wasn't that hard once you know where the cameras are. I had easy access too. One of the family's trusts owns the hotel."

"And Rose?" I said, trying not to let the anger rise again.

He smiled. "Wish I'd been a little faster and hit you a little harder with the Toyota. That would have saved me a lot of trouble. Still, you came in handy."

"You could track the investigation through me." I began to understand.

"Exactly," he said. "And eventually you'd start looking for Boyd."

Mia stamped her feet, struggled against her restraints.

"Once Boyd was located," Blaine said, "I could take care of him too. Then everyone who knew about 1994 would be gone."

Except for the daughter, the ultimate piece of evidence. And Rye.

"The biggest problem of course was Rose's child." He seemed to read my mind. "But just a little while ago, I received an unexpected gift when I called Tito Mullins."

I tried not to react to Tito's blunder.

"He was more than happy to tell me all about your hunch regarding this house." Blaine grinned. "The McFadden name generates envy in some people. A desire to curry favor."

"You need to listen to me, Blaine. You have six hostages. You can't kill all of them and get away with it."

"Do you know how much I hate it when people tell me what I can't do?" he asked, his eyes lidded.

I didn't speak.

"Blaine, you can't run for office. Blaine, you can't go to that college. You have to do what *the family* tells you to do, Blaine. That's the McFadden way." A vein in his temple throbbed as he spoke.

"Too many moving pieces." I shook my head. "Whatever you're planning won't work."

"Yes, it will," he said. "In addition to Rose, you just killed another innocent person, Jax Connell. Not that big of a stretch to see you and Rose's current husband shooting each other."

"What about the others?"

"I have plans for them." His pupils were dilated, his tone ominous.

I wondered what he was on or if this was just the crazy coming through. I had to keep him talking. Tito and the knife were the only chance any of us had.

"Keep me but let everyone else go," I said. "Your grandfather's not around to clean this up for you."

Oops. Wrong thing to say.

He snarled like a rabid dog and pressed me against the wall, squeezing my throat until my head started to swim.

"Don't you mention that old pervert to me. Ever."

I managed to nod, and he let go.

Oxygen flooded my lungs.

"Where is Rye?" he asked.

Where is Tito?

"Who fathered Rose's child?" My voice was a croak. "You or Rye?"

The question appeared to knock him off course. He leaned back slightly, a wary look on his face.

"I know you engineered the whole thing," I said, "suckering your brother into taking the three of them from the camp. A rich boy looking for some kicks."

"You're not as dense as I thought." Blaine sat on the bed by Caleb. He slid a cigarette lighter from his pocket.

Please, Tito. Hurry.

"Rye preferred hurting the boys," Blaine said. "His wires got a little crossed after spending so much time with my dear grandfather. Sweet little Rose was all mine."

I swallowed the revulsion I felt. He had molested Rose. And now he was planning to kill his own child.

"There's still a chance for you to walk away from this," I said. "No one else has to get hurt. Let Mia and the baby go, and I'll be your hostage. We can look for your brother together."

"You sound like Rose, all those years ago." He snickered. "Leave the boys alone, she said. Take me. Don't hurt my brother."

Mia began to sob, tears streaming down her face.

"Didn't work for her then," he said, "and it won't work for you now."

C'mon, Tito.

"I'll start with the kid here. You're not that tough, Dylan. Nobody has the stomach for what's about to happen."

"I don't know where Rye is. I swear." Cold sweat dripped down the small of my back. Blaine flicked the lighter. A flame appeared. He pulled the car seat toward him.

And that's when the door opened.

Blaine's jaw dropped as Rose Doucette's daughter stepped into the room, holding Tito's pistol. He extinguished the flame.

"Who are you?" she asked, lips trembling. "Why did you break in and tie us up?"

Silence.

"Why did you kill that man?" She took a step closer, gun held high, breath coming in heaves.

"I was trying to keep you safe," Blaine said. "There's so much I need to explain."

"He's going to kill you," I shouted. "And Boyd too."

She looked at me, fingers white on the gun's grip.

"And who are you?"

"He's a very bad man," Blaine said. "He killed your mother."

Mia squealed from behind her gag.

"My mother?" The girl grimaced. "You knew my mother?"

I nodded. "I knew her very well. And I would have never harmed her for any reason."

"Oh, when will the lies stop?" Blaine made a *tssking* sound. He slid off the bed and held out his hand. "Give me the gun, sweetie. I don't want you to hurt yourself."

"Call 911," I said. "Tell them shots fired, officer needs assistance."

Blaine eased closer to the girl, his hand out.

She looked at Blaine, and then at me. Her teeth chattered, arm shook.

"We're all going to die if you don't make the call," I said.

"Don't believe a word he says, dear." Blaine smiled. "He's just trying to—"

He lunged and ripped the gun from her hand. The action diverted his attention from me.

I stepped forward as he gained control of the weapon. I kicked his knee, a toe punch like it was a soccer ball and I needed to score a goal, or the game was lost.

He screamed and fell to the floor, the gun slipping out of his hand.

I took a gulp of air and kicked him in the stomach with everything I had. He curled into a ball, struggling to breathe.

I turned to the girl. "Call the police. Hurry."

She gaped at Blaine for a moment and darted from the room.

I sat on the floor, rocked backwards, working my bound hands over my hips and legs so that they were in front of me. Then I retrieved the gun.

Blaine was struggling to stand. He'd made it to his knees, blood dribbling from the corner of his mouth. He pulled the semiautomatic from his pocket, tried to aim at me but his arm wavered.

"Who do you think you are?" His voice was weak.

I pointed Tito's pistol at his face.

"I'm a McFadden." He managed to steady his arm. "You have no idea what I can do to you."

"This is for Rose." I pulled the trigger.

CHAPTER FIFTY-NINE

Sarah was her name, Rose's daughter.

Tito had been unable to cut through his restraints with my knife, but Sarah was younger and more agile, and she'd successfully freed herself.

She'd then cut loose Boyd, who had called the police before trying to hack away Tito's plastic handcuffs.

Sarah had taken that opportunity to grab a gun from the shelf and head to the bedroom in the back. She had moxie, that Sarah. Just like her mother.

I freed Mia, who immediately scooped up Caleb. Jax had given him Benadryl and he was slowly coming awake.

Tito burst into the room and saw what had happened. He cut me loose and asked if everyone was all right.

I nodded and sat on the bed, holding onto Mia and Caleb until the first two responding officers arrived.

Tito gave them a very abbreviated version of what had happened and told them to call Detective Larry Weeks.

Weeks arrived ten minutes later, along with a patrol lieutenant and the medical examiner.

They took a quick walk-through of the house and then returned to the living room where everyone had congregated.

Mia was sitting on a chair in the corner, holding Caleb. Boyd and Sarah stood nearby.

Tito and I were by Jax's body.

Weeks surveyed the scene in the living room one more time and then said to me, "What happened?"

Before I could reply, Tito said, "My client was involved in a shooting after having been held hostage by the two decedents."

Weeks pointed at Mia and said to me, "I thought she was your lawyer."

"Ms. Kapoor and her infant were kidnapped by the two decedents," Tito said. "They've both been through the wringer. I'll be speaking for everyone here."

Weeks jerked a thumb toward the rear of the house. "Dead guy in the back is Blaine McFadden. You better start speaking fast."

"We need paramedics," Tito said. "After everybody gets checked out, we can talk about what happened."

Weeks chewed his lip for a moment before pulling a radio from his belt and calling for an EMT.

Boyd took a step forward, his head low, shoulders hunched like a dog who was afraid someone was going to swat his nose with a newspaper.

He stared at the carpet and said to Weeks, "Do you want to see the video?"

"Why, yes I do," Weeks replied.

Boyd picked up a tablet computer from the dining room table. He told us he had cameras in the living room and in the front yard, inconspicuous little things he'd bought because they were so cheap. They recorded to the cloud, and he showed us what had happened, clear footage of Blaine and Jax breaking in, Jax tasering me and Tito, and finally Blaine killing Jax with my pistol.

"Thanks for showing us that," Weeks said. "What's your name, son?"

Boyd told him.

"This your house?" Weeks asked.

Boyd nodded.

"This is Rose's brother," I said. "I'll explain later."

The expression on Detective Weeks's face softened. "Rose was my partner."

Boyd stared at a corner of the ceiling without speaking.

"Being somebody's partner is like being family," Weeks said to Boyd. "That means you're like my family now."

Boyd wiped his eyes as the first of the crime scene investigators arrived.

*　*　*

While the house was being processed by the investigators, Sarah and I sat at the kitchen table with Mia, who had Caleb in her arms in a vice grip.

"How did you know my mother?" Sarah asked.

"I was married to her for fifteen years."

She was silent for a moment. "Daddy told me she died."

"Boyd?" I said. "That's your father?"

She nodded. "Why would my mother not want me?"

"She was very young when you were born," Mia said. "Not even in high school."

Sarah closed her eyes for a moment, her expression indicating she had a lot to think about. As did we all.

"How did you end up living here?" I asked.

"I've always lived here." She told us her last name was not Doucette, but one I recognized as Gloria's maiden name.

Since childhood, she'd been told to never acknowledge the Doucette name if anybody ever came around asking.

She also told us she worked at a clinic and one day she wanted to be a nurse.

"That sounds like a fine idea," Mia said.

"Sometimes I think I might want to be a police officer," she said. "Like my Aunt Rose. She used to tell me what it was like to be a cop when she came to visit."

Mia squeezed Caleb tighter and looked away.

I walked to the sink. Stared outside at the yard, blinking back tears.

The lawn was green and well-tended. There was a small brick patio with a charcoal grill and several outdoor chairs. A wind chime hung from the branch of a Bradford pear tree in the corner of the yard.

I tried to imagine Rose sitting in one of those chairs, nursing a glass of wine, talking to Sarah. Lying to her.

From out of nowhere a new emotion came over me, anger at Rose for keeping this life secret for all those years. From her two husbands. From her daughter. From everyone. The anger vanished as suddenly as it had appeared, replaced with a deep sense of melancholy.

"That's a great idea too," Mia said. "I bet your . . . Aunt Rose would like that."

I debated how much to say right now. Should I tell Sarah that Rose was her mother and she was now dead, killed a few days before by the man who I had shot only an hour ago, a monster who just happened to be her biological father? Eventually it would all have to come out. But for now, perhaps taking things slow might be better.

One of the crime scene techs came into the kitchen and asked a question about the house. Sarah left with him, and Boyd crept into the room, arms crossed, not making eye contact.

"You doing okay?" I asked.

He stared outside. "Rose told me you could fix this."

"I did my best. Unfortunately, a lot of people died. Why was she meeting with you in the parking lot across from the stables?"

"She wanted me and Sarah to leave town. Josh, he was the other one with us that summer, he was going to blow the story open. She didn't think we'd be safe."

A sound idea. If they had left, I wouldn't have encountered Sarah puttering in the yard, her presence lodging in my subconscious. The uncle's old address would have just been another dead end.

Yes, a sound idea except it wouldn't have stopped Blaine McFadden's relentless search.

"When she was a minor," I said, "what was her custody situation?"

"My aunt and uncle took her in. My mother, well she didn't need to raise any more kids."

"Why did you move in?" Mia asked.

"My aunt died. And my uncle was old, so he moved to Denver where his children lived." Boyd paused. "Seemed like the right thing to do. We're family after all."

Mia nodded. "Why didn't you leave when Rose told you to?"

"Where would we go? This is the only home Sarah has ever known."

No one spoke for a few moments.

"I told Rose years ago that you should know," he said to me. "About Sarah and all. I'm sorry."

"Why are you sorry?" I asked. "None of this is your fault."

He was silent for several seconds. Then he said, "I told her she should tell Sarah too."

And what good would come of that, I wondered? There were no right answers for this situation, only ones that appeared less bad than others.

"What was Rose and Sarah's relationship like?" Mia asked.

"Good, I guess. Rose loved her and tried to be there for her." He paused. "But then she wouldn't come around for a long time."

The child represented a failure, I realized, a time when Rose had been unable to control something. The real Rose Doucette became more and more clear in my mind, the hard place she found herself in. The best thing in her life, the person she loved most in the world, was a constant reminder of the worst time in her entire existence.

Mia sighed. "What a terrible situation for everyone."

Footsteps from the hallway. The three of us stopped talking.

Sarah came back into the kitchen, sat down at the table, and looked at me. "Would you tell me about my mother sometime? What she was like?"

I smiled. "I'd be happy to."

EPILOGUE

We had a small ceremony officiated by Olive Ramirez, the judge who had granted me bail when I had been booked for the murder of Rose Doucette, a charge that had since been dismissed.

Tito served as the best man. Caleb, now almost eighteen months old, was the ring bearer.

Mia was the most beautiful I had ever seen her, wearing an ivory dress and a double strand of pearls. I felt a deep sense of peace and contentment standing beside her.

Only immediate family attended, plus Boyd, Sarah, Larry Weeks, and a few close friends.

Mia's mother cried during the vows. I liked to think they were tears of joy.

I was sure the location of our nuptials raised some eyebrows—the hotel where Josh Gannon had been murdered by Blaine McFadden—but I didn't care.

The way I figured it the McFadden family owed us. Mary McFadden and her aunt and several of her uncles understood that and comped the whole thing, including the presidential suite for the newlyweds.

Much like the incident at Camp Eagle Bluff in 1994, the family had managed to keep out of the press most of the details about what had occurred at the house off of Audelia Road. Part of the news blackout was making sure I was happy and non-talkative.

After the ceremony and a brief reception, Mia's parents took Caleb to their home, and a small group of us retreated to the bar where I'd had a drink with Rose six months before.

Tito ordered two bottles of Cristal and started making toasts. Here's to the bride, here's to the groom, here's to their life together.

Much drinking and laughter ensued.

I sipped champagne to be polite, while Mia nursed a club soda and lime. She was three months along, and the dress was starting to fit a little snug.

When Tito ordered the third bottle of Cristal, I stood and told everyone we were going to our room.

Tito pulled us aside and raised his glass. "One last toast then. Just for us."

I slid my arm around Mia's shoulders.

"Here's to Rose," he said.

I shook my head. "Here's to the future."

ACKNOWLEDGMENTS

As the years roll by, I find myself experiencing more and more gratitude, especially for two things: Being alive and healthy; and being able to exercise the talent I've been given, i.e., writing books like this. Regarding the latter, I would like to thank Bob and Pat Gussin, Lee Randall, Faith Matson, and everybody at Oceanview Publishing. Also, many thanks to Richard Abate for helping make this novel possible at the outset.

Several people generously provided their time and expertise in helping me research certain aspects of the story. For their help with police procedures and the intricacies of the criminal justice system, I would like to thank Lance Koppa, Jim Born, and Paul Coggins. And for providing me with insight into Indian American culture, I would like to thank Jason Thomas.

For their help with the manuscript, I would like to offer my gratitude to Jan Blankenship, Victoria Calder, Will Clarke, Paul Coggins, Peggy Fleming, Fanchon Henneberger, Alison Hunsicker, Brooke Malouf, Julie Mitchell, David Norman, Glenna Whitley, and Max Wright.